Belvedere Woman

By the Author

Previous Novels

The Lawyer and the Libertine

The Coroner's Conscience

Appointment at Amalfi

The Missing Masterpiece

The Russian Master

After the Monsoon

Betrayals

Dislocation

The Only Case

Plays

Brazilian Blue

The Cellophane Ceiling

The Acquisition

A Hero's Funeral

The Old School Tie

Belvedere Woman

IAN
CALLINAN

ARCADIA

This work is one of fiction. There is no person alive or dead who is in any way to be identified with any character in the novel. If a reader thinks that such a person can be identified that reader is mistaken.

The author thanks Carl Harrison-Ford for his editorial assistance and encouragement. Errors, incongruities solecisms and the like are entirely those of the author.

First published 2016 by Arcadia
the general books' imprint of
Australian Scholarly Publishing Pty Ltd
7 Lt Lothian St Nth, North Melbourne, Victoria 3051

tel 03 9329 696 / *fax* 03 9329 5452
aspic@ozemail.com / www.scholarly.info

ISBN: 978-1-925333-60-2

Cover design Amelia Walker

[ASP]

Contents

Chapter 1
Wednesday Evening

Sandra sat in the wicker chair on the verandah: five thirty and tipsy, two hours ahead of schedule. That lunch. Only wine. White wine shouldn't count. She felt slightly giddy. Were her feet, in their Ferragamo sandals swelling, or were they, like the rest of her, just a little larger? She reached for her glass and leaned back in the chair. Marvellous, comfortable, old chair, re-caned, re-wickered until you didn't know what was original anymore.

Belvedere, five thirty on a Wednesday afternoon and she was already half-pissed. Mother hated that sort of language. Typical. Mind you, Sandra's use of coarse language was only a recent innovation. Slightly genteel, her mother, not like her robust well bred, oh, so well bred father. To be genteel was déclassé, he always said. Her generation, attuned to Knightsbridge fashion as decreed in two-months-old, by seamail, English magazines, preferred conduct or language to be U, not Non U. That dated her. The children wouldn't know what she was talking about.

She wondered whether the wine made her intelligent. She thought different thoughts when she'd been drinking. Come to think of it, these days she really didn't have many thoughts when she'd been drinking: just a bundle of instinctive actions and reactions. What was the word Lucy had used at lunch today? Automaton, that was it, automation. She knew what that meant. What a good word, the sound told you the meaning. When she wasn't pissed, or on the way to being pissed, that is, at any time when she hadn't had two drinks, she was an automaton. But when she was drinking, the thoughts, even ideas welled up in her head. And she came out with things that people sometimes said were witty. It wasn't that she needed drink to give her confidence. She was usually confident. People in her, yes, she'd say it, station, nice word too, station in life, always had confidence. She had been brought up that way. No, alcohol didn't give her confidence. It stimulated her though, gave her ideas, thoughts that she didn't know that she could think. She sipped the wine and wondered why she felt so very sad tonight. Inkie, the children's melancholy, black Labrador, slow and ancient, snuffled along the verandah and put his heads in her linen skirted lap.

Lunch had rather gone on. They did seem to these days. Benny was so nice though, the freshly cut flowers he brought to their table, the specials, his discretion about their diets and their departures from them. And, yes, let's face it, like any good restaurateur he went for the big margins on wine. Plied them with it. They all protested of course. But he knew how they liked their tipple. 'I won't let on how much you're all drinking if you don't let on you know how much I'm overcharging you for it' was the unspoken conspiracy.

Five thirty, no, five forty-five now on a Belvedere evening in early December and she was almost fifty years old. Inkie looked more than fifty. What was the dog equivalent, seven to one? Inkie would be seventy in human terms. She fondled his ears. Dear old Inkie. The children's last pet, or at least their last pet here. They were gone now. Their wives or mistresses or boyfriends or lovers, whatever you called them these days, didn't seem to like pets. Too hard to get into a two-door Beemer she supposed. Anyway, who wanted the trouble of feeding and washing and grooming a dog or cat? Who was going to look after them when you went skiing at Aspen?

Well, she was the one who'd introduced them to Aspen. Some of her friends went there and came back and told her about it. She'd been an English-type person before then. If you wanted to ski you did it, like the English, in Switzerland, St Moritz, perhaps France. They'd insisted she go. So the whole family had gone. It had been one of their best holidays, until, until Jack. No, she wouldn't think about that, not today. She tried to drink from her glass. It was empty. She stood up, needing a little more effort than was seemly and standing on poor Inkie's tail as she did. He yelped in pain. She was immediately apologetic. She kneeled on the floor, gently stroking the dear old fellow and becoming maudlin at the sight of his rheumy eyes and rickety old body. As she stood up and walked towards the kitchen and the refrigerator, she could feel unaccountable tears stinging her eyes and rolling down her cheeks. Poor Inkie.

Last night's bottle … or two, was finished. And that bloody Jack hadn't put a bottle in for tonight. She was angry now. She went down the back stairs carefully holding the railing as she descended. Then, underneath the grand high old Queensland house, she turned right towards Jack's cellar. Cellar. Yes, he'd been pleased to call it that. But it was really an old concrete blockhouse with apertures for ventilation and shelves for bottles, hundreds of them. He used to talk about buying some barrels and a bench, giving a dinner party there, perhaps, in summer, when it was hot outside, but cool there. It had come to nothing. It was just a storehouse.

'Damn,' she'd forgotten the key. She turned around and nearly stood on Inkie again who had followed her quietly down the steps. She sat down on the concrete path heedless of her cream linen skirt by Carla Zampatti and fondled the dog's thinning coat. He snuggled up to her responsively. 'This is no good.' She struggled to her feet careful not to bump him. She found the key, exactly where she must have left it last night, on top of the refrigerator. She admired the dog's stubbornness as he lay on the landing refusing to follow her down again. 'God,' she felt tired, how tired.

Still she wasn't going to be thwarted now. She wrestled with the lock and eventually the door swung open: dozens of square metres of wine. Some must be better than others. There'd be Christian Diors, Chanels and Schiaparellis of wine no doubt but her rules for wine were much simpler, 'choose the white wine closest to the door with the plainest label: Chenin blanc, pinot, chardonnay, who gives a damn?'

Happier now she bore two bottles back up the staircase gently nudging Inkie in his ample stomach as she carefully stepped over him on the back landing. He grunted in pleasure rolling on his back and sniffing her ankles in ecstasy.

'Now, where's the bloody corkscrew?' She tried to solve this latest problem as she peeled away the metal wrapping around the top of the bottle. 'Damn.' She'd broken her left index fingernail in her anxiety. An angry, sharp, crimson line of blood opened beside the nail. 'Did alcohol make the skin thin and soft?' When she was young they used to say what a beautiful complexion she had. She couldn't recall even one adolescent pimple. Mother, in some things Mother was ahead of her time, used to say, 'be careful of the sun, it's not for delicate Caucasians.' Now where did Mummy learn a phrase like that, 'delicate Caucasians'. It wasn't said condescendingly. There was nothing unique in this country about being a Caucasian then. It was just a health or beauty thing. She hadn't thought of that for years. She must remember those words. They would have some impact today. 'Probably an offence nowadays.' She never read those tedious articles about discrimination. Didn't have to. There was only one rule, don't speak openly anywhere or anytime, except among your real friends, and precious few of those she had, near the beginning of her sixth decade.

She found a paper handkerchief and wrapped it tightly around her finger. The blood was already seeping to the surface of the paper. 'Press it harder, get another handkerchief.' She did, and the bleeding slowed down. She located the corkscrew on top of the refrigerator near where she had found the key. 'That's logical. Must have been functioning all right last night.'

At home Daddy had always opened the wine. He didn't care for it much himself. He was a whisky man. They were a whisky generation mainly. Wine was pansy stuff. Besides, whisky, even whisky bottled in Scotland, was better value. How Daddy would be surprised at her dexterity in inserting the corkscrew, gently, but firmly—she giggled—'What did that remind her of?' She felt sad again. There wasn't too much of that these days. 'Still the job in hand, must concentrate.' She neatly drew the cork out, making only the faintest plop. 'Not bad for someone half pissed. Probably wasn't, not now, perhaps five eighths way there. Look at the clock, six ten already.'

It was growing dark as she took her full glass, a canister of ice cubes and the opened bottle back out to her favourite chair on the sweeping verandah. The house had recently been repainted over Jack's protests.

'Who does he think he is,' Jack complained, 'Rembrandt?' Still, he paid the bill when it came. Fresh white paint on the wall with green trimmings. The verandah floor was fresh and cool. Lucy said they could have been at a well-kept Resident's house in the Punjab 70 years ago.

It was better sitting down. Those lunches, bit unnecessary, still—the day had to be filled in somehow. It was a mistake to have Mother there though. She was reverting. The hat, and then the gloves. My God, the gloves. Sandra could not recall packing them when she moved her into the retirement village. You'd think they would not let her out wearing them and she tucked her napkin into the collar of her dress. Still, that wasn't so stupid when you thought about it. All those coloured sauces that Benny made. The all tasted the same, of course, but how they ran and spattered. Perhaps she should have followed suit, like Lucy. That Lucy, she could still surprise her, sensitive and considerate one minute, arch bitch and main chancer the next. No wonder Alex left her and she'd buried the next. It hadn't clipped her wings though. There just seemed to be some women who needed a man on her arm, and some who didn't.

Where was she? Mother, yes, reverting. She had carried a look of disapproval throughout the lunch, except, surprisingly, when Lucy spoke. Lucy's language made no concession to the older woman. If she, Sandra, had used language like that her mother would have reproached her. And her mother's dress? It was different when Daddy was alive. He'd insisted that she go to the sisters Nelson, dressmakers by appointment to the elite of Belvedere.

Those Nelson sisters were pretty scary. They'd become very grand in the end with their fine old Queenslander just down the road, full of gilded European and oriental porcelain, and large canvasses by the fashionable Australian artists of the thirties. She used to know the names. Daddy was a kind of a collector himself. Sometimes alcohol did help. She began to recall some of them, Ashton, Sir William Ashton, Fred Leist, and Hans Heysen of course. Daddy liked them but he'd liked best Norman Lindsay, all those ugly buxom nudes with hips like Amazons, lush black hair everywhere and breasts like udders. Her uncle protested when Mother had sold them after Daddy died. There'd been a heated argument. Her mother said they were vulgar.

Sandra secretly agreed with her but they had been Daddy's. It was sacrilege to sell Daddy's personal things. Mummy won.

Those sisters Nelson were ruthless but presented an appearance of censorious Calvinism. What a joke that was. Everyone knew that both of them were the mistresses of old Fred Lucas, the investor. They shared him. That's where they got their real money, from old Fred and his tips, not from running up outfits for the district. Mind you they deserved everything they could get there. Putting up with that old lecher. Everyone said it was difficult to make a business pay in Belvedere. Belvedere people knew the value of money.

Long after they left their city store, they still worked, from home, employing seamstresses who sewed their hearts out. Sweated labour, some people in the district said. They still had the sisters run up their costumes and their dresses though.

She sipped her wine and thought of the first dress the sisters had made for her. Could it be so long ago, thirty six years, 1939? Yes. She was fourteen, sweet fourteen they used to say. 'Sandra's so pretty, she's got such beautiful manners.'

The sisters Nelson, and their business at that time, were in transition from the city to their residence. The preliminary fitting was at their house. She had been overawed by the occasion. Her first evening dress, not full length of course, ballerina type with a flared skirt. That was the fashion then. Daddy usually had as much confidence in his social position and standards as Robert Menzies in his infallible political judgement. Nonetheless, in matters of taste, even though he might not personally like their choices, he would still defer to the sisters. The Nelson sisters were, for Brisbane then, special. Some of their furniture was plain and straight, fragile looking and patinated to a faded golden honey colour, Georgian she now knew. It was so different from the heavy, carved, toffee apple coloured mahogany and cedar she was used to. Daddy said it had been in their family for generations. It wasn't just the furniture and paintings the Nelson sisters had, there were also the tapestries, frames that should have been wrong but were somehow perfect for the pictures they contained. She remembered best their Ashton snowscapes that she was surprised to learn were painted in the Australian Alps. They looked so European. The pictures were all bright and light, not modern of course, but they seemed so, so tasteful.

The Nelson sisters didn't act like dressmakers. They could have been mistresses of the Universe. Now where did that come from, rather clever that? Then she vaguely recalled reading it in a book she couldn't finish, set in New York about an investor or something like that who got himself into some dreadful trouble with some negroes and the legal system. He called himself, a Master of the Universe. It was something about a bonfire. She couldn't remember the name. Now why had she thought of it at all? Free association, the Nelson sisters, their lover an investor, a book about someone involved in the investment business. The mind, she had discovered late, was a strange and unpredictable apparatus.

She stood up, deliberately careful to avoid standing on old Inkie. She was distressed to see spots of blood on her skirt. She had quite forgotten about her poor finger. She refilled her glass. Inkie groaned as she resumed her seat. It was quite dark now. From the verandah, without even getting out of her chair she could see the lights of the container port at the mouth of the river. She could also see the street lights running down the hill to Equitation Road.

Belvedere was small in area. People kept on trying to extend it like arriveste vigneurs in the champagne district of France. A newcomer would buy a house just outside its undeclared but well understood precincts and then would give his address as Belvedere. That never washed. Yes, the mailman might still deliver his letters but the cognoscenti knew that he was not, and would never be a Belvedere man.

Belvedere was not just a suburb. It was an enclave of about twenty to thirty blocks, bounded by streets with English names: Thirlmere, York, Spring, Lincoln, Bayswater, Durban, Beattie and Conan. The best street was Thirlmere where Sandra had lived almost all of her life. It ran up from Equitation Street to an eminence that looked towards the sea. It was favoured by cool breezes whose only disadvantage were the swarms of mosquitoes they carried in the hot humid months of January and February. The soil was fertile and produced vivid and luxuriant purple jacarandas, infernal red and purple bougainvilleas and flaring red poincianas.

Belvedere was only seven kilometres by road to the centre of the city. One corner of it extended to the river where the broadest reach occasionally harboured grand ocean liners. However, you needed care when you approached the river. That was the only point of ambiguity, a point at which the anointed of the city might, if they were not careful, rub shoulders with waterside workers, or even encounter foreign looking sailors from unkempt cargo hulks.

Thirlmere Street was well away from the danger spot. Thirlmere Street stood at the centre of the enclave, and as with a walled area of an ancient city, within walking distance of the best churches, the best schools, and, axiomatically, the best people.

People were out walking. How fashionable that had become. She looked to check whether any lights were on. That was one of Belvedere's few faults. People did tend to drop in unannounced. She was guilty of that too. She tiptoed—why was she tiptoeing—to the kitchen to turn off the light there. 'Might as well top up, while I'm here.' She refilled her glass, surprised that the bottle was below the halfway line. She made a ceremony of squeezing the mangled cork back into the neck. 'That was it then, no more until Jack comes home.'

Back in her chair she asked herself where she was. 'Free association' and they used to say she wasn't bright. 'Free association' wasn't the sort of expression the ignorant used. But before that? Yes, the Nelson sisters and her first dress.

She had resisted, but her mother had insisted on the yellow, mustard more like. Totally unsuitable, repellent, hideous colour. The Nelson sisters thought so and said so. Mother, though, despite that superficial appearance of hesitancy, was as unbendable as a bar of iron when she made up her mind. The sisters weren't used to being contradicted on matters of taste. That haughty indifference of the superior tradesperson whether you patronized them or not didn't impress Mother. So it had been the mustard. Had she known then what she knew now, she wouldn't have been worried at all. Little did she know then the awe that a silken clad, scented, outwardly assured, high heeled, lustrous haired, soft, curved young woman could inspire in adolescent youths.

Thirty-six years. Where had they all gone? Was she becoming a philosopher? It was the wine. What was it that someone, yes Lionel, the witty Lionel had told them at that dinner party the other night? Churchill had defended his alcoholism by saying he could guarantee that he'd taken more out of alcohol than it had taken out of him. That was pretty good. 'He'd lived almost forever hadn't he?'

Her glass was finished. Her resolve wobbled a little but prevailed, as much because of the effort of getting up as of purpose. She closed her eyes but she didn't sleep. Alcohol didn't always make her sleepy. It sometimes set her mind off, sending her back down avenues and byways that she'd forgotten all about. Thinking of the past could make her sad, not always though. Tonight it was nice to think about that first dance.

It wasn't only the effect of young pubescent female flesh upon adolescent youths that made the mustard colour of her dress irrelevant. By no means was hers the brightest. Pastels must have been out of fashion. The colours were primary ones, across the spectrum. One girl wore purple, another cerise, and a red-headed girl—what was her name—even wore bright orange. They must have looked like a bunch of dancing jelly beans.

It had been fun though. God she'd been nervous. Lucy said no one would have guessed she was nervous. Daddy's training again. And talk about supervision. You weren't allowed to go to the lavatory without a chaperone. She giggled to herself at the thought. Not such a lot had changed. The rules of the Stradbroke Club, the exclusive women's club in Brisbane, laid down that a member must always accompany a non-member to the lavatory. Why, frightened someone might knock off the soap? She giggled again.

The rules had been strict for dances. Parents and teachers were ceaselessly vigilant to intercept a hurried assignation in the dark. What a joke that would be today. Her own children refused to believe anyone could ever have taken those sorts of rules seriously.

At first their only dancing lessons were at the school, given by the Music mistress. There were no boys. The danced with other girls, blushing and imagining boys on their arms.

She had stood there in the mustard monstrosity, pins everywhere, while her mother flittered around. The Nelson sisters walked with firm strides. They were like a tag team exchanging pins and words but never getting in each other's way.

All the girls at school knew about them, or thought they did. Could it be true that a man could have two sisters as mistresses, at the same time? How was it that Lucas could get away with one mistress, let alone two? In books the mistress always lived on the other side of town. Belvedere, back then, and old Lucas unashamedly kept them both in their house on the hill in the heart of the suburb. At school the girls almost became delirious over their speculations about the sexual mechanics of the dual relationship. Today Sandra, yes, she and all of her friends, would simply pass it off as a threesome as if it were the most natural thing in the world.

When the fitting was almost finished, Lucas had turned up. He was dressed in a well-cut summer suit and incongruously wore a black beret as if he were an artist from Montmartre. Her mother spoke politely to him as Sandra changed in the other room. What was their secret, those Nelson sisters? They were fleshy and notorious. But they got away with it, as did Lucas, she reminded herself. Why hadn't there been a scandal? And when Mrs Lucas was alive why hadn't she tried to do something about it? The secrets of a marriage. Who really knew anything about anyone else?

It was the custom those days. Her mother and her mother's cousin Merle, from whom she took her second name, dressed her as if she were a sacrificial virgin. How they kept their double standards in those days. Rouge, powder, perfume, nylons, silk, high heels, satin underclothing, and a dress tightly drawn against rounding breasts and straining thighs. Having put her in this man trap she was enjoined, on pain of death, disinheritance and expulsion not to allow any boy to get closer to her than dancing distance, let alone to touch any forbidden places. First time dressed as adults, they had entered the hall trying to keep their eyes downcast. What a joke that had been.

Sandra dozed off with Inkie beside her lying contentedly on his back and growling occasionally in a dream of some long lost, probably imagined, engagement. Belvedere was closing in on itself, finally battening down for the night. Husbands were home now, walks finished, porch lights turned off, cars garaged and locked, and watchdogs turned loose behind high fences.

She woke up in fright. Where was Jack? Her right wrist felt sore. She had been leaning her weight against it, leaving it caught between her hip and the cane armrest of the chair. She was disoriented. What was the time? She held her arm up and peered at her wristwatch. Why weren't watch-faces luminous the way they used to be? Eight thirty, where was Jack? Her throat was as dry as, what was it Lionel said, as an Arab's armpit. Naughty Lionel. It was only in their circle you could get away with a remark like that today.

With great resolve she stood up, cleverly as she told herself, avoiding Inkie, as she did so. She went to the kitchen cabinet, selected a glass, tottered to the refrigerator, opened a bottle of Perrier and poured herself some water. She retreated to her chair, pleased with herself for resisting more wine. The mineral water prickled her tongue.

She supposed she should be worried about Jack. Five years ago, as recently as two years ago, he would at least have gone through the form of telephoning. Had it rung she would have wakened. Her hearing was very good and she was a great user of the telephone. The children said she never heard anything unless it suited her but she always heard the phone. No, Jack hadn't called.

Whenever she went out to lunch things seemed to go wrong. She went to lunch a great deal these days. For her group there were really only three possibilities now, lunch, golf or bridge. She had tried bridge. They were so precious about their bridge. They had said lots of things about Sandra over the years but no one had ever said she was competitive. The bridge table had struck her as a forum for failed hopes and unrealized ambitions. It was silly, she had thought, for serious middle-aged women to set such store by the chance of a coloured card. Besides, she had often found herself the object of the fury of her partner. She and bridge had parted company for good.

There had been times when she had enjoyed golf. Rarely, she played a round of nine holes on a weekday, without a partner or a caddy. Daddy had been a good golfer. In the end she had decided that regular golf was not for her though. It was the ritual and the maleness of it all that repelled her. The women who played had such muscular arms and wore shoes in the brogue style with sprigs and thick-fringed tongues. They spoke in loud voices and were as brown as Indians.

So she drifted into the luncheon set. That was another thing about Belvedere, whichever set you chose, you would always find people, girls you'd known from school, just as you'd see their husbands, if you went to the city, at other tables massaging clients, and occasionally, if they were stupid or intentionally making a public declaration, at a table for two with a young blonde or brunette doting on their every word. Thank God Jack generally spared her public humiliations. How long?

Now that she had woken up and her eyes accustomed to the dark she could see clearly along the length of the verandah. It was about twelve-foot wide and floored with Tasmanian oak. Here on the eastern side it took particular punishment from the sub-tropical morning sun. She waxed it herself, every month, rejecting the hard plastic spray polish Mrs Simpson her cleaning lady tried to press on her.

She could just make out the colours of the velvety orchids suspended from the ceiling. There was a new moon, riding high just below the line of the guttering of the roof. It was white as face powder and she could see the soft glow of the flowering jacarandas clearly in its light. The jacarandas flourished at examination time in Brisbane. Put away your racquets and your bats and your dancing shoes, they used to say, when the purple and mauve flowers bloom. Now's the time for study. It was different today with their semester system which she didn't fully understand. Daddy had saved her much of that, of examinations and worries about studying and passing and graduating. Daddy held clear views about the role of women. 'I don't want my daughter vexed by all of that,' he would say. 'They're enough blue stockings in this world as it is.'

The point with Daddy was that he was infallible. Sandra accepted his word on everything. She wasn't the only one. His friends always seemed to agree with his opinions.

She looked at her watch. It was nine o'clock. Where had the last three hours gone? Her mouth was dry again and she could smell sour wine on her breath. She regarded herself as a fastidious woman, and here she was, waking from an alcoholic slumber, foul-breathed, bloodstained, her skirt crumpled, maudlin and cold in the south-easter that had ruffled her hair in her sleep. She looked for Inkie. He had deserted her for his basket at the far end of the verandah, his nose buried in his tail and his body curled upon itself for warmth.

She was disgusted with herself. Despite everything, she would have been ashamed if Jack had come home and had to wake her, not that he hadn't done it before.

Sandra went into the bedroom. She looked at the bed where her children had been conceived, the bed where—well that wasn't something she was going to think about tonight.

The bedroom furniture was à la mode, Brisbane, circa 1936. Daddy had personally ordered it, after telling Mummy his intentions of course. He had gone where everyone in Brisbane went in those days, to Rosenstengels. He had stood up to the old man and insisted on his own choice of timber and design. Rosenstengels pressed upon their customers heavy, solid, carved furniture in oak, mission oak, they used to call it, although to Sandra it didn't look much like the mission furniture she saw in the Californian houses illustrated in *Architectural Digest* that Lucy had shown her.

No, Daddy had insisted on maple, Queensland maple. It had to be coloured and polished, of course, but not in that dreadful black mission colour. And the style—he had chosen a replica of a bedroom suite made for the visit of the Prince of Wales and installed in Yarralumba. It had turned out to be the best furniture in the house, much nicer than the heavy, carved Victorian pieces in the other rooms. Just as well their bedroom was a large room because otherwise the bed, the bedside tables, the wardrobes, the chests of drawers and her dressing table and stool wouldn't have fitted.

She went to her chest and took out a pair of fresh pyjamas, silk, like something from a Noel Coward play. Before taking off her clothes she turned on the hot tap in the shower. As the room steamed up she looked around it.

In obedience to the decorating imperative of the day, her father had somewhat reluctantly built on the verandah, immediately beside and communicating directly with their bedroom, an en-suite bathroom. It was the best he could do. A second, even a third bathroom had come to be regarded as indispensable, especially when you took into account that all those project houses in funny suburbs you'd never heard of before, like Eucalypt Close or Roseland Heights, with their second bathrooms.

So, in addition to the two bathrooms already in the house, he had commissioned the en suite. The bidet insisted upon by his wife did trouble him. He practically never mentioned a sexual matter to her in public but she knew that he thought there was something immoral about the whole arrangement.

Sandra took off her shirt, her bra and skirt, then her pants, kicking them towards the wicker clothes basket for Mrs Simpson to pick up and wash tomorrow.

As she sat on the lavatory the steam started enveloping the room. No bath for her tonight. She'd probably fall asleep in it. Before the steam became impenetrable she looked around the little room remembering her pleasure in the forays that her mother and Neil had undertaken across the city to find the pieces that were just right. Neil was such a perfectionist. Everything must be right for the period, she had lectured. 'We should try for authentic old pieces but if we can't get them, there are some places now where you can buy half-respectable reproductions.' The detail that man went into. Sandra and her mother had gone to Paddington for the catches and fittings. She'd thought of that suburb as a slum in the past. There'd certainly been some odd people around but there were also some stylish ones. She saw elegant dress shops beside smart cappuccino bars, places she hadn't dreamed existed on that side of town. And many of the houses, old wooden ones clinging to steep slopes, had been restored and painted in their original colours.

Neil said that, even though it was against his interests, he was against all this—what had he called it—gentrification. 'The unrestored houses looked more real with their peeling paint and drooping boards. And where are all the poor going to live?' That was a good one coming from him.

'You and your bloody interior decorator and his fancy boy. What am I supposed to do, keep them in genuine gold lame cloaks for life?' Her father became very angry.

The tiles had been the hardest. You could get them anywhere today, that is, reproduction. They only came to reproduce Federation style tiles after their addition. They'd had to comb second-hand shops and go to demolishers' yards. Neil wouldn't have been satisfied anyway with repro tiles even if you could have got them then. He had been like a bloodhound. They'd finally found the white ones that he wanted, not square, but rectangular, like the tiles in old butchers' shops, and black and white ones with geometrical patterns for a frieze. Yes, they'd done pretty well.

She stood up and turned on the cold tap until she had the right temperature, put on her shower cap and stepped into the bevelled-glass interior of the shower recess. How good the water felt. Already she was beginning to feel less sleepy. She soaped herself and stood under the torrent for five minutes. One of the many magazines she read had recommended banishing everything from your mind for at least five minutes each day. She did that now, quite successfully she thought.

She got out of the shower and towelled herself in front of the full length mirror. That was something else that Daddy didn't approve of. After a minute she stopped, took up another towel and wiped the steam from the mirror. At forty-nine her figure was still very good if a little less so than two years ago. She had to be honest with herself. She had aged more in the last two years than in the previous ten. But then she'd always looked young. She was just starting to catch up with time. She lightly powdered herself and washed off the last vestiges of make-up. She no longer felt sleepy. She was hungry and still thirsty. Her self-inspection was brief. She had no need to examine herself at length in the mirror. She knew what was there. She knew now, whatever the formula was, that for the present at least she had it: that men had regarded her as attractive and still did. She could see nothing remarkable about herself. She was taller than most of her generation, five feet nine, in the old measurements which were the only ones she understood, long dark amber hair, straight and lustrous, incongruously light, hazel eyes, thick eyebrows, and a long aristocratic but elegant nose, thick, firm lips, a large laughing mouth and a jaw that was a feature but not a promontory. She always stood straight, and her breasts, if only modest in size, were still firm and accentuated by her good posture. Her legs were long, shapely, but not fleshy and free entirely from any hint of varicose veins. She had small feet and high arches. She dressed well, and, these days, very simply, sometimes in long and rather shapeless dresses with sandals to show off her pretty feet. The mixture somehow added up to a cool, almost aloof but beautiful femininity.

No, she had no need to linger in front of the mirror. She dressed quickly in the clean pyjamas, slipped her feet into soft leather slippers, and wrapped a light wool dressing gown around herself. She then took three minutes to clean her teeth, methodically following her dentist's instructions.

Sandra went into the kitchen. She toasted two pieces of bread and made some tea. The moon was riding far above the roof now. She took the toast and the tea back to the verandah and sat down again in her chair.

In her childhood the picture theatres had run the same film over and over again. Her mother had always been careless about time. They would often arrive well after the film had started. They would wait, over interval, until they reached the point at which they had entered. 'This is where we came in.' It was a very unsatisfactory way to see a film but she had become used to it. These days thoughts crossed her mind in the same way. She would think of an event in her life halfway through it and then would have to go back to reconstruct the beginning.

The appointment at the house of the Nelson Sisters was not the beginning of that story. The beginning was the announcement by their form mistress that their brother school was conducting a dance for pupils of their age and that they were invited to attend. The brother school was, naturally, Daddy's old school. She instinctively knew that he would be torn when it came to deciding whether she could go. She was so young, boys today were, less, less—considerate, than they were in his day. Still it was his old school. She would be permitted to go.

An image of Daddy being obstructive and judicious flashed through her mind. Daddy in his prime. Daddy, six feet one tall, still relatively slim and vain about his figure. Daddy in a good, tailored suit: dark grey with a fine chalk stripe in winter during the daytime; in summer, lightweight wool in a sharkskin colour and texture with brogues heightened by an occasional application of ox blood polish to the colour of old Cuban mahogany, Daddy in a tweed sports jacket and flannel trousers at the weekend. Daddy confidently driving his car and giving them the benefit of his opinions on the road system, the government, the economy and women drivers as he aggressively overtook a grey-haired 'little old lady' in a Morris Minor.

Earlier Daddy had been an even more striking figure. Daddy had been a war-time soldier, a handsome, muscular, brown, khaki-clad figure, mentioned in despatches, effortlessly able to hold his little girl high in the air when he marched afterwards on Anzac Day.

Daddy had at first been of the considered opinion that Sandra was too young to go dancing at night. She had fought with him over the right to have outside dancing lessons. Today girls not much older seemed to fight over everything else, harassment, equal opportunity, abortion and politics. A fight over a mere dance should be unthinkable. If she thought about it too much now she would become giddy again.

Her first cause had been the right to go to Gwen and Mark Linton's dancing academy where many of her friends and the other girls from Belvedere went. Gwen and Mark Linton. It sounded rather like Marge and Gower Champion dancing to 'Life upon the Wicked Stage ain't what, ain't what it used to be…?' She was reminded of that graceful, energetic couple dancing across the deck in 'Showboat'. What a film that had been, hinting at dark infidelities, but all coming right in the end for everybody except Ava Gardner. She had seen it, when? It must have been the year before the dance.

Gwen and Mark were no Marge and Gower Champion. Mark was a tall cadaverous man who danced with precision and utter joylessness. Gwen, on the other hand, décolletaged, was enthusiastic and prone to snuggle up a little too closely to the older boys. The air-conditioning was unreliable and the ruder boys complained about Gwen's body odour.

For all that, the academy was an exciting place. It wasn't frequented just by the boys from the brother school. The business depended on numbers rather than on a few elite pupils (as some saw themselves), so that Gwen and Mark charged a small price to encourage adolescents to come from all quarters of the city. This had alarmed Daddy. He had, however, ultimately yielded because the classes were in daylight hours, Tuesdays and Thursdays after school. The preferred class was the later one at four thirty, because it was attended by the boys who'd had to train for sport before learning to dance. 'Jocks', they would call them today. All those American expressions. There used to be a flutter of excitement when they arrived, red faced from their exertions and their warm showers, bringing with them a kind of adult carnality that the conscies couldn't project. 'Conscies'. She hadn't used or even thought that word for years. In books they'd call them swats. An English word from English comics and stories. She wasn't quite Americanised yet.

The breeze was becoming stronger, a wind almost. She was warm now wrapped in her dressing gown after her shower, and not even slightly sleepy. She returned to reverie, the place where she spent so much of her time now.

She very quickly learned all the popular dances at the Academy, the Jolly Miller, the Pride of Erin, the Foxtrot, the Quickstep and the Waltz. Old Mark thought she had a real aptitude for ballroom dancing. He began to teach her the rumba and the Tango. Daddy put a stop to that when he arrived early to pick her up one afternoon. Unnoticed, he had watched from the side door as the totally asexual Mark had carefully inserted his knee between her dancing thighs and had leaned over her as she arched her back towards the floor in the climatic of the sensual Argentinean rhythm. Daddy had come close to forbidding any further attendance. By promising to abandon South America, forever, as she told the story to her friends, she persuaded him to let her continue.

Jack was one of the jocks. 'Jocks.' Now where did she first get that? In what book or film had she seen or heard the word? Certainly not an English one. He didn't pay her any attention at the Academy. But Daniel, Dan, was no jock not in those days, or at least not in the conventional sense in which the word was used. They might well call him a business jock today, or whatever higher order of male title his achievements demanded. The most striking thing about him then, and later, was his intensity. On his second day he had come up to her at the Academy. He was wearing the undistinguished uniform of Morcom High, a state school on the outer marches of the southern side of the city. Usually the few state high boys who came to the classes were afraid to approach the girls from the private schools. If the girls didn't make the state school boys uncomfortable, pretty soon one of their private boys' school protectors would, and usually in a threatening way.

He was not a boy to be easily deterred. Dan Bencham was tall at fifteen, five feet ten high and, until he danced, a little on the awkward side. He never grew an inch after fifteen. He was thin, quiet, black haired and black browed with a jutting jaw, wide dark eyes and a look of determination. Still it must have taken quite a lot of courage for him to approach her.

Her feelings about such a boy were always going to be coloured by her upbringing and her associations. She reproached herself for being surprised by his forthrightness, and over cleanliness and neatness. He had a scrubbed look. Strange that. She had been told that she too always looked wholesomely clean, as if she had just stepped out of an antiseptic bath. All that business about opposites attracting. They'd had wholesomeness in common, more fools they. Everything else, though, was then polarized.

She hesitantly agreed to dance with him. It was a waltz and old Mark Linton looked approvingly on as they moved in harmony to the repetitive Strauss music. She had accepted as much out of an uncertainty as to how to refuse, as a desire to be his partner. But as she danced she appreciated that there were a subtlety and a strength about his movements, quite different from the hardness and roughness of the sportsmen.

So on that day they danced together several times until a boy from Daddy's old school, the Anglican College, St Mark's, cut in. Dan had yielded, reluctantly, out of good manners only.

During the war, as a little girl, her mother had explained, only American Negro servicemen were confined to the south bank of the Brisbane River. They were in deep trouble if they crossed the bridge. Sandra's school days were a little like that. High School boys ought not cross the great social divide. Catholic boys didn't consort with protestant girls and vice versa. She felt guilty then for dancing repeatedly with Daniel, Dan.

It was that sort of thing that Lucy had talked about at lunch. 'I can't believe how restricted it was: everything; religion, schools, suburbs, colour, sex and money. The last is the same though, money. That's important, but the rest …'

Helen Kent had taken it up. 'What d'you mean about sex, about a division there on social grounds?'

'That's exactly what I do mean. Just think of the opportunities we missed. Do you remember your wedding night? My God I do. Well, I'm not going to talk about it, that's the point, nothing much to talk about. Let me say this though. I wish we'd had more of what our children have.' Sometimes it was difficult to know whether Lucy was serious.

There had followed the usual inconclusive debate. Sandra had kept out of it. She usually did nowadays. They always covered the same territory, what might have been, what it was then and was now for their children, whether, like their marriages, it was better or worse. There had been a time when she had been an enthusiastic participant in these discussions. That was part of the trouble. She had gone AWOL with the wine. It wasn't the first time that had happened either.

Her tea had long since cooled and she had lost track of the time again. The suburb was deathly quiet now except for the sound of the wind that was still strengthening and the rustling of the trees. Even Inkie had ceased to grunt and grumble in his basket.

Her watch was inside. She went to get it and noted it was eleven o'clock. Where the hell was Jack? Who cared? She cared. Did she care?

Jack, Jack Rentle was an obstetrician stroke gynaecologist, the Peter Pan of the profession his contemporaries called him. A number of his professional colleagues had died, retired or become part-time consultants. Not Jack. He wasn't going to lie down. He thrived, he said, and his good health proved it, on the early and the late calls out, the difficult births and the Caesars. The mothers and the grateful fathers extolled his efforts. There were a few fathers who might have done well to be less grateful.

It was unlike him not to call if he was to be as late as this. That was a matter of form he did observe. Was this some kind of silent declaration, no letter, no telegram, no call, no word, no hope? It was possible that there might be a particularly difficult labour. But what about the adoring theatre sisters? They'd swim in molten lava for him. Surely he could have asked one of them to slip out to call her.

'It's not as if I'm here waiting powdered and perfumed to welcome him,' she conceded. 'Perhaps I've overdone it a bit lately.' Still, when he did come home he'd been happy enough to join her drinking the wine, up to two bottles some nights except for an inch or two left, a vouchsafe to moderation in which neither of them really believed.

She told herself she was being ridiculous. Thinking too much was bad for anyone.

She took her cup into the kitchen and rinsed it. She surveyed the room to make sure everything was in order. It had been refitted three years ago when the suburb had been swept by the new fad of Thai cooking. As their children forsook the kitchen for the takeaways and the bistros, the local mothers returned to their kitchens armed with coffee-table recipe books and primed to stir and marinate by the local cooking schools.

For the first time it struck her how incongruous this space-age kitchen contrasted with the rest of the house (except for the en suite). The walls on three sides had been clad with gleaming stainless steel and the benches were thick black Belgian granite. The stove looked as if you could navigate it to Mars, and the refrigerator, microwave, dishwasher and the hand-held appliances were of the same rocket ship design. It ought to look streamlined. Her mind still reeled at the expense of it, eighty-five thousand. Much more, Jack had shouted, than the fit-out and equipment for his surgery. She'd thought herself clever when she'd responded, 'Babies have been coming into the world since the beginning of time, we've only been cooking with gas and electricity for less than a hundred years.'

Jack didn't have much of a sense of humour these days. Come to think of it he'd never had much of a sense of humour other than about physical things, slapstick things. That was the right way to put it, slapstick: a half-drunk friend forgetting where he'd parked his car and trying to unlock a stranger's vehicle, and car chases in old silent movies. But then she wasn't so clever, she acknowledged, as to be a wit like Lucy. When Lucy spoke in that deadpan way, clearly articulating the most filthy jokes, the men swarmed around and laughed and laughed. Lucy was one of the few women she knew who were able to be scathing and sexy at the same time. Once Sandra had tried to crack a joke when Jack was straining and thrusting above her, and for a moment she had thought he would strike her. He didn't, but subsided into detumescence.

She was fiddling now, re-hanging a tea towel, wiping down the sink, squaring up some tablemats for the morning. The morning. What was she doing tomorrow? In the morning when she woke she would decide upon a programme with a clear head. Better to do that then.

She thought of the pile of books on the bedside table on her side of the bed. No, not tonight.

Sandra had become a reader, a late reader. Books were now a consolation. She often wished she had had a disciplined education in what to read. Now, all she could do was read the reviews, listen closely when her children's friends spoke of the books they were reading, and browse through the bookshops. Reading and dreaming and drinking. These had become her life. She deliberately omitted lunching. No, she would not read tonight.

She cleaned her teeth again and broke a Mogadon in two, taking half with a sip of water. She was in a drugged sleep when an hour later Jack arrived home, undressed and slipped into bed, being careful not to touch her as he rolled over to sleep.

Chapter 2
Night Reflections

Sandra always dreamed when she took a sleeping pill. She sometimes thought that her dreams were the most logical part of her life. Bizarre events that happened in her dreams somehow still seemed to occur in an orderly way.

It was a month before her wedding, twenty-nine years ago. The Nelson sisters were giving her the last fitting. Because of the colour of her hair she had insisted on Ivory satin. Her mother had argued white lace but Sandra had learnt to stand up to her. The bridesmaids were all present for their fittings: Lucy, Prudence and Kath. What an absurd business it had all been, the fittings, the shoes, the going away dress, the other honeymoon clothes, the presents list at Rowles who proudly proclaimed that they were the vice regal jewellers and the leading purveyors of crystal, silver and porcelain.

There had been bickering about the guest list, not, as so often happened, between the respective families, but between her mother and her father.

So far her dream was running like a perfectly synchronized film reel. She could hear her father's loud voice. It sounded condescending in her dream, like real life. He was lecturing her mother.

'Dawn, we simply cannot have that team of camp followers you call relatives.' He flicked the ash from his cigar as he spoke.' You never see them these days anyway.'

'Through no fault of mine.'

'That's quite right. They obviously feel uncomfortable here. I don't think they'd even want to come to the wedding. It would be too grand for them, the Archbishop, the Cathedral. No, I don't think they'd want to come over here.' He made the journey from Blue Field on the south side, to Belvedere on the north sound like the crossing of the Limpopo in flood.

Sandra woke up. She knew that notwithstanding the sleeping tablet, it would be some hours before she would fall asleep again. God how she hated not being able to sleep. She could sense her heart palpitating. Jack in that robust way in which doctors discuss family fears and illness told her not to be stupid, she had a heart as strong and as regular as a Melbourne Cup winner. She lay in the silent dark only gradually becoming aware of Jack's steady breathing beside her. He would, she knew, be naked as always, when he slept. That nakedness didn't have much to do with her these nights. 'Much! Nothing at all.'

Her mother could be a very determined woman. Sandra came to know that she wasn't just eccentric, she was also shrewd, much more shrewd than Daddy. She used to tell herself she'd lost out on the genetic lottery by inheriting her father's genes. He always managed to look so wise. People had deferred to him. She now knew that they did because he was rich and socially confident but not clever.

She turned to lie on her back. She hadn't thought of the wedding and what had happened before it for a long time. How ridiculous for civilized people to carry on that way. It was all very well for primitive people to bring the bride dressed and adorned like a fatted female calf to the slaughter, but for so-called sophisticated people in the nineteen century?

But they still did it, and it was more unbelievable today that they would go through the hypocrisy of the white dress and the presents' list. They'd all lived together beforehand, now, had set up home and already started up the treadmill. 'Was it a treadmill? Where had that word come from?' Jack breathed on easily beside her. 'What a constitution the bastard has.' He had been up at six o'clock in the morning to do his rounds. And then he would have attended some confinements during the day, seen patients in his surgery, and afterwards, no doubt, almost fucked his latest female registrar to death.

She asked herself whether she cared. As she told herself she didn't, she could feel the tears on her neck. For a moment she thought of throwing the bed clothes off, jumping out of bed, turning on the lights, shouting at him that she knew, knew everything, of packing, and telling him coolly as she walked out the door that she'd send for the rest, and he'd be hearing from her lawyers.

Several of her friends had done just that, or something like it. Lucy had been the first but then it was easy for Lucy, she had intelligence and an energy and skill that she'd been able to turn into a thriving business.

Sandra wiped her cheeks and thought again of her wedding.

Her father had strongly encouraged the match. The Rentles were old Belvedere stock. She suppressed the giggle, out of habit. On no account should Jack be woken unless it was for a call out. 'Old Belvedere stock.' There was practically nobody who'd lived in this town for more than three generations, Belvedere or elsewhere, and if they had their forebears were almost certainly convicts.

The Rentles didn't work. They owned property, some blocks of shops, a small city building called Rentle House, and a share of a sheep station outside Longreach. Among some people, the last gave them a special cachet. In social circles, then, to be a doctor, a barrister, preferably a Queen's Counsel, an architect, a stockbroker, or a very senior bank officer, was to be highly respectable and acceptable. Only a member of the judiciary however could trump a man with long connections with a sheep station, particularly one with a well-known name like the Rentles' place, 'Rosalind Plains', named after the wife of the Rentle who had first taken up the selection seventy years before. The name and the connexion stood them in good stead although imprudently large families and a failure to observe the rules of primogeniture had heavily diluted Jack's father's share in the property.

Attitudes to sheep farmers, that's what they were, although it was permissible only to call them graziers, had changed a great deal too. In the past, at Christmas time, or during Show week, the city outsiders would pore over the social pages to read of the graziers' holiday revels at Surfers Paradise, and to look at the photographs of the beautifully gowned daughters at the Show Balls, of which there seemed so many. Two or three only were the special ones to attend though. God and a few insiders only knew why. They were just further occasions for the boys to get boorishly drunk wearing hired tails and stiff white waistcoats that softened as the night grew late.

It was the law that alcohol could not be served, or even brought into a place, where a dance was being conducted. Like prohibition in America it acted as an irresistible inducement for young people to get as drunk as they could, initially at pre-Ball parties in hotels, and then to carry leather bags full of spirits to the dances themselves. During Show week the law was quite unenforceable. She remembered one particularly unpleasant ball at the city hall at which broken glass crumpled under her sandaled feet as she had slipped and stumbled in the sea of spilt liquor that covered the dance floor in a shallow pool.

She turned to the luminous clock on the bedside table. It was only two thirty. She tried to compose herself for sleep. The images kept coming.

At lunch today Lucy had described the period between her engagement and marriage as a phoney war. At Sandra's question Lucy explained: the interlude between the declaration of war by Hitler and the invasion of France. Sandra had been ashamed that she had had to ask the question.

'Everybody, all the world leaders and the armies were standing off, waiting for someone else to make the first move. People lulled themselves into a false sense of security. They thought that Hitler might call the war off.'

'We didn't want our marriages called off. Anyway it's a bit thick to compare marriage with war.'

'Speak for yourself, lady,' Lucy had replied. 'To handle Alex I needed a vocabulary like a nuclear arsenal, and I didn't have it … then. We were like, I was about to say, soldiers, going to war. No, we were more like conscripts, compulsorily enrolled in marriage by our teachers, our parents and society itself.'

At that point Kath intervened. Kath claimed to be happily married. Sometimes after they had finished the first bottle of wine Lucy would begin to bait her.

'So what's your Bill been up to lately, promised to take you to Switzerland for skiing instead of that golf holiday you've done every Christmas since your honeymoon?'

Kath objected to anyone calling her husband Bill. 'William and I haven't decided yet. We'll talk it over like we've done every year.'

'And Bill will reach the same decision he's reached every year for the last twenty five or so. Kath, why don't you wake up to yourself? Put a stop sign up when he comes near you and don't listen to a thing he says.'

By the time that the second bottle of wine was empty and Sandra's mother was safely dispatched to her retirement village, the gloves were, as always, right off. As Sandra reflected on lunch she thought of the expression 'gloves off' that had passed through her mind. Even the language was the language of the men's locker room. Who was that writer Lucy was always talking about, Marilyn … Marilyn French? That was it and her book was, The Women's Room. Well, Lucy and Marilyn French, whoever she thought she was, could have their women's room. It didn't sound like much of a place to her, not even tonight. Kath had read the book, in secret almost, and was ready to attack Lucy about it.

'I'm beginning to wonder about you, Lucy.'

'What are you talking about?'

'The way you're always going on about Marilyn French, her book, The Women's Room. All those bad men, worse than any we know. The real thing is, it's full of lesbianism. Do you like that Lucy? Are you a lesbian?'

Lucy had smiled a deliberately secretive smile. 'I thought you'd never ask Kathy my dear.'

Kath was speechless. If it hadn't been for the wine and curiosity she might have flounced out. She found some words. 'That's, that's disgusting. To think, after all this time.'

Lucy began to laugh, that rich loud deep laugh that drew men around her like thirsty hunters around a waterhole. 'Don't worry old thing, it's not an invitation. No, your old girlfriend hasn't gone over. I only batted for the other side once.'

Sandra remarked to herself, male imagery again. She really was becoming more perceptive. Lucy's confession meant the end of argument for that day. They pushed her to tell them about it. Who was it? When, why? Was it long ago? Finally, hearing herself ask the question with surprise, Sandra said, 'What was it like?'

‘Long on foreplay, short on consummation?’

Kath had daringly observed, ‘Sometimes I wouldn’t mind some of that myself.’

‘Not with a woman, you wouldn’t,’ Lucy had replied. ‘Somehow heavy breathing’s only convincing when it’s done by a man.’

‘When, where?’ Sandra pressed her.

‘It was a long time ago, after Alex left for the first time. I went on a cruise, do you remember that? To the islands, an expensive cruise on that American ship full of facially uplifted widows and check-trousered octogenarians. There was another woman who had made the same mistake as I had of thinking she might meet some interesting men who wouldn’t need a block and tackle to get it up. We used to sit together drinking after dinner while the old people played a rubber or two of bridge as a bedtime treat, and afterwards when they were all tucked into bed at nine o’clock. One night we literally fell into my bed together. Both utterly and irredeemably pissed of course. We only went into my cabin because it was the closer and we couldn’t have walked any further anyway. We were rolling around laughing and she accidentally touched me on the breast. I then put my hand between her legs and she did the same to me. One thing led to another. Next morning we agreed it hadn’t been a success. First and last time for her, she said, as it was for me. No Kath, the book’s not just about that, it’s about getting on the front foot.’ Male imagery again, the language of the playing fields, Sandra thought proudly to herself.

That was the high point of the lunch which meandered on until half-past three. They had been making a habit of being the last in the restaurant after lunch. When they did rise, Sandra, who had vowed last time that she wouldn’t do it again, silently counted the bottles, forgetting the complementary Drambuie liqueur the proprietor had urged upon them, with their coffee.

Outside, the sunlight was unusually bright. Sandra put on her Palomo Picasso sunglasses and said she might do a little shopping before she went home. The truth was she knew that it would be unsafe for her to drive the mere mile and a half to her house. She would walk it off, she told herself.

It was only in recent times that a dress or shoe or gift shop had been opened in the suburb. Previously the only storekeepers were the greengrocers, grocers and butchers who appealed to the vanity of their customers by their highly respectful manner of address that masked their exorbitant prices. Little did the customers know how they talked about them behind their backs, about the conflict between their parsimony and their snobbery. 'She never buys more than half a pound of steak at a time and makes me cut off all the fat before I weigh it. Thank God she's too mean to drive to the next suburb to compare their prices with mine.' The shopkeepers would swap war stories about their impossible demands for the best when they gave their dinner parties. 'Dinner parties. I don't know why they don't all live in a commune together. They might as well. Dropping into and out of each other's houses ...'

'And beds,' the greengrocer would interpolate.

Sandra walked very carefully along the footpath from the restaurant to the little shopping centre. There was, of course, the inevitable gift shop, with gift paper as much per metre as a cheap summer dress, hand-knitted sweaters, incense candles, greeting cards, soaps, somewhat amateurish craft pottery, and silver-plated spoons with handles wrought in the shape of lyre birds and kangaroos. It was not a very interesting shop but it was, after all, the gift shop for the suburb. Loyalties must be observed. There were hundreds of people all over the world who had received as Christmas presents or tokens of appreciation for a short stay, a piece of the silver plate, or a mottled pottery biscuit jar from their premises.

She had felt a little wobbly at the time. Then she had tottered into 'Claire's'. Sandra liked Clare. Sandra wasn't sure Claire was in. She was unable to see her, lurking behind a reduced, previously inflated rack of winter fashions. Claire was immediately sympathetic when she saw Sandra. She pulled out a chair and sent her assistant Rose into the back room to make tea which was, Sandra decided as she sat down, a sound idea. It was one of the good things about Claire that, although you knew she was really trying to sell you something, even if you didn't buy, she would still treat you as a valued customer.

Sandra would have been horrified if she had known what was passing through Claire's mind. Claire was tall woman with hair dyed unashamedly bright red. Her lined face showed that life had taken its toll on her. Her attitude proclaimed it was she who would be making the decisions in the future rather than having them imposed on her. Poor spoilt, no, not rich girl, or rather not girl anymore, although there was still something disarmingly young about Mrs Rentle—No, poor, spoilt, slightly stupid, slightly rich, snobbish Mrs Rentle. A nice woman, adrift, victim of her upbringing, struggling to get away from it all. More to be pitied than disliked. It was true that as a dress shop proprietor, although she never received the confidences of a hairdresser, she still had a pretty good idea of what was going on, and you'd have to be blind not to know how Jack Rentle was going on. And look at her. Sandra Rentle. She must be fifty but she didn't look it, not just yet; still attractive, beautiful even, some men would say, dressed in her linen skirt, simple shirt, leather belt and expensive sandals. Claire reflected how elegant such a simple look could be. However, at the same time as she concealed her disdain, she resented that fate required her to bend to these women.

Rose brought out the tea, camomile to soothe Sandra who had only bought perhaps three or four items in the last two years. 'They really were a useless lot, lunching, gossiping, dressing, gossiping and drinking. She had little time for them, except, inexplicably for Sandra. Snob that she was, she was still kind. She remembered one day when the little Greek boy, son of the local fruiterer, had fallen off his bicycle and cracked his skull and grazed his knees, how Sandra had left her group of friends and rushed over, using her scented handkerchief to wipe the blood away, soothing the boy and helping carry him into his father's shop, heedless of the staining of her dress.

Sandra drank the tea gratefully and moved on. Her car was in the car park in front of the newsagent. As she carefully manoeuvred herself into the driving seat, she noticed a billboard that stated in large letters, 'Bencham Takeover to Succeed'. Her head reeled as she read it.

And her head reeled again now, in bed, as she remembered reading it. They said she had no intellectual discipline. No doubt they were right. But if your mind brought various strands together and placed them all in context, was that, she asked herself, illogical?

She had been recalling the period of the 'phoney war' as Lucy insisted on calling it. There had been that curious, now obsolescent ritual of a shower tea. Someone had said its purpose was to provide an occasion for the giving of presents to enable the new bride to give afternoon teas for her friends: others said it was an occasion for guests to give the prospective bride tea towels and other like presents to enable her to run an efficient kitchen. Whatever the purpose, lost as it may have been in its distant bourgeois origins, it had been, Sandra recalled, a singularly boring event. Present had been her mother, all of her bridesmaids, Mummy's 'Blue Hill sisters', as her father called them, Daddy's formidable sisters, some school friends, and the women of Jack's family. They brought gifts, mostly useless, and sometimes duplicated, to be excessively gushed over. All of this she had done perfectly, much inspired by the example of those who had gone before.

Finally she had been able to get away. She had walked down the long foyer of Rowe's, the tea-house where the tea had been given. Rowe's was both a restaurant and tea-house, furnished and finished in Tudor imitation-oak panelling in an acceptably antipodean way that no one mocked. The fare was plain and filling at mealtimes, and the afternoon tea consisted of perfect triangular sandwiches of ham or tinned asparagus, with China tea served by waitresses in black crepe dresses, stockings, white aprons and waitresses' caps. It was a responsible, respectable, solemn place, indeed, the place. Sandra smiled to herself again. Why did she return to the licensing laws? Only three restaurants in the city had been granted licenses to serve liquor. Rowe's had not even applied.

Rowe's Restaurant was in Edward Street, next to the men's wear store named Rothwell's, then owned by a small public company, latterly much discredited by having its shell taken over by a Western Australian entrepreneur, converted into a merchant bank and bankrupted, events all then totally unforeseeable. Edward Street was the hub of Brisbane mercantile activity, with insurance companies, oil companies or banks on all of its corners, and solicitors and accountants on the upper floors of most of the buildings.

Sandra had made her excuses and left her mother and mother-in-law to gather up the pre-bridal offerings, pleading a longstanding dental appointment that she had already decided to miss. It was cloudy when she came out on to the footpath. She was already short-sighted and it was only when she almost bumped into him that she recognized Daniel Bencham: Dan Bencham in his white shirt, sombre navy tie and Rothwell's charcoal, fifty-fifty suit. That's how they advertised them: fifty per cent wool and fifty per cent synthetic. They conducted an advertising campaign featuring photographs of two men, oh so sophisticated, in their early thirties, dressed in Panama hats and Rothwell's suits, described as Mr Porous and Mr Style, the height of young executive fashion.

Daddy refused to shop at Rothwell's. Once Sandra had bought him a tie there. He had contemptuously looked at the label, and lied that it was just what he needed. He never wore it, and quietly told her mother to give it to the gardener. Rothwell's was not even for the nouveau riche, he confided later. It was the sort of place where young men, clerks mostly, who would have been sent to India or Africa in the old days, would go beforehand to be pretentiously and cheaply outfitted. Not all of Daddy's pronouncements made complete sense.

Dan paused and stared at her. 'Sandra,' he continued to stare at her. 'You look, look …' Shyness overwhelmed him. He tried again. 'You look beautiful.' The incongruity of the words and the passion with which he spoke them, with his plain accountant's clothes, and his shy but still intense manner stopped her in her tracks. He stood perfectly still, openly, wondrously admiring her. The shoppers and business people had to step around them to pass by.

It was as if that last unhappy meeting had never taken place.

'Hullo Dan. What are you doing in Edward Street, taking time off on a Thursday afternoon?' She was aware that she was pleased to see him. He ignored the question, still too shocked and excited by the encounter to reply.

'I spoke to you. Didn't you hear me?'

'Sandra, you're so, so … beautiful,' he finally untied his tongue.

For a moment they stood there looking at each other. Then, 'Will you have tea with me?' he asked.

She had drunk a great deal of tea in Rowe's and her bladder

trembled at the mention of more. 'Tea? Yes, why not? Where?' She looked behind her to make sure that none of the crowd who had been at her shower tea was witnessing this meeting. To make doubly sure she took his arm, hurrying him across Edward Street, feeling the tension in his muscles through the Rothwell's fabric, guaranteed by its maker to breathe in the hottest summers.

Immediately opposite Rowe's was the Shingle Inn, rival of Rowe's, with a pedigree as long as the former, and, as it turned out, a much greater staying power. There too the waitresses wore white aprons and comb caps but their dresses, in a kind of anachronistic and eccentric obeisance to the Tudor past, without a hint of an ankle, let alone a knee.

She ushered him into the restaurant and they sat on the bench seats, at one of the black vitrolite tables, opposite each other. She was wearing gloves, 'gloves, and a hat, turban-style hat, that was the rage. For God's sake a hat and gloves.' She marvelled now. It wasn't those that had saved her, or spoilt it all in the end, depending upon how you looked at it.

She could see that he was not familiar with a place like this, a place so powerfully genteel. A waitress approached them to tell him to look at the menu. He did, and then he had asked her what she wanted. She hesitated. She couldn't order just water. 'Coffee, white please, and, and a biscuit.' The waitress turned to Dan. He seemed to be reading without seeing. Sandra prompted him, 'Dan, would you like some coffee, or some tea, something else, a milkshake?' she had laughed.

'Black tea, nothing to eat,' he announced finally.

'Chinese or Indian?' the waitress interrogated.

He looked at Sandra who offered, 'Indian, I should think. It's darker and stronger. That's what you'd usually drink I'd say.'

He had nodded. The waitress snapped her order book shut, annoyed by their slight and boring orders as she walked away.

Sandra peeled off her gloves and put them in her suede handbag. 'Well, Dan, you still haven't answered me. What were you doing in Edward Street in the mid afternoon in your charcoal suit with your business-like briefcase?' She had already noticed that it was of plastic, patterned to simulate leather. She was not going to be daunted by that.

'I was returning to the office after doing an audit.'

'All that ticking and adding, must be exhausting.'

'Oh, the adding's all right. We've got adding machines. They're portable now. I've got one in my briefcase. Would you like to see it?'

'No thank you. Is that all you do, auditing?'

A distant look had come into his eyes. 'For the moment, yes. It's all part of a learning process you see.'

'Learning process, what do you learn by auditing except auditing?'

'But that's just the point you see. You learn so much. You learn about waste, how businesses could save money. You learn about assets they own that they're not using, some they should sell, to invest the proceeds, and others that should be made productive. I'm not going to be just an auditor all my life.'

'But are you an auditor yet?'

Had she been then able to see into Daniel Bencham's mind she would have seen an unbounded ambition: obsession, money, power, North Brisbane, Brisbane, Queensland, Australia, the World, and Sandra. She would have seen a maelstrom of slights actual and imagined, a mind so conflicted and determined that it almost hurt.

He would show them. He would break out of this little ghetto of iconoclasm and snobbery. He would fly beyond them and above them. His mother would wear a Hartnell gown. She would have a dozen of them, and those others, those exotic French ones, Chanel, two each or more of those. And the Club, that club where they met and condemned everyone else, why, they'd beg him to join and he'd refuse. They could drink their whisky. He and his mother, and Sandra too, they'd drink champagne all the way from Reims.

At the centre of it, and in the deep recess of his mind, was Sandra. She had been there all along. She would be there always. He had seen the look on her face that day at Creekdale. Well it wasn't the place he'd choose to live in either. He could understand that. He wasn't going back to Creekdale, even if his mother, a widow now, would not want to be moved. He'd convince her. She'd see when he had the means, when he built her a mansion, and hired help to do the work she'd uncomplainingly done all of her life.

'But are you an auditor yet?' Sandra repeated the question.

'No, I sit for my finals in two months.' He explained to her the process for qualification as an accountant. He reminded her that it wasn't necessary to go to university at all, certainly not full time, as she knew, not that he wouldn't have liked to. You could be, he told her, either a public or a chartered accountant. She hadn't been able to understand the difference then and didn't now.

'But you say that each can do exactly the same work?' He had reluctantly agreed. 'Then what's the difference?' He had throughout the conversation kept his eyes fixed on her. His eyes had not even wavered as the waitress slammed down their cups and the plated jugs and pots, and presented Sandra with five chocolate-tipped biscuits arranged in a fan pattern on the plate. He asked her a question, without answering hers.

'You look so dressed up. What were you doing?'

'I've been to a shower tea.' He had looked at her questioningly. 'A shower tea's a kind of afternoon party that the friends of a girl who's about to be married give for her.'

'A shower tea, who's getting married?'

For a moment she though the question disingenuous. Nobody who read the social pages of either of the two daily newspapers, or the two Sunday ones, could possibly have been unaware of her and Jack's forthcoming nuptials. They had been photographed repeatedly: at the races, at various balls, at garden parties, at their engagement party and, it sometimes seemed, a thousand parties since.

'It's my wedding.'

He was about to pour his tea. He dropped the pot with a force that should have shattered the vitriole and a crash that reverberated around the small restaurant. An old couple at the table across the aisle glared at them, and a waitress moved as if to approach the table to rebuke him. He looked at Sandra longingly and futilely.

'Let me take that,' she said. 'It's a woman's role to pour the tea.' She had wrapped the small, ironed, linen cloth provided to insulate the pourer's hand from the heat around the handle, and poured him a cup of tea. The waitress had brought a half of lemon wrapped in muslin. 'Would you like lemon,' she asked. He somehow indicated yes.

Then in a flood of words he had spoken. 'You can't get married, not now, not yet. Who is he? Why do you have to get married? You can't, never, you can't.' He had continued until she had had to hush him. As he spoke she observed how he had changed. He had filled out and was muscular without being muscle bound. His face had developed a remote, avian look, not particularly handsome, sharp featured, a little forbidding. The readymade suit fitted him well. In smart clothes he would look, she had searched for the word, no, not 'aristocratic', that was not a word for an accountant, but 'elite', as if singled out for some great purpose. She told herself that was fanciful as she quietened him. She asked herself what she was doing here. Then she finished her cup and tried to bring the occasion to an end.

'It's getting late. Don't you have to report back to your office?'

'Not necessarily. Usually I wouldn't when I'm on a job. It's only because I finished unexpectedly early that I was going back. I don't have to go back.'

'Do you still live at,' she had fumbled to remember, 'Creekdale?'

'No. I share a flat with two other accounting students at Stone's Corner.'

'High jinks at Stone's Corner,' she had laughed but nothing she said to him could be treated as a joke.

'No. We're all studying. Besides, they don't pay us much you know. By the time I feed myself, help my mother a little, dress, pay out fares, there's not much over. And I'm saving what I can. One day I'll have some investments, I can tell you.' He forgot his anguish for a moment in his enthusiasm for investments.

He was, she then thought, rather a bore, a prude, but not, as her daughter's generation called the ineffectual, the halt, the lame, the short-sighted, the spectacled, the short, the bald, the dandruffed, the sandaled and the abstemious, a 'nerd'. No nerd could project the aura of energy that he projected.

Dan signalled the waitress. Sandra was fearful that he might commit the gaffe of scrutinizing, querying the bill and taking out a purse to pay it. She almost loved him there and then when he took out his wallet, extracted a ten shilling note, and without even appearing to look at the bill, left it on the table, stood up, and said, 'Will we go now?'

'Go where?' she had asked herself. He was off to Stone's Corner and his accountancy books: she was for home ... What was there at home? More wedding talk, more clothing talk, more guest lists, more presents to be opened and made the subject of extravagant thank you's. She wondered whose wedding it was sometimes. Perhaps Jack might look in. That should have excited her.

On an impulse, as they left the restaurant and came out on to Edward Street, she asked, 'Have you got a car?'

'No such luck,' he replied. 'Still, Stone's Corner's not very far out, lots of trams pass through it, Belmont Hill, Coorparoo, Mt Gravatt and Holland Park.' He sounded like a speaking directory.

On an impulse she said, 'If you really don't have to go back to work I could drive you home.'

'Oh I couldn't do that, take you out of your way, you'd have so much to do, with the wedding, and all that.'

She pushed aside his protests. Then she remembered her insistent bladder. 'You'll have to wait here. Just stay there.' She had darted again through the peak hour traffic now jamming Edward Street and had re-entered Rowe's, which did have lavatories. After she relieved herself, she had sat silently in the cubicle. It was not too late to back out. There could be a forgotten appointment, a fitting, a rehearsal of the damned ceremony itself, a family dinner. There were a thousand excuses if she needed them.

When she came out of the cubicle she examined herself in the mirror. She scrubbed her hands and then washed her face, removing the light makeup that she wore. She opened her hand bag and reapplied a little powder and some lipstick. She took out her comb and a small brush and redid her hair so that it fell straight and long down to her neck and about her ears. Then she took out the little atomizer of toilet water that she always carried in her bag. She had looked quickly around to reassure herself that she was still alone, and had dabbed the perfume behind her ears, and then lightly between her breasts. She straightened the top of her dress, checked her appearance once more, and, satisfied, left the room and re-crossed the street.

He was still there, of course, standing straight, like a sentinel on lookout. Relief washed over his face as she came up to him. 'Now,' she said, 'My car, I've parked in Elizabeth Street, in the car park. Let's take our time collecting it, so the traffic will clear …'

'It's not really fair, taking you out of your way. I could get a tram.'

'I've got time to fill. I'm beginning to think you don't want me to drive you home, that you're ashamed of me or something.' As she said it, she thought exactly the opposite, that perhaps she was the one who was ashamed. She couldn't help herself. Even now she could still withdraw. She walked on beside him. Now and then she stopped to look into a window to admire the contents. Once she stopped in front of a small men's store in where there were displayed some silk ties with foulard patterns, quite bright patterns. She heard herself talking like a wife. 'Foulards, now they're nice. They would look good with a dark suit.'

'You don't think they're on the bright side?'

'There's nothing wrong with bright ties so long as they're tasteful. Those are. A man can always wear colours if he's confident about them and the patterns aren't vulgar.'

'Vulgar?'

'Yes, vulgar. You'll know when you do it for a while. It's a kind of an intuitive thing, although you need to practice. You can be confident though if they're Foulards, silk of course, imported and by a good English maker, you'll be all right.'

She never talked to Jack about his clothing. She had never had to. He dressed like a mirror image of his father. When she came to think of it, their taste in ties wasn't very good either: always club or old school ties, which, because they tended to be made of inferior and synthetic materials, became spotted and frayed.

The office workers crowded the footpaths. They were unlikely to be any of her friends at this time. Then she paused. This was the commercial side of town. There might be articled law clerks or young solicitors about at this hour. She took his arm and quickened her pace. They turned into Elizabeth Street, and he stood back as she paid the parking fee and arranged for the attendant to bring her car out to the street.

It was a new Laurette, dashing in appearance and unreliable in performance. The colour was bright blue and its chrome parts gleamed in the street lights that had now come on.

He had sat awkwardly with his case on his lap until she told him to put it on the back seat. She cautiously nosed her way out towards the flow of the traffic in the street, vainly leaving her spectacles in her handbag. As if men cared, she now realized, whether a girl wore glasses or not. She had overheard one of Jack's friends saying once, 'Just another item to take off.'

She had begun to feel a little desperate as they approached Victoria Bridge. 'I'm not too familiar with this direction. You'll have to help me.' The trams made loud clattering noises and were dangerously close. All the people on them seemed to be staring down at her and her passenger. The lights changed and she moved off quickly, spinning rubber from the tyres as she did. They crossed the bridge.

'Just get in the left lane,' he had said. But it was too late. The line of traffic in that lane was continuous and unyielding. She became more confused and drove straight ahead, missing the left turn and heading towards West End. Light rain began to fall and it blurred the windscreen even with the wipers on.

'Damn, I've messed that up.'

'No, it'll be alright, I can get you back to Stanley Street and then Logan Road. Once we're on that, we'll be right. It's just straight ahead.'

She should have worn her glasses. She could only see the streets to the left when she came close to them, too close to cut in front of traffic and enter the left lane. 'You'll have to tell me, quickly,' she had said. 'Give me time to make a turn. I'm not a racing driver you know.'

It had been a humid day and it started to rain in earnest, big drops falling slowly, and then bigger drops pounding heavily and quickly like a frantic drumbeat on the roof of the car. 'I can't see a damn thing.'

Through the gloom he could see Davies Park on their right and a lay-by at the end of a lane beside it. He screwed his head around. There was nothing too close behind them, and there was a lull in inbound traffic. 'Quickly, pull across there just, before that street light.' She swung the car across, dangerously fast in the wet. She stopped under a Moreton Bay fig and turned the engine off. Intermittently, the fruit of the tree, dislodged by the torrents of rain, spattered on the roof of the little car.

They sat in silence for a minute or so. She spoke first, 'I couldn't see a damn thing out there.' She didn't disclose to him how short-sighted she was without her glasses. 'And I've got no idea where we are now.'

'We're at Davies Park, a park beside the river. Have you never been out this way?'

'I'm not in the habit of prowling round the south side. Where's Davies Park?'

'I told you, beside the river. We're at West End. You missed the left turn at the interstate railway station. And once you did that we were always going to end up at West End.' He laughed nervously. Sandra made no response. 'I'm sorry, it's my fault. I should've given you more warning. If you're not used to this side of town, you couldn't have known.' Sandra continued her silence. 'Look, I'm sorry, I've caused you so much trouble. I'll get out and I can get a tram back to the station and then change to take another one to Stone's Corner.'

'Yes, you're lucky aren't you? What did you say, you can catch a Coorparoo, a Camp Hill, a Mt Gravatt or a Holland Park?'

Her face was turned from him, and although his eyes were becoming used to the dark he couldn't tell whether she was laughing at him or with him. He decided instead that she was very annoyed.

'Look, I'm sorry. I'll go, but let me just guide you out of the lane here.' He reached for the door handle.

It was suddenly very important to her that he not leave. She reached out her hand across his body and pushed it away from the door handle. 'Don't go. If you really have to I could at least drive you back to the station.'

'I'll stay as long as you want. Anytime, anywhere,' he had said.

Sandra did not know what to say. She did not even know why she wanted him to stay. The silence lay between them like a warm, deep ocean, into which they knew that had to plunge. Out of nervousness, he did so, first again.

'The man you're marrying, he's not, not that fellow ...?'

'At the Ball, Jack? Yes. Don't you ever read the social pages? No, you wouldn't. He's a junior doctor. He's going to be a gynaecologist and an obstetrician. I'm going to have to get used to interrupted nights.' He sounded far removed from a chartered accountant.

'He's older than you?'

'Four years. Our families have known each other forever. They live only a few blocks away. Most people know one another in our suburb.' It was becoming hot and close in the little car. She rolled her window down an inch. The rain, if anything, had become heavier. 'What will you do when you become a chartered accountant? Will you stay with the firm you're in now?'

'I don't think so. There's no opportunity there. I told you before how I see so much waste. I'd like to go into business. I'm sure I could run businesses economically.' He paused and blurted out, 'Why are you marrying him?'

It should have been an impertinent question. She thought seriously about an answer. None immediately came. 'I hardly think it's any of your business. How long is this rain going to last?'

He ignored her question and put his hand on her knee. She flinched and put her hand on top of his. She felt a slight tremor in her back. He turned towards her, and with his other hand gently stroked her cheek. Then he passed his hand over the rest of her face like a blind man trying to commit each curve, each eyelash to memory. There was nothing aggressive or rough about his actions, and she felt herself responding to his movements by stroking the back of his head with her free hand. Actions were being performed by her as if she were remote from them. She was relaxed and excited in a way in which Jack had not moved her.

Jack's style was quite different. As if by rote, he would feel down the top of her dress, sometimes he would unfasten her bra, sometimes not. It was better when he did, otherwise he sometimes hurt her as he pulled it down to her waist where he would unfasten her skirt. She had determined on her mother's, her aunt's, her headmistress's, and most of her girlfriends' advice, and Daddy's unspoken assumption, to be a virgin on her wedding night. Girls, well, some girls, saved it up like a precious treasure. Jack wanted it, but at the same time, had she yielded, he would have been the first to be critical. Girls weren't supposed to do it. Men were supposed to make them try to do it. Jack followed the ritual. The next move would be his hand inside her pants. Sometimes she would take off her skirt or pull it up over her waist. He would try to pull down her pants. No, he might probe inside them, but until the big night, the pants would stay on like armour.

Dan was too shy to make any further move. She moved his hand from her face on to her breasts. She struggled to undo her bra but desisted when she couldn't reach the clip behind her back. She wanted him to move his other hand up her leg. She took her hand off his, and he began to knead the inner flesh above her knee.

She heard herself say, 'This is hopeless. Quick, get out.' She opened the door, shut it behind her and got into the back seat. He followed her, mesmerically, being pelted with rain as he fumbled with the doors.

'Now,' she had said. There was not very much room in the back of the little car, but there were no impediments like pedals, a steering wheel and a gear lever. Methodically, she took off her shoes. Then she undid her blouse and folded it. Each item she placed on the front seat. She undid her skirt buttons and lifted her bottom to slide out of it. She wore stockings with suspenders which she unclipped. For a moment she sat there in only her pants. Then she looked directly at him. He could see her eyes shining even in the dark and the curves of her white body made a pale silhouette against the navy blue upholstery. She then slipped out of her pants and held them where he could see and feel them, between her thumb and forefinger, before dropping them on the bundle of clothing on the front seat.

She turned to him and pressed her naked body to the charcoal wool and synthetic fibre suit so strongly endorsed by Mr Porous and Mr Style. Knowing that she sounded like something out of a music hall, she had said. 'Take it off.' He was so intoxicated by her scent, her softness and her willingness as not to understand at first what she wanted. 'Aren't you going to take your clothes off?'

At last he had done so, heedless of where anything was being put. He caressed and kissed and fondled every part of her. But not for long. He spent himself in his urgency. She felt the warm sticky fluid on her legs and inner thighs. She had panicked then. She had heard how, with some couples, even the slightest trace of semen anywhere near the vagina was enough to impregnate the woman. She had pushed him away roughly. He apologized.

'For God's sake stop saying you're sorry.' She felt a mixture of disgust, relief and frustration. 'In the back of a car,' she had thought. 'How sordid. A month before her wedding, with a state school boy, like a, what did they say in the books, like a common little shop girl.'

Chapter 3
Thursday

At this point her tiredness, the alcohol and the sleeping tablet locked her into a sudden deep sleep. She rolled over and dreamlessly slumbered on into the morning.

Sandra slept far into the morning, oblivious of Jack's preparations for the day. After he got up, he dressed in a tennis shirt, shorts, socks and joggers. They were all Reeboks and of matching designs and colours. As a pièce de résistance he added an elasticized towelling head-band with a logo on it to hold back his longish, soft hair. When he returned from his run, he showered, shaved and dressed in a lightweight English wool suit of a pepper-and-salt colour to match his hair. He drank a glass of trim milk, ate a rice biscuit and left for work. He was gone long before Mrs Simpson had taken up her place in the laundry.

Mrs Simpson, after she had bundled one load of clothing into the washing machine and turned it on, headed for the kitchen to tidy up there. She made no attempt to be quiet. Mrs Rentle wouldn't hear her, and if she did, it served her right. She should have woken long ago. She looked disapprovingly at the wine bottles as she emptied the contents of the kitchen rubbish bin into a black plastic bag.

There were times, she said to herself, that that silly woman could be sweet, very sweet. She was doing herself no good though. She had seen it with others. She was the type. Their looks, when they went, evaporated like the sheen of water on a flat road on a hot day. And she was a woman who needed her looks.

Sandra slept on while Mrs Simpson washed and dusted and scrubbed and ironed and hung clothing out to dry. She slept on while

Mrs Simpson polished the hardwood floors and vacuumed the rugs and carpets. Still she slept as Mrs Simpson mopped the wooden floors of the wide verandah which clung to the front and sides of the old house. The walls would need painting again soon. Sinks of money these grand old Queenslanders. Give her a brick veneer with a tile roof and plaster walls any day.

It was eleven o'clock when Sandra woke. She could hear Mrs Simpson as if she were at the other end of a metal pipe. Sandra felt dull and leaden-headed. She was hot and her bedclothes were crumpled. She had no idea what the time was. She stretched each leg and foot, gingerly, and felt her sore head. She caught sight of her bedside clock. Five past eleven. Jack was long gone of course. It was now more than twenty four hours since they had exchanged a word. It was no good blaming it on his profession. That wasn't what made her sleep insensibly on as he readied himself for his day. The nights though, they were his fault. One in every two, sometimes more, he was very late. When he was early … she put that thought aside and threw her bedclothes off. She stumbled to her feet and then sat down on the side of the bed. She tried to remember whether she had left the curtains open last night or whether Jack must have pulled them back when he got up. She squinted at the bright light. It was going to be … it was, she corrected herself, a hot day.

She had woken about this time yesterday. Then she had promised herself an early visit to the health centre, for 'step' and running, and then stretching in her new leotards. She would go tomorrow. Meanwhile there was today.

Sandra made her way out to the kitchen. Mrs Simpson looked regretfully at her. 'You need black tea.'

'I thought I might have coffee.'

Mrs Simpson disregarded her choice and started to prepare the tea things. 'Coffee's bad for you, all that caffeine, when you've slept late, with sleeping pills I'd say.' Twelve years faithful attendance, of hearing but ignoring arguments, of washing their dirty linen, of observing their privileges and indulgences, of coming to see their lives for what they were, gave her rights and authority.

Sandra drank the tea seated at the kitchen table looking out across the tennis court in the back garden. Her appearance of concentration was intended to discourage any further advice from Mrs Simpson, who, as always, stood ready to be a confidante.

Sandra finished the tea. She thought about a piece of buttered toast but her stomach told her that would not be a good idea. She looked at the kitchen clock, still only eleven twenty: at least twelve hours to go before bed again. Her mouth felt dry. She waited until Mrs Simpson left the kitchen and then drank a long glass of water. For the first time that day she felt a little better.

She went back into the bedroom and dialled Lucy's work number. She was surprised when Lucy, rather than her answering machine, answered.

'I didn't expect to get you. I thought you'd be out on a job.'

'I'm about to go. You don't sound too well. What's wrong?'

'I thought we might have morning tea?'

'Morning tea! The morning's over. I'm a working woman. I haven't got time for morning tea anyway. That lunch yesterday was a mistake as it usually is.'

'It was fun though.'

'Fun. To hear the same old stories, women bitching away about their husbands, and then getting half-pissed in the middle of the day. That's the sort of fun I can do without 364 days a year. Now look Sandra I do have to go. Is there anything else?'

'Could we meet for lunch then?'

'Sandra, I told you. I don't want another of those this year.'

'Not with the other girls. I thought we could have a talk about old times. We don't have to drink. It could be a very quiet lunch.'

'Listen Sandra, I've got to go. I've got a major decorating job at the Coast, and I've got to call in at a fabrics wholesaler first. If you really don't have anything to do we could meet at the Coast for a salad and a mineral water, nothing else. You'd better make up your mind quickly. I should have left half an hour ago.'

'A light lunch, we could meet at the Grove.' Sandra named the most fashionable bistro at Noosa.'

'I said the coast, not Noosa. Stop thinking on railway lines.'

'The Coast, oh, the Gold Coast. Haven't been there for ages.'

'Now listen Sandra, I've got no time to behold how the Gold Coast has slipped and how you never go there now. I've got a sixty-year-old retired dress manufacturer from Melbourne who's decorating his new penthouse for his new bride, his third in fact. He's got half a million to spend and I am to be the one to do it for him. I'll be one of the hundred eating a salad and sipping a Perrier at the Mirage Promenade Café, at the Mirage shopping centre between one thirty and two. If you want to meet me for lunch then that's where you'll need to be. Have to run. Goodbye.' She replaced the hand-piece loudly.

As Sandra stood under the shower, she deliberated whether to go to the Gold Coast or not. There was no point in turning her mind to the alternatives. There weren't any. 'What to wear?' She knew how those Gold Coast women, those who weren't Japanese, dressed. She had gold sandals and a white shirt but no white slacks. She tried to do a mental inventory of any chunky gold jewellery she owned. The result was disappointing.

She did her best, choosing the lightest pair of slacks she owned, a pair of fine linen and light wool in ivory. She put on the little heavy gold she owned and combed and brushed her hair to give it a slightly bouffant look. For once she applied some bright make up, choosing a Marilyn Monroe vermilion lipstick.

She called goodbye to Mrs Simpson, not waiting for a reply, and descended the steps to the garage underneath the house. Her car bore the nicks it regularly fielded these days, but they were slight and the vehicle still looked clean and safe as she got into it and clipped on her seat belt. She carefully backed out and turned into the street. She pressed a button and the driver's window slid neatly down into the door. It was pleasant to smell and look at the bougainvillea and the other bright tropical flowers that grew along the verges of the wide-trimmed footpaths. It had rained recently and the grass was green and thick.

Sandra's headache had gone. The Gold Coast. Lucy was right, she hadn't been there for years.

At first she had some trouble getting on to the freeway. Then when she did, she kept looking for, and not finding, any familiar landmarks. The city had become an elongated sprawl stocked with shops and grandly signposted warehouses which were really retailers under other names. Here and there a resolute resident had kept his house, still fronting the highway and enduring the never-ending noise and fumes. She remembered that in the old days you had to drive through Stone's Corner, Holland Park and Mt Gravatt to get on to the Pacific Highway. Those suburbs, those damn suburbs: Belmont, Coorparoo, Holland Park and Mt Gravatt, and Stone's Corner. She had dropped him off there, that night. Both of them were full of shame, but each had different reasons. Now the freeway made all the suburbs anonymous until you reached those areas with addresses that no one she knew lived at.

As she drove down the highway she recalled how in the distant past, before Noosa, they had taken some of their holidays at the Gold Coast. Daddy's father owned a house at Broadbeach just south of Surfers Paradise. It had been a quiet, exclusive area then; that was until the new hotel was built there. It had stood several stories high overlooking a flat sandy plain fronting the sea with balconies facing north, a pill-box-like intrusion into the formerly quiet residential area. After a time the trees and gardens had taken root and the hotel became part of the landscape.

The traffic, although steady, was not heavy at this time of day. Sandra accelerated and her little red Mercedes picked up speed. It was still new. She had bought it out of her own money. There was still quite a lot of money but it did need rationing and she knew that she should have gone for something cheaper. Jack had offered her a Japanese car—bloody cheek. He drove a Mercedes, a big one. He got into it every morning like a German general putting on his uniform. All the doctors drove big Mercedes. They said they did it on grounds of safety: safety my eye. Look in any doctor's car park at any hospital, and you'd see them, with their personalized number plates, but no caducis badge, which the doctors used to put on their cars as a status symbol before the days of drug break-ins. No, if Jack could have a GEL, KEL, BEL or an SEL or whatever he called it, she was entitled to her more modest model of the species.

She pressed the radio button. There was a talkback program playing. She tried to concentrate for a while. The Deputy Prime

Minister telephoned in and was berating the announcer with a flood of statistics that made her head swim. Jack only ever listened to news programmes that discussed health benefit schemes and gave the stock exchange report. Enforced listening to those had quite turned her off the radio except for light music. She found the second ABC station and turned the volume up.

She was by-passing Beenleigh now. She used to have to drive through it. What a bottleneck it was in holiday periods. The roadside shops must have thrived then. Now it was a huge dormitory suburb for Brisbane and the Gold Coast.

They'd had a lot of fun at the Gold Coast, before it was ruined by the high rises, the hotels, the theme parks, the traffic and all those Japanese tourists. Not that there weren't areas that were already tainted when they went there. None of their set would ever go to Coolangatta. The most southerly in the State of the beach resorts, it was one of the first places in Australia to provide packaged holidays. The shop girls, the junior secretaries, their mechanic boyfriends and all the rest turned the place, as her father used to say, into an Australian Blackpool with hot weather. They played a dance game on the beach. She racked her brain to remember the name. Then it came to her, the 'Hokey Pokey'. They used to wiggle their hands and legs and gyrate their bodies as they sang. It became quite famous. She could recall her father's surprise when some of her friends said their parents had driven them down there to watch. Her father certainly wouldn't have done that.

Their days at Broadbeach were slow and always the same. No one worried too much about skin cancer. They would coat their bodies with oil and tanning creams anyway. After all these years she could still feel a thrill of sensuousness at the memory of herself, like the other girls, slowly and deliberately applying the oil in front of the boys on the beach in the hot sun. First around the ankles, then the calves and ever so slowly right to the tops of the legs. What had Dan said, on that one occasion when they had sat alone on the beach together? 'I watched you. You applied that oil like a girl from a seraglio applying a sweet and warm unguent.' She had had no idea what he was talking about. He explained to her what a seraglio was and what an unguent was. She had listened in amazement. He asked her what she was studying in English. She told him the basics of her syllabus. Then he began to talk about poetry and books. She thought at the time that it was rather dull except for the intensity of his interest. They were more interesting though than the accountancy he turned to later.

After that, she was always conscious of the impression that the sunburn oil ceremony, as she called it to herself, created. These were the days of the two-piecers, an inch or two less would have made them bikinis. Not that they suffered for that. She struggled to remember something else that Dan had said that summer. She must be becoming old for it came back to her in a way that recent recall never did. It was, she thought, a couplet, part of a poem by one of those English Romantic poets.

'Heard melodies are sweet,
Those unheard are sweeter.'

Dan explained it carefully to her. 'You can make things too obvious, you can spell everything out, but what is better is to leave things to the imagination. That's what the poet was talking about. It's like your beauty. You leave some of it covered up, and the rest is for the imagination of the onlooker.'

What an unlikely person he was to be sprouting poetry. He was, she understood now, a romantic about everything except money, or perhaps even that too. The money was a Holy Grail rather than a means to dominate people and crush their business. How could an accountant be a romantic? Perhaps he could. His figures could be translated into visions, materializing into masonry and factories, hotels and buildings, shares and gold.

Sandra drove on. A few days of a beach summer. How had they contrived that? She struggled to remember the details. Perhaps she was becoming a poet herself. If she was, she was the only one in the family. She thought of her children, and Jack. Jack. Jack the poet? That cap didn't fit. Her mind returned to that time so long ago, at the Gold Coast. How long ago? She was sixteen. That was the fifties, decades ago.

She tried to recapture the sense of the time. She was young, that was clear. Could it really be that sixteen was the best age? What a disappointing life she must have had if she could think that, even entertain the thought for a moment. It had been a good time though. She and her friends were the cynosure of every male between twelve and fifty as they had held court on that sub-tropical beach.

She would rise in the morning. 'Rise in the morning.' That sounded nicely aristocratic. There would be a light family breakfast although she always ate heartily. Then she would make her toilette. 'That's another nice phrase.' She thought. 'And the only person who would appreciate it would be someone like Dan.'

The next delicious task was to select a swimsuit out of the half dozen or so she owned, a towel to match, the beach umbrella, a little portable metal ice-chest with cold orange juice in bottles, and ice inside it, the magical sunburn oil and, last, the latest thing, the battery-operated portable radio to play the current hits, usually sentimental songs, long before hard rock and grunge.

Sometimes her parents accompanied her to the beach, sometimes not. When they did, they were gone by 11.30, up on the terrace of the house nursing their gin-and-tonics and whisky sodas, talking of their neighbours and listening to nothing that anyone else said. Not that it mattered. Their Broadbeach neighbours were, for the most part, Belvedere neighbours. What was it that Dan had said? Her mind once again traversed the past and produced the answer. 'Your lot don't travel, they just relocate the enclave.' She had only vaguely understood what he meant at the time.

Sandra had now reached the turnoff to Sanctuary Cove. She had never been there. Some of Jack's golfing friends, mainly doctors, had bought residences there. Jack said that was the sort of place they might like to end up at. He didn't say it by way of consultation. It was, like most of Jack's statements, a pronouncement, like a Papal Bull. 'What the hell exactly is a Papal Bull,' she had asked Lucy. 'Something pretty serious that you can't go against.' That certainly described anything Jack said or thought.

He had gone on to describe the area: 'Villas, that's what they call them. You can have one of three types, absolute waterfront, golf-course front or other.'

'What's other?' she had asked. He didn't know. 'What's the

difference between waterfront and absolute waterfront,' she then inquired. He couldn't answer that either. If there was one place she didn't intend to end up at it, was a place called Sanctuary Cove. Still, she was curious. She would like to see it: on the way home perhaps.

She continued. Once it had been a matter of great excitement as they approached the ocean. There was always a competition for who was the first to see the sea. Daddy cheated of course, claiming a glimpse long before the breakers and the distant blue horizon lay open and unobscured beyond the road ahead. It was all so settled now. At a place called Helensvale, the road configuration channelled her to the west. It was only after driving for a few minutes that she realized that she had been diverted from the old road that turned east and which they had used to travel.

The new road was a bypass highway, six lanes, and fast cars and loud trucks dashed past as she started to look for sign posts pointing east. There were none in view. The highway stretched ahead and she returned to her thoughts.

Broadbeach used to be the place. There were others too. Main Beach she omitted for the moment. Surfers Paradise, and Coolangatta forever, Miami, Northcliffe, Currumbin, Tugun, Burleigh, and all the way to Tweed Heads in New South Wales. Surfers Paradise was a forbidden fruit, exciting, tempting. She remembered how Jack and his medical student friends used to spend their days during vacations in the beer garden of the hotel, deliberately, slowly getting drunk and boorish. How silly she and her friends were. Sometimes they would sit there with them. God knows why, sipping a crème de menthe soda and ice, or some other technicolour drink, as if they were enjoying themselves.

Her parents never came to grips with the freewheeling Surfers Paradise standards. They tried to prevent her going there but, in view of those who did go, Jack and his friends, and eventually the children of most of their set, they never brought themselves to the futility of forbidding it completely.

She had moved ahead of herself. She remembered now. One holiday Dan, with two of his schoolmates, had camped on the reserve at Beenleigh. Large parcels of land with absolute beach frontage, as they would now say, were reserved for campers. What an eyesore they had been. Tent cities, row upon row of tents of all shapes and sizes, some caravans, communal bathing and lavatories, and the constant smell of cooking and bad drains. She shook her head at the recollection. Dan and his friends had borrowed a tent from somewhere and pitched it at the north-eastern corner of the reserve. They were on a little bluff, with the beach immediately below. Some rough ground around them deterred other campers so that they had a measure of privacy denied to most of the other campers. For some reason most campers didn't seem to mind being huddled close to one another. Glimpses of camp-stretchers and pots and pans, clothes hanging on makeshift lines, and other intimate scenes of improvised domesticity seemed to provide a reassuring feel of close suburban comfort. She had visited Dan's tent once, when the others were out, Dan had sensed her distaste and taken her for a walk on the beach.

Sandra almost overshot the left turn to the east. The little Mercedes responded quickly to the brakes and she turned off the freeway. Driving due east now, she was surprised by the density of the development, acre after acre of little brick veneers with concrete tile roofs, playing fields, small industrial complexes, and vast arid fields of flat clay sand cleared, waiting for yet more development.

At last the sea was in sight, the still waters of the Broadwater with the northern sandy lip of Main Beach behind. She was also surprised by the yachts moored on the other side, long, sleek, white vessels bristling with antennae, and more than one with a helipad and helicopter on the back. There were others that rode high in the water with cockpits as tall as castles. They all shimmered on the blue water like a stage set for a Hollywood extravaganza.

She turned south again and travelled beside the still water. The traffic was busier and she had to attend to the road. She came to the Nerang River. The towers of Main Beach and Surfers Paradise in all colours of the pastel spectrum dwarfed the shops and the few old houses that remained. There should have been a limit to the height of these residential towers but it seemed that there was not. They competed for height with one another by adding bizarre cones, helmets and turrets to their tower tops, and curlicues to balconies.

There were straight, curved, converse, concave, enclosed and open buildings. The newest-looking towers were the most elaborate. Sandra wondered how the next builder would ever be able to do something more bizarre.

The hotel and shopping complex where she was to meet Lucy looked new and inviting though. Its former owner had fled to Majorca from where Australian extradition proceedings had been unable to dislodge him to return to face major corporate fraud charges. But his development, set in tropical gardens and with a low profile, was rather elegant.

Because the day was now very warm, she parked in the cavernous basement under the shopping complex. One of the few blots on it was the thirty-feet-high wire-fenced atrium extending from the basement to the second floor, in which some sorry Australian native birds were photographed by the Japanese tourists who thronged the expensive designer and Australian craft shops. Various food stalls and restaurants made up the majority of the other tenants.

She found Lucy already seated at a table overlooking the water and the yachts. She waved to Sandra to join her. She was drinking Perrier. 'A Perrier day only my love,' she said to Sandra. Sandra thought about chardonnay but wasn't prepared to argue, not yet anyway. 'I've only got three-quarters of an hour. I have to meet them at the penthouse. At two o'clock.'

'Them? I thought he was the client. Is the fiancée coming too?'

'And a friend of his who is thinking about buying an apartment in the same building. He wants to talk about how he'd decorate it if he did buy it. This is pretty important: two for one. I could make a lot of money out of this.'

Sandra was not concerned about making money, never had been. Nor had she, so far, been concerned about where it would come from. Enough always seemed to be there. She had persuaded herself that she still lived a simple life, just like when she was young and the Nelson sisters were her dressmakers. She had deluded herself into thinking the well-cut clothes with simple lines, and natural materials like silk and wool, and real linen and cotton, were bound to be cheaper than those synthetics. They didn't travel overseas as much as most of their friends, and the Mercedes, well, you had to drive a strong car for safety.

Lucy resumed where she had left off when the waitress had served Sandra her Perrier water. 'I don't think you're listening Sandra. This could really set me up, the money from this, perhaps two jobs, not to speak of other commissions I might get as a result.'

'You know I'm interested Lucy. Tell me about it.'

'Have you any idea how it works?'

'No, not really. Well, not at all.' There was a hint of condescension in her voice which Lucy recognized but chose for the present to disregard. 'I charge the owner a commission of twenty percent based on the total cost of the work. That covers design advice, finding the furniture, the materials, the trades' people and the upholsterers. So for this job, if it goes ahead, I'll also get my percentage from the suppliers: could be as much as a hundred and fifty, all up.'

Sandra had lost interest in the numbers. She was instead concentrating on the fashionable people who were lunching at the bistro. It too was à la mode, à la Gold Coast: unglazed big Portuguese terra rosa tiles on the floor, clean white lacquered walls, an exposed kitchen with stainless steel surfaces and wire baskets of fresh vegetables dangling from hooks, long-legged, short-skirted, enthusiastic, incompetent waitresses, and a maitre d' oozing charm in an unconvincing European accent. Lucy was completely at home. She had recently dyed her hair straw blonde and Sandra wandered whether her breasts may have been assisted by some surgery. Perhaps it was just the cut of her halter blouse and a new bra that were doing the trick. She would ask her later. Lucy wore a gold chain with large links as a belt around her waist and her pants were white with a gold strip, like a bandsman, down the outside of each leg. Here she seemed a different person, more obvious, racy, or as Sandra's mother would have said, 'fast'.

Lucy began to discuss the people. 'See those two women over there.' She discreetly nodded her head towards a couple dressed not unlike herself except more expensively. They looked about thirty-five to forty years old, and were a tribute to the art of the manicurists and the cosmeticians as, in the same way, in a few years, they would be testimony to the skills of a plastic surgeon. Each had a green salad and the ubiquitous green bottle of Perrier water in front of her. Other people looked at them from time to time as if they either knew or thought they should know them. They were both blonded. They were very sure of themselves and acted as if they were accustomed to being looked at. They did not have the x-ray figures of Tom Wolfe's New York hostesses but they were very, very slim and obviously highly body conscious.

'They,' Lucy said, 'are two of the three best-known courtesans of the Gold Coast.' By using the word 'courtesans' Lucy was paying Sandra back for patronizing her about money matters. She waited for the inquiry.

'Courtesans, what do you mean by courtesans?'

'Ladies of style who for large sums of money or property are prepared to sleep and consort with the rich and famous. There might be some rich here. I don't imagine there's anyone famous. *Grandes horizontales*,' she added, further in condescension.

'Just high-class prostitutes, that's what you mean?'

'No, I don't. These are different. They don't go with more than one man at a time. I don't understand it. They seem almost to be passed around. If one developer or entrepreneur has had one of them for a time, then some other businessman slightly lower down the property food chain will take her on, almost as if she'll give him lustre, kudos I suppose they'd say.' Lucy thought about what she had said for a moment. 'They don't look especially attractive to me.'

'I'd describe them as a little on the thin side. And look at those faces, those artificial smiles at the wine waiter. Damn it, I think I'll have a glass of chardonnay.'

Lucy held up her hand. 'Don't, you're driving. You don't need it.'

Sandra was angry but she still wasn't prepared to argue about it. 'What's the fiancée like?'

'She's gone against the run of play. She hasn't been passed down. She's gone upwards. My client is one of the wealthiest men to come up from Victoria for years. He hasn't been here long, not long enough to learn about any of these women's pasts. He wants a name, the social pages, charity functions, a luxurious apartment that will be featured in a popular magazine. Cindy, that's her name, will get him all of that.'

'Cindy, no one's called that.'

'You had better believe it. Cindy she says she is, Cindy she is. If there can be a New York Holly Golightly, there can certainly be a Surfers Paradise Cindy Spark.'

'What's your client's name?'

'Frank Mosca.'

Sandra's nose turned up, as it always did at the mention of something third world or Mediterranean. To her there was little difference between the two. 'Mosca, that sounds foreign.'

'He is rather swarthy. He's got no accent, though.'

'Lucy, don't you think you ought to be careful about the people you're dealing with in this business? Do you really know anything about them?'

'I know everything I need to know, and that is that Frank is conservatively worth about two hundred million dollars and he's reached a stage in life when he'd like to begin enjoying it. Come on, eat up, your salad and you can come with me to meet him.'

'I don't think I'd want to do that.'

'Loosen up, live a little. The world isn't Belvedere's little acre.'

They wrangled about it even longer than they wrangled about the bill, Sandra demanding to pay, with Lucy saying she was being condescending now. Sandra thought of the long afternoon ahead of her. She thought of the lonely drive back home, the hour or two before she would have to think about dinner, of waiting for Jack, wondering whether one of her children might call, and of the indecision about when she might take her first drink. Lucy clinched the argument finally.

'I can leave my car in Frank's parking space and come home with you. He has to come up to Brisbane tomorrow to fly back to Melbourne. I'll ask him to drive it up. Then I can go back with you.'

'Will he do that? You must be on very good terms with him.'

'He's my client, good client.'

'It isn't only interior decorators who have clients.' Sandra mouthed the words almost inaudibly as they left the restaurant.

Lucy swung round on her. 'What did you say?' Her voice was loud and a nearby diner looked up, startled.

'I just said, do you have many clients?'

Lucy did not believe her. Poor Sandra, half the time she didn't know what she was thinking, let alone saying. It used to be the same at school.

Sandra followed Lucy's little Japanese car along the Pacific Highway looking for places familiar to her youth. The old Surfers Paradise Hotel with its stuccoed and tiled corner tower had long gone, gone with the beer garden and the old Chevron Hotel across the road. Most of the shops on the highway were duty free shops, or Australian souvenir shops. How shocked Daddy would be if he could see the Japanese characters on the windows, and even the street names in Japanese. Daddy had always had strong views about Orientals, especially the Japanese, and not just because Daddy had fought them in the War. Daddy had done his bit, more, despite his mature age when he enlisted. He had been a Captain. Daddy had been lightly wounded in the left arm at Lae. Afterwards from time to time he wore the arm in an immaculate white sling making little of the old war injury that sometimes troubled him. No, Daddy had no love for the Japs.

Lucy turned towards the beach and stopped in front of a pink and purple masonry efflorescence that stood thirty stories high in a landscaped garden, of transplanted, tall trees, an artificial beach around an irregularly shaped swimming pool, and large false rocks and boulders made out of fibreglass.

Sandra stood beside her car surveying the monstrosity and the long, sharp shadow that it made over the real beach and across the rows of breakers as they spent themselves on the sand. 'My God, it's hideous Lucy, hideous.'

'It is, isn't it? It's a bit better inside though. Come on, we'll go up. Frank will be in the apartment.'

They passed through the foyer, a reading room without books or papers on one side, a bar on the other, and a reception desk beside the lifts. The floor was paved in a mutton-fat marble and the walls were finished in a pink-suede wallpaper. 'It hasn't improved yet,' Sandra whispered.

The penthouse occupied the twenty-ninth and thirtieth floors and enjoyed the exclusive use of the roof. A private swimming pool was suspended into the top floor from the roof and had walls of thick glass on three sides looking into the apartment. There were some workmen's trestles, a couple of old plastic chairs and a paint-spotted pine table in the anteroom leading off from the lifts. An olive-skinned thick-haired man in his early sixties was seated on one of the plastic chairs. His hair was too sleek and black. He wore cream espadrilles, jeans, an open-necked cream silk shirt and a heavy gold chain around his neck. His face lit up when he saw Lucy.

There was another man, perhaps five, perhaps ten, years younger, restlessly prowling around the apartment. He had made no attempt to dress in the Gold Coast style and looked uncomfortable in a business shirt, unbuttoned at the collar, a lightweight checked sports coat and tailored light-wool trousers. The third person, standing beside the windows, was a nervous slim woman of forty or so, dressed just as the two courtesans were in the restaurant that Sandra had just left. They were introduced. The other man, whose name was James Speed, told them to call him Jim. The woman, who didn't wear a wedding ring, gave her name as Mrs Spark.

Lucy explained that Sandra was an old school friend. 'Did Frank mind?' No, Frank didn't mind. Ever since the death of his first wife Frank had made it his business to be in the company of as many attractive women from twenty to fifty as he could. He thought Sandra to be in her early forties and undoubtedly attractive.

Lucy said the best thing to do would be to go through the place room by room, explaining her ideas. She had with her rolls of plans and samples of materials and carpet, colour charts and photographs in her brief case. They should start in the main living room beside the reinforced bullet-proof plate glass of the suspended swimming pool.

Frank said the pool made him feel good. It made him think he was in the movies. 'Remember that James Bond film when Goldfinger, or whoever he was, had that great aquarium as a wall to his living room. That's why I bought this apartment,' he told them. 'I knew I'd have to get a good decorator to do it up and I got the best.' He blew a kiss at Lucy. Mrs Spark looked on impassively.

Sandra was surprised at how professional Lucy was. She made even wall-paint sound like an exotic fluid: glazes, semi-glazes, rag finish, granocite and two packs. 'That sounds more like a beer than a paint.' They all laughed at Sandra's joke.

'I think we shouldn't have any carpet on this floor at all except for Oriental rugs. We should have parquetry throughout except for the kitchen and bathrooms.'

Frank nodded but stated a reservation. 'The wood sounds good, but I don't know about those Chinese rugs. Two a penny, big thick things with patterns cut like mown grass cut out of them.' He was pleased by his contribution to the aesthetic debate.

'Frank, Oriental, as in rugs, doesn't mean, at least it doesn't usually mean, Chinese rugs. The English used to say the Orient begins at Calais, so rugs from North Africa, Turkey, Persia, further east, even parts of Europe, the Caucuses are all called Oriental rugs.'

Frank put his arms around Lucy. 'This is what I like about this woman. She knows so damn much about as many things. Tell me some more about those Oriental rugs.'

Mrs Spark said nothing, just watched. Lucy spoke about a magnificent and rare antique Isfahan she had seen in Sydney. 'I've never seen bigger in Australia,' she told them. 'Twenty-five feet by thirteen with ten borders and a motif taken from the Caliph's rose garden on a faded pale-orange field.'

'Poetry,' Frank laughed. 'Poetry. This woman could make a refrigerator sound like a space turbine. She's going to give this apartment more class. I don't know where she gets her ideas from.'

Lucy was measuring a window sill. She asked Sandra to help her. Sotto voce she spoke to Sandra. 'From *Architectural Digest*, *Maison Francais*, *Home Beautiful* and every other magazine I can plagiarise.' She turned towards Frank. 'You flatter me too much.'

Lucy was a different person in this setting: confident, just coquettish enough, knowledgeable, and obviously very expensive. Mosca dwelled on her every word.

'Biedemier is the latest thing on the West Coast. Of course that simply means that it was everywhere else ten years ago, and won't become de rigueur in Australia for five years. We'll be the first at the Gold Coast to have it. Northern European, light timbers, beech or faded pale mahogany, inlaid ebony or ivory in spruce, clean lines, columns and black feet. I know where we can get a beautiful bureau. And other pieces, a sofa, wine table, and a couple of casual chairs.'

Frank was looking at her, open mouthed in admiration. 'Biedemier?'

'Yes, Biedemier,' she responded. 'In German, means Mr Conventional, Mr Smith. 1840 say, a little later. The growth of a middle class, plain furniture for plain middle class Mr Smiths. That's what we're talking about. Mind you, when it comes to the point, not too much of it is middle class. Frank.' She swung round on him and took his hand, 'there's quite a lot of the aristocratic touch in the best of it. You'll like it, I promise you. I've got a vision for this apartment.' Lucy, unnoticed by Frank and Jim, winked at Sandra. Then she returned to her purposeful stride. 'But Frank I'm rushing ahead. You're the client. What does the client want?'

Frank looked at her trying to think of something to offer. 'Do you think I should have a billiard room?'

Lucy repressed a shudder. 'No Frank, you don't need a billiard room. A study, with green billiard table felt and bookshelves on the wall, yes. A billiard room, no. For God's sake Frank, you don't play billiards. Who does these days?'

Mrs Spark spoke for the first time. She had, for a thin woman, a deep voice.

'Why the hell shouldn't he have a billiard room if he wants one?'

'It's a big apartment Lucy. How are we going to fill it?' Frank, encouraged, asked.

Lucy ignored the other woman and looked at Sandra. 'Not with billiard tables. What do you think Sandra?'

'Daddy had a billiard table at home,' Sandra recalled the big room at home. 'Daddy loved billiards.' Sometimes she thought she could still smell the whisky and the Velazquez cigars that Daddy smoked.

'Different time, different place. Who the fuck wants to play billiards now?' Lucy spoke deliberately.

Frank and Jim, with their friends, freely used obscenities and profanities, but they were shocked and thrilled by Lucy's rehearsed roughness. Frank laughed, and said, 'All right, no billiard table. Tell us some more of your vision.'

'I can't pretend that this is going to be straightforward. You can hardly regard the intrusion of this,' she pointed at the bullet-proof glass wall of the swimming pool, 'as an architectural triumph. If I had my way I'd cover the glass, but you don't want that do you Frank?' Frank shook his head.

'I know what you're thinking, beautiful naked nymphettes swimming into your living room. Got it Frank, haven't I?' Frank shook his head again but couldn't conceal the smirk that passed across his face. 'Well let me tell you that a wall with a few good paintings on it and a Louis XV commode against it would be a hell of a lot more chic than a few naked women trying to do the Australian crawl. Still,' she held up her hand, 'the customer's always right, we'll keep the pool and even light it both inside and out for different effects. Pure MGM. I'll ring Hollywood and see if Esther Williams is still around.'

They gradually moved through the large apartment with Lucy talking about periods and styles as in a foreign language, Frank and Jim nodding in bewilderment, and Mrs Spark silent in contempt. Sandra was bored now. She looked at her watch. 'Three thirty, I must go.'

Frank seized the opportunity. 'We've done enough for one day. Let's have a cup of coffee.' He turned to Sandra, 'before you go. We can have it downstairs.'

'Not for me,' Mrs Spark turned on her heel and left.

They descended to the ground floor and entered the coffee lounge off the reading room. Lucy explained that she wanted to travel back with Sandra. Could Frank drive her car up? 'No,' he said, 'he could do better than that.' He would drive his own car to Brisbane and leave it with Lucy while he was in Sydney. She would be free to use it and he could drive her back to collect her car when he returned from Sydney.

'I couldn't drive your car. People would ask all sorts of questions.'

'Not the Bentley. I'll bring the Range Rover up. It's not conspicuous.'

Over their coffee, Jim, for the first time, showed some animation. He talked about his own business. Unlike Mosca, he had not simply been an investor. He still managed the large clothing manufacturing business he owned in Melbourne. It was easy to see that he was impressed by Sandra. He could not believe, he said, that she had children well into their twenties. Heavy handedly he told her she must have been a child bride. Sandra's barely disguised disdain for him seemed to make him more eager to engage her in conversation. She gave as little information in answer to his question about her husband, her interests, her house and her holidays, as she could. He began to wonder whether he really should buy an apartment at the Coast. Apart from Frank he had no friends here. Still, he could make them, he supposed.

'Do you or your husband ever come down to the Gold Coast?' he asked.

'Not these days. The place has become so, so, raffish.' She was proud of the word. She had read it only recently. 'All the Japs who are here, the big buildings, the traffic, the commercialism, and the people, the people.' She made a gesture with her hand of infinite weariness. She made no effort to exclude the two men from the 'people'. We go north these days, have done for years now, to near Noosa. Before the place was spoilt, we came here with our friends and relatives. They're all gone now.'

'Took their money and ran, didn't they Sandra?' Lucy interrupted. 'Sold out for lots of money to the first high-rise developer to offer them their thirty pieces of silver.'

'They'd decided to move. The whole place became impossible! I'm sure I don't know what prices they sold for. That wasn't the point. It was a time to find, a, a more congenial place.'

'You said Noosa, did you?' Frank asked.

'No, not Noosa. Noosa's all right for the restaurants but not as a place to stay.'

'Sandra and her husband have a house at Inchcape Beach. It's a small settlement, what, half an hour from Noosa, Sandra?' Lucy asked the question in a conciliatory tone, but before Sandra could answer, Jim interrupted. 'Inchcape Beach. I used to know a poem about the Inchcape Rock. Any relation?' No one responded to the attempted joke. 'Inchcape Beach. It sounds exclusive. What would it cost to get in there?'

'I haven't the slightest idea. Nobody I know would sell.' She made selling sound like contracting yellow fever.

'I suppose this area's better for me anyway. I can use the airport here if I want to. Besides, I like the city life aspect that's here.'

'I'm sure you're right,' Sandra sniffed.

'Will you come down, with Lucy, again? I mean. If I buy, I'll get her to decorate my apartment too. You might like to help. I wouldn't mind paying.' Jim was impervious to social sensitivities.

Sandra ignored him as she gathered her handbag and her keys. 'Lucy, it's time we left.'

'I've just got to make arrangements about my car. I'll see you at the front.' Lucy left the coffee lounge with Frank.

Sandra looked around feeling trapped. She noticed a door with a plastic silhouette of a female figure with a parasol mounted on it. She nodded to Jim and hurried to the sanctuary to emerge five minutes later when the coast was clear.

On the drive back, Sandra began to interrogate Lucy. 'You and Frank ...?'

'Yes.'

'Well, are you, do you? You're very familiar with each other.'

'And?'

'Are you his mistress?'

'No, just his occasional bit on the side. So what?'

'How could you, all that gold and tan. And I wouldn't be surprised, face surgery.'

'How could I? Sandra have I ever told you before, you make me sick with all your sanctimonious bullshit, snobbery and money. Perhaps I'd be sanctimonious if my old man had left me loaded and I had a husband who, when he wasn't bonking them, was looking up his patients' vaginas at $200 a time, twenty times a day. But I wasn't and I didn't. So what if I do give Frank a little on the side at the same time as I'm teaching him how to spend his money, and perhaps, just perhaps, get on to the fringe of polite society.'

'Lucy, you're a snob too. 'Fringe of polite society.' I think you're just a courtesan, like one of those other women, his fiancée. You're just using him.'

'Why not? Apart from the money, he's not a bad fuck for his age, and everything else considered. You ought to think about it yourself. That Jim Speed. He would have done anything for you. I don't understand it, that little girl put-on voice of yours ought to infuriate them. It seems to attract them like flies. I thought he was almost going to ask you how much you'd do it for. You ought to think about it Sandra old girl. Turn the other cheek, metaphorically, get square on Jack.'

Sandra was not one to stay offended at anything said by a social equal. It was different with other people. Her friends said she could wither with a glance if she was so minded. She was silent for a few miles. Then she replied. 'He's not my type and Mosca's not yours.'

'You're still waiting for Mr Right to return. You could be miscalculating there. We're almost in our fifties now. Perhaps not the last lap but there's not a lot to go.'

'Somebody like Mosca would never marry you.'

'Nor I him. I'm just making a down payment on an independent future. I've tried the other, didn't like it much, either time.'

'What about his …? Does she know?'

'No, and wouldn't want to hear it anyway. Inconvenient. If she made an issue of it he might drop her. She's far too worldly for that. She's been in my position, that is, supine under some other woman's man, a hell of a lot more often than I have. People like her and me treat men like neutral territory. You can pass through it so long as you don't damage it and don't settle there.'

'You know all the rules then?'

'Instinctively, they're not difficult I can tell you. Even you Sandra my dear would pick them up quickly. It doesn't matter Sandra. It's just a matter of a tingle of a nerve. Sometimes it tingles, sometimes it doesn't.'

It was becoming dark as Sandra drove the car through Oxenford. Lucy spoke, 'Own up, you had an interesting day and a teetotal day. That was good for both of us.'

'What you're doing interested me. I'm glad I saw that. I can give you some advice. If you're not careful you'll end up with a dreadful name.'

'At my age, that mightn't be a bad achievement. Come on Sandra, I know what's in your mind. I know about you. You've forgotten you told me what happened in the past. Don't try to be holier than thou with me.'

Sandra made a point of concentrating on her driving. She accelerated and the powerful little car picked up speed. She told herself now was not the time to talk about that, or for that matter even to think about it. Later. She spoke of generalities. Lucy asked about the children. Sandra didn't want to talk about them. They were on the freeway into the city when Lucy apologized. 'I'm sorry for saying what I did about Jack. It was an exaggeration.'

'Don't apologise. I've got a pretty good idea about what goes on. In a way I'm like Frank's fiancée. I simply ignore it.'

Sandra dropped Lucy off and was surprised to see Jack's large Mercedes parked in front of the house. He was sitting, agitatedly, in the living room. Impatiently, he asked, 'Where have you been?'

She ignored the question. 'What are you doing home at this hour?'

'I've been asked to do some consultations in Cairns. Very unusual cases and quite urgent. They want me to fly up tonight.'

She did not believe a word of it. 'Short notice isn't it?'

'You've been married to a doctor long enough to know that nature never gives us much notice.' He said it in a way that she used to think responsible but now knew to be hypocritical. 'I'll pack a few things.' He went into the bedroom. A few minutes later she followed him in there. She pretended not to see the sports shirts, shorts, casual shoes and bathing togs that he had packed at the bottom of the case.

She asked him how long he would be gone.

'It could be a few days. I may have to operate or assist. And Jensen, you remember Ralph Jensen, we met him at that conference in Perth a few years ago? He's got a yacht. He asked me to sail with him for a few days on it. You don't mind do you? You could take a holiday yourself.'

To tease him she mused, 'Perhaps I could join you for the cruise?'

'Look it's all too uncertain for that. It depends how long the work takes. We mightn't even get a chance to sail. You'd be awfully bored hanging round Cairns.'

'They tell me it's very attractive now, that there are plenty of things to do. Rainforests, golf tours, trips to the reef, and good restaurants.'

'It's approaching the worst time of year. It will be very, very hot.'

'All right then. I'll give it a miss, on your say so, thanks. Just watch the heat yourself though. Don't get overheated.'

His relief was palpable, so much so that he missed the barb at the end.

'You should go away yourself. Look, I'll pay.'

'I don't require any money from you simply because you're going on a trip and I'm not.' She didn't realize that whenever she spoke of money she did so in a haughty tone with her head tilted back upon her neck, and without looking at the person to whom she was speaking.

Jack hurriedly shut his case, touched his pockets to assure himself that he had his keys, wallet and credit cards, blew Sandra a tentative kiss and walked down the hall with his case. It was only when he was on the top step that she called out to him. 'Aren't you taking your medical bag?' In confusion, he returned, picked up his shiny leather doctor's case, waved and clattered down the steps.

It was quite dark, and Sandra went around the large house turning lights on in alternate rooms. She passed through what had once been Daddy's billiard room. It was, now, more accurately, the family room, converted after she and Jack moved in. She was disappointed that she couldn't smell any cigar smoke.

She knew that she should be continuing with her reading programme. Tonight though, no, not tonight. She went into the bedroom and changed into a light shift and flat sandals to prepare herself for another solitary night.

Chapter 4
The Dinner Party

The difference between yesterday evening and tonight was that it was seven thirty and she hadn't had a drink. She was hungry. Unlike most of her friends she could eat voraciously and still not put on weight. She made herself a large sandwich which she sat on a plate in front of her. Otherwise, everything else was the same as last night. She was in her favourite chair on the verandah. Inkie had companionably made his way up the steps to join her. The suburban noises were beginning to subside. The joggers and walkers were going home. She was alone. There was an opened, as yet full bottle of chilled chardonnay, and a wine glass in front of her.

For a time she watched the vines of condensation making uneven descents down the cold glass of the bottle, before she poured herself her first glass of wine. She bit into the sandwich and sipped the wine. 'Solitary. I like being alone. Sometimes I just want to drink and think, think and drink.' She composed herself to let the past come back.

She and Jack had been married for about twice seven years at the time: seven years was supposed to be the limit of a man's fidelity. Christmas, New Year; it had been eventful for Jack. He and his colleagues railed against the Labor government that had replaced the conservatives after more than fifteen years. Not that the conservatives, with their high tax policies, had been conservative enough for Jack.

It had been a very hot Christmas and suddenly the rains started. Most of Belvedere, the part that counted anyway, had been safe. But much of the rest of the city was flooded. Roads had been closed without warning. Suburban bridges had collapsed. Babies still insisted upon being born. Jack had cut rather a heroic figure.

He owned a four-wheel-drive vehicle at the time, a Range Rover, as well as a Mercedes. He had gone out in the Rover with its high clearance. 'I have to get through,' he said. He had even been shown in some television news fording a swollen creek in water almost up to his armpits and holding on to a rope stretched taut across the stream. He was also photographed making urgent house calls. Sandra had been proud of him.

The flood had certainly dislocated their lives. Its effects were to be felt for more than three weeks. He had to stay at the hospital overnight sometimes. He would warn her of the possibility before he left in the morning. There was a great demand, he said, for doctors, and that was true. He claimed that there were more premature births in that period than there had been for a decade. In a way, it had been rather nice for a time: living a fairly basic life, with an edge of danger, people helping one another. It must have been a little like that in the London blitz, she told herself.

They weren't the only things that the times may have had in common with the blitz. She had found out, as people usually do, by accident. George, their son, had developed a sore throat and a high temperature. She had been panicked by some sensational stories in the newspaper about how, as the floods receded, they would leave behind contagious diseases and germs that could defy diagnosis and cure. At one o'clock in the morning she finally called. She had put it off because, like most doctors, Jack was sceptical about any complaints of illness by any of his family. She knew his direct number in the small bedroom allocated to him at the hospital for overnight stays. All the doctors insisted on a direct line so that they could take calls from other patients if they had to stay overnight.

No doubt had he been in the room he would have answered the telephone himself. If it had not been late, and had she not been startled into wakefulness by the urgency, Jean Ghent would probably have ignored the ringing. Perhaps she might have thought it was an internal call for her. It might even have been a wrong number. She picked up the hand-piece.

'Jean Ghent, Dr Jean Ghent speaking.'

Sandra would still have recognized the clear, confident voice if she had not given her name. She could associate the voice immediately with its owner: a clever, long-brown-haired woman of about thirty, on the way up, temporarily a registrar, heiress apparent to a leading consultancy and university professorship. She was one of the new women, not a woman just preening herself on qualifying as a doctor, but a woman who would always be going places. She had an adequate figure, good regular features, and rather large legs with strong rounded calf muscles accentuated by expensive court shoes with high heels. She always seemed cool and controlled. She dressed for work as if for an exclusive luncheon. She was unimpressed by any of the senior doctors except those she needed to cultivate. She lived in no fear of the doctors' wives, whom she looked down upon for their vacuous lives and extravagance. Sometimes Sandra contrasted herself with Jean Ghent. She had met her a couple of times at hospital functions. What would it be like to be Jean Ghent? She must have a lot of independence.

Sandra struggled for an innocent explanation for the woman's presence in the early morning in her husband's bedroom. There was none. She spoke, as she did when she was distressed or uncertain what to do or say, in a high drawling affected tone that Daddy had encouraged her to use.

'I'm looking for my husband. This is Sandra Rentle. Would you please go and find him. It is urgent. His child is ill. I'll hold the line.'

For once the unflappable Jean Ghent hesitated. There was silence on the line, and then, 'I'll see if I can find him.' Sandra held on to the telephone while she speculated whether he was there or whether he had in fact been called out to look at a patient. It seemed to take forever for him to come to the telephone.

'Is that you Sandra?'

'Who the hell do you think it is, the wicked witch of the west? I'm only calling you because your son and heir is running a temperature of about a million degrees, has a sore throat, and could be dying for all I know, while you're making newsreels wading through swamps and humping your registrar ...'

'What are you saying, what are you talking about?'

'If you're not home to look at your son within half an hour I'm calling an ambulance and your eminent colleague, Dr Symes, to meet me at the hospital to examine my child. Please yourself.' She dashed the hand-piece against its cradle so violently that a chip fell off it.

What she had discovered was confirmatory rather than revelatory. It nonetheless infuriated her, for its tastelessness, its insensitivity, its grossness, its, its … She struggled to find the words, if predictably. And as she did so she realized that the word 'jealousy' never crossed her mind. She had sat back on the stuffed couch in the living room to analyse her feelings. Among all the emotions the one that she should feel, jealousy, continued to elude her. She asked herself, what residue of even mild affection she retained for Jack? Poor Jack. She thought on. Poor Sandra.

He arrived within twenty minutes, well groomed, hair too neat, and obviously on the defensive. 'Your son's in his …' she emphasized the 'his', 'bedroom. You may know where that is. Go and look at him.'

Jack paused, as if to offer an explanation. Sandra turned away and walked towards the kitchen. 'When you're finished, I'm having tea. You can join me if you wish.'

She put on Daddy's walk. It required loping military strides, as if she were on parade, serenely ignoring everyone but aware that others would be looking and gaping.

Later, George's temperature dramatically reduced by aspirin and the infection weakened by the liberal administration of antibiotics, they sat in the kitchen drinking tea and assuring each other that George would recover soon. Neither spoke of the events of the last couple of hours although each knew that a turning point in their lives had been reached. Suspicion has been translated into certainty. The unspoken had been spoken.

'I should get to bed. Rounds start at seven tomorrow.' She watched Jack as he made his way to the bedroom. From the back he still looked the trim young man she had married. He had always had a healthy, fit body. As a medical student he had managed to roister with his contemporaries but still keep fit. She recalled nights at the Victoria Park refectory when they were students. The refectory was a large fibrolite, asbestos cement building with a wooden floor built in the park across the road from the General Hospital, the Queensland training hospital for aspiring doctors. Local lore had it that the female students and other women, especially the nurses, who attended the regular Saturday night dances conducted there were all sexually depraved and determined to ambush the medical students. Local lore also had it, they were Jack's words at the time, fleetingly overheard by Sandra, that the nurses were so randy that you could hear them panting at twenty yards. She hadn't noticed it herself.

After he qualified he became more boringly health conscious. He was one of the first of their group to do so. Lucy said that he had pioneered designer joggers and the towelling headband for the whole of Queensland.

Lucy was no respecter of people and certainly not of Jack. 'You think you're going to live forever don't you? You think you're always going to be fleet and golden limbed, the Adonis of the medical profession.'

Sandra had wondered for a time whether there was something between them, that perhaps their badinage was a device to conceal affection. She started to watch Jack carefully. Nothing could be further from the truth. He hated Lucy's comments. Like a foreign country under bombardment by a superior air force he tried to fight back with ill-considered, limp salvos until his frustration at their failure pushed him into sulky withdrawal.

So he had, as Lucy said, jogged and fornicated on, as if his life depended on it. 'Perhaps it does,' she had added afterwards to Sandra. 'It's a little like martyrdom. You're only alive if you're in pain. Sandra, let's be frank, how the fuck could you have married a pig like that?'

They were at a lunch together after. Sandra had described to Lucy what she had discovered on the night of the high temperature. 'It seemed the right thing to do at the time. We had known each other for a long time. He was clever—You didn't do so well yourself.'

'Clever! He took seven years to pass.'

Sandra recalled how students were permitted to continue their university courses even if they regularly failed their examinations. 'That might be right. Say what you like, he's a very good doctor now.'

'He's a very fashionable doctor. I'd as much let him near my nether regions as a black widow spider. Society doctor whose only advantage over other society doctors is an intimate knowledge of the target area because of expansive, personal navigation.'

Sandra listened quietly to Lucy's demolition of her husband. A year ago, she might have been at the barricades, defending him. Now, her disillusionment was complete. Besides, despite all the vicissitudes of her life Lucy was still one of their privileged group. It was hard anyway to hide anything from Lucy and she did seem to have Sandra's best interests at heart. 'I admit it did come as a shock.'

'Shock! You've known all along what a two, three, four-timing little bastard he was. It's just you wouldn't admit it to yourself. You should treat this as a liberation. You owe him nothing. You ought to leave him.'

'And do what? Go where?' Sandra tried to visualize what it would be like, confronting life on her own, life without a husband. She wasn't brought up for that. Men made the important decisions. You couldn't always rely on them. Her mother, admittedly a dubious source, had said, 'Never trust any other woman. Men can, usually do, cause pain. But if you're clever, you can handle them. You can't handle other women.' Lucy said much the same. Well, it was all right for her. She hadn't had to handle Jack. She didn't have a son at St Mark's Anglican Boys' School and a daughter at the sister school. She didn't have to do tuck-shop duty and organize fundraisers. She'd lost her man, men? Lucy's advice didn't even work for Lucy.

They attended a dinner party together a week later. The usual crowd was there, Lucy and some handbag for the night called Ivan with a surname ending in 'ski'—he was quite out of place—Paul and Ruth Dawson, Ken and Andrea Lisa and their hosts Simon and Jessica Round. What was pleasant about their dinner parties was the proximity of their houses. Simon and Jessica lived only two blocks away in the same sort of house as Sandra's, although smaller of course. It was pleasant to walk slowly in the early evening waving to those of their friends and neighbours who were still about, and afterwards, after midnight, when the party was over, to return home tipsy and unworried by a motor car or the police preying on drunk drivers.

And you could talk in shorthand to your friends. When you mentioned the beach, everyone knew which beach you were talking about. Sometimes, when she joined in the gossip about those who were not present, she wondered what others were saying about her. You could be certain that this wasn't the only dinner party in Belvedere that night. What would they be saying at those others as the candles burnt low, the night lengthened and the alcohol took effect? Better not to think about that. Better not to think about lots of things these days.

Simon was a successful solicitor in a major city firm. Jessica had recently graduated as a mature-age student. She had taken, of all subjects, geography as a major. Now she was about to start a course to lead to a Master's degree. She had not been a school friend of Sandra's. She had attended a different school although she had always lived in or on the edge of Belvedere.

Jessica became very self-assured when she had gone to the university as an adult student. For a time she had even dressed like a university student, long straight bleached hair, shorts, a knapsack, sleeveless shirt in summer, and boots, with black socks. She would sometimes do some shopping at the local shopping centre dressed that way. At night she continued to dress in her designer labels. She spoke about getting a job, using her learning, she said. No one asked her what the current demand for geographers was.

Simon was middle-aged in a way Jack wasn't. Simon had always been middle-aged. He was a particular friend of Jack's. They went back a long way, to the first day at St Mark's prep school. Simon was a jogger. Almost the whole world except Sandra, and Lucy, were joggers. He tended to make proclamations rather than speak. Lucy said he would make the transfer of a cottage sound like the conveyance of the Rockefeller Centre. At weekends, he still dressed in the tweed sports jacket of his youth, summer and winter. He had inherited his place in the firm from his father. He was Jack's and her solicitor. It always seemed to Sandra that he was more interested in his own investments than in other people's legal problems but Jack swore by him. His hair was beginning to thin so he grew it long to have more of it to spread. As well as continue to jog with Jack, when Jessica took up university he took up physical fitness as if it were a penance. He went to the gymnasium every day. Sandra saw him there when she occasionally used her subscription. It was impossible to miss the way in which he showed off, in the early morning sessions, in front of the young housewives, the local matrons, and the young secretaries in leotards who somehow found their way to the Belvedere Gym.

Simon and Jessica had become very rich. Unlike many of their friends they had both applied themselves to increasing their inheritances. Now they could have stopped work altogether and travelled whenever and wherever they wished. Simon had a goal, though, which kept him on his home ground. He desperately wanted to be President of the Law Society. He claimed it as his right. He had tried unsuccessfully twice before. He told the party that this would be his year.

If you had to list your criticisms of Simon and Jessica you would have to include, no, not meanness, an aversion to extravagance perhaps. The guests sat or stood on the traditional verandah when they arrived. The choices were of inferior Scotch bought on special, an Australian gin, mineral water from a returnable bottle, or a sparkling Australian wine at seven dollars ninety a bottle. The savouries, 'nibblies' as Jessica called them, were ageing potato crisps, bottled olives and a slab of sweating cheese to be taken with a cracker biscuit. No one expected anything to be different. They all set about getting drunk with the means at hand.

Simon was more full of himself than usual. There had been a council of war that morning to plan his campaign for the Presidency. You could be forgiven for thinking he had just won the New Hampshire Primary. 'I've got a treat for you all,' he announced. 'I've got three,' he was pleased about the three and repeated it, 'three bottles of Grange Hermitage for dinner, 1970.' The others had to hide their surprise at this extravagant generosity.

'Have you opened them yet?' Lucy asked.

'Of course I have. Everyone knows you've got to let Grange breathe, an hour for each year,' he replied in his self-satisfied voice.

'I didn't ask for that reason. I thought we might get something decent to drink before dinner.' Lucy said. She had made some inroads upon the gin by now. Simon pretended he had not heard her.

To prove how democratic he was, Simon asked Ivan what he did for a living. He was rather shocked when he replied in a central European, presumably Polish accent.

'At present time I work as brickie's labourer.'

Really, Lucy was too much. A labourer. He did have a suit on though and his white shirt was clean and starched. 'Usually, I compose music.' The others and Simon relaxed. This was art then. Artists, musicians, sculptors, they all went their own way. He would add some exoticism to the party. Simon could imagine himself telling his partners about his colourful guest on Monday.

Jessica, as the acknowledged expert on cultural affairs, took up the questioning. 'Music, what sort of music do you compose?' He looked at her as if she were stupid.

'I compose music. What do you think I compose, pop songs, rock and roll? I am musician.' He drained his glass of gin and tonic and passed it to Lucy to be refilled. He was a tall solemn man, perhaps five years younger than Lucy, very serious, and with a dangerous, tragic, impulsive air about him. The men, none of whom was as tall as he, were more formal and careful with him than they were with men who were members of their own set.

Jessica tried again, 'which musicians do you admire?'

'There is only one truly great musician, Wagner.'

This surprising response from a Pole stopped the conversation. Ivan was unconcerned. He cut himself a huge slab of cheese and drank the replenished drink that Lucy brought him. He seemed content to eat and drink and remain outside the conversation.

Sandra pulled Lucy aside, 'Where did you get that?'

'He lives in a little flat near the river. I ran into him from time to time at the shopping centre. He carried my parcels to the car once and we struck up a conversation.'

'Are you …?'

Lucy laughed. 'No, not yet anyway. Probably not at all. I don't think he's very interested. I just thought it might be fun to bring him along here. Kill two birds with one stone, shock that pompous ass Simon, and make sure Ivan gets a free feed. Although, given Simon's tightness, that's a bit chancy. A few bottles of a decent red are a change. We should be grateful for small mercies.'

They went into dinner shortly afterwards. Jessica has passed out of her ethnic cooking phase, thank God. Sandra could remember the succession of stir fries, satays and buckets of rice that they had to eat on past visits. Jessica had simply done this time what they all did. She had telephoned 'Porcelain and Silver'; the local caterers who had suggested, and delivered in good time, a cauliflower and blue-cheese soup, a roast, and an Italian ice dessert. Simon liked roasts. He was very good at carving them and always cracked the same joke, that he should have been a surgeon.

As Sandra sat down, she experienced the same sensation of disembodiment as she usually felt at about this time at any dinner party. Not that she would be alone in that regard. In this set on Saturday night, unless the joggers were running in a veterans' half marathon in the morning, none of them would have stopped at two pre-dinner drinks. Sandra had counted five but knew that she was probably one out, and the others would have kept up with her. Ivan pretty clearly though had outstripped them all. He looked more gloomy than when he arrived and was a little unsteady when seated. Lucy brought him a glass of mineral water which she put in place of the gin he had brought to the table with him.

Simon made a great fuss of putting Sandra on his right. The Dawsons were placed at the far end of the table with Jessica. Beside her on the other side he sat Ken who engaged her in conversation for the first time that night. When he spoke his voice was slurred. Jack and the others would shake their heads as they whispered to each other that Ken wouldn't hold it: a matter of serious masculine dishonour.

Ken was the chief executive of a small local public company that manufactured special heat-resistant earthenware tiles and pipes, and other practical ceramic products. He and his wife lived six blocks away, just, if only just, within the inner circle. He was a short corpulent man who was an outstanding dancer. The evening would probably end, as most did when Ken was present, with dancing. Someone would suggest that the rug be rolled up and a record be played. Until then Ken would seem, indeed would be, hopelessly drunk. He would miraculously sober up and execute the most dexterous and elegant steps begging each of the women in turn to dance with him. Afterwards they would practically have to carry him to his car so that

Andrea, herself under the weather, but not as deeply so, could drive him home. Heaven only knew how she got him out of the car, if she did. She herself as an unfailingly cheerful woman, totally preoccupied with her children.

At the time they were all absorbed in their children's schooling. Not that there were any serious questions about where they would go, to the expensive Anglican or the Presbyterian schools that were members of the Great Public Schools Association. They knew lots of Catholics of course. They all had some best friends who were Catholics, but while the children were being educated their schooling tended to keep them separate. Sandra was pleased she was some distance away from Andrea. There was a limit to how much anyone could listen to stories about tuck-shop duty and school uniforms, of fund drives and raffles and school dances and new headmasters and headmistresses.

Simon was being mean about the wine. Did he really have the bloody stuff or not? Sandra had a good mind to ask for a white. Lucy got in ahead of her. 'Simon, I'd like a glass of white wine with the soup.' Displeased, Simon looked up. Reluctantly he went into the kitchen and returned with a bottle of chardonnay. Sandra could distinctly remember the brand because she had bought half a dozen bottles of it herself at the local pub where it was offered at a reduced price of five dollars ninety-five a bottle. When she had got it she had been in two minds whether to finish the first bottle. It had grown on her, she had found. 'Hurry up,' Lucy asked, 'We'll be finished the soup before you've opened the bottle.'

Everyone demanded white wine and Jack had to open a second bottle. When he had gone to get it, Lucy mouthed across the table, 'I hope he doesn't use that as an excuse to hold back on the Grange.'

Simon's good humour was restored by the sight of the roast that Jessica brought in on an old blue-and-white serving plate that had been in his family for two generations. His good humour increased as he delicately sliced the meat into large, thin, perfectly cooked slices. Jack pre-empted the joke to give Simon more pleasure than if he had spoken himself.

'I swear Simon I'm going to take you to the theatre to do some of my surgery for me next week. Beautiful. Perfect.'

The conversation was tirelessly and unashamedly gossip. This was the generation of spouses who tried to stay together, often making each other miserable, and wondering whether they would be less miserable single, or with someone else. The problem was they were all so alike that any change would be illusory. They would just live at different addresses. Some of them were beginning to wonder about the example of the generation between their's and their children's. Were they happier with their changing alliances, shattered marriages, divorces and valiant second, even third attempts?

'What would Daddy have made of all this?' Sandra asked herself. No doubt they had had their pieces on the side. At least if Daddy did he was totally discreet. Look at the Nelson sisters. They still kept up the façade. Were they happy with their façade? Sandra wasn't. She struggled to hear what Ruth Dawson was saying from the other end of the table.

'She finally up and did it.'

'Who?' Sandra called out.

'Rose Losey.'

'What did she up and do?'

Ruth had the attention of all of them now. 'She ran off with Miss Druid.'

'No one could be called Miss Druid,' their cultural leader Jessica called out.

'I tell you there is and she did.' Miss Druid was her daughter's music teacher at St Cecilia's, a rather large, hairy woman, 'You must know her, all of you. I'm sure she taught Nicola.' Ruth was referring to the Rentle's daughter.

Jack pronounced his usual diagnosis of any discontented woman. 'Obviously Jeremy wasn't giving her her greens.'

The whole table laughed except for Ivan, Lucy and Sandra.

'I don't know about that Jack. You think a few thrusts and a grunt are every maiden's and mature woman's delight. It's not the same as jogging.' Lucy took him up.

'Well, I'm glad she didn't get her clutches on Nicola,' Jack would defend his daughter's honour to the death.

'How do you know she didn't? They give them a liberal education nowadays.' Lucy was well on the way now, and fearless. Jack reacted angrily.

'You're talking about Sandra's and my daughter.'

'Take a cold shower Jack.' Lucy turned away from him. He half rose in his chair. Ivan, as if awakened from a deep sleep, acted, clamping a huge hand on Jack's shoulder, pressing him back into his seat.

Simon jumped up. 'I've forgotten the Grange. Hold your horses everyone. He darted over to the sideboard to decant the wine, making a great ceremony of it with candle and the decanter, talking all the while. His expression of holiness was heightened by the reflection of the flame in the cut glass.

'Wonderful wine. Particularly good year, too. God knows what it would cost if you could find it in the shops. Look at that colour.' He sniffed the decanter which was now full. 'Beautiful, old fruit, heavy, musky.' He spoke like a wine magazine.

No sooner had he half-filled Lucy's goblet than she picked it up and drained it. 'There's too much ceremony about wine. God, after what we've drunk so far, who'd know the difference anyway.' Simon tried not to hear her but she insistently held out her glass for more. 'I know it's bad taste to fill the glass but let's have some bad taste, eh Simon.'

He half-filled her glass again and passed on to the others. Then he resumed his seat at the head of the table beside Sandra. The beef was good and Sandra, intent on it, thought she was mistaken. That surely was not a hand on her left knee. She shook her leg and the hand went away. She looked and saw Simon's right hand return to the table top and pick up his knife.

'Jack seems to be very busy these days, long hours. I suppose a surgeon's got a shelf life. Reflexes fade with age.'

'Don't solicitors?'

'No, not really. Solicitors just got wiser as they get older.'

Sandra could see out of the corner of her eye the look of disbelief on Lucy's face. She shook her head to quieten her and to her surprise that was effective. Sandra turned to talk to Ivan who had already eaten every scrap of the food on his plate. He was no longer content with water and picked up Lucy's red wine and drank it. Lucy gestured to Jack to fill both of their glasses. He had to decant the third bottle to do so.

Paul Dawson was a general practitioner. He was usually a quiet, thoughtful man, overawed by a garrulous wife. He had not been brought up in the district and often asked himself why he lived in it now. Emboldened by Lucy's outspokenness and too much of the Hermitage himself, he said to Jack, 'Three bottles down, must be three to go. I don't see them. Where are you hiding them?'

'There's no more Grange.' The response was sharp and final.

By eleven o'clock they were all, except Simon, drunk beyond redemption. Wives adrift from husbands were talking familiarly with other men. Seated on a couch beside Sandra, Simon had wedged her against the arm rest. She didn't mind. She was experiencing fatalistic feelings of indifference. No one was sure whether Simon drank less than the rest of them out of a determined abstinence or meanness. By comparison with the others his voice was unslurred.

'I know what happened between you and Jack the other night.'

She struggled to clear her head. 'Between Jack and me? What do you mean? Nothing happened.'

'Look, you've got nothing to be ashamed of. It's not your fault.'

'Simon, what are you talking about?' She finally managed to sit up straight. She wriggled her body to move further away.

'Jack, and the hospital, how you caught him out.'

'How the hell do you know that? What is this, a boy's confession?'

'Well, yes, Jack did tell me. We're very old friends. You know that.'

'The bastard. I'll … I'll …'

Simon took her hand and gently rubbed it between his two hands.

'He just came out with it. I didn't encourage it. I suppose he felt guilty; he just wanted to tell someone about it.'

'Who else was there?'

'No one. I swear it.' He moved closer to her and had placed one hand on her knee. The disjointed conversation, with occasionally raised voices and the clink of glass coming from the verandah seemed a long way away. No one had any idea what they were drinking now, or cared. 'There can be nothing more humiliating for a woman, a beautiful woman and a mother to be cast aside for a mistress. And how obvious, a mistress who is a subordinate at the place where he works.' His hand had moved up her leg and he was kneading her inner thighs through the silk of her dress. She pushed his hand away.

'And I suppose Jessica wouldn't be humiliated by this.' She pointed to his hand and pushed at him to move away.

'You must know about Jessica, when Jessica went on campus. That changed a lot of things for us. Not my doing. I can assure you. Running round out there like a refugee from hippiedom. I know she smoked pot. And she did other things, worse things.'

Sandra was interested now. 'Is pot any worse than that white wine you served us?' Inhibitions reduced by the alcohol, she quoted Lucy. 'She said it had the refinement and potency of camel's piss.'

'Lucy thinks she can play around in the men's room. She's very lucky we all tolerate her after she went through two husbands.'

'For God's sake one walked out on her and the other one died.'

'That may be, but her conduct didn't help.' Simon was like a randy adolescent rubbing his body against hers now.

'You don't know how my heart goes out to you.' He had his arm behind her back now and was gripping her bare shoulder. 'I mean it, I want to sleep with you, cherish and comfort you a little.'

'Simon, you sound like a script for a bad movie.'

Sandra and Jack stumbled home through the silent suburb. Overhead a late 747 broke the curfew to come in to land from the Bay. Its engines sounded like muted thunder as they prepared themselves for bed, where for a little time they dutifully made clumsy and unsatisfactory love. It was, in all respects, a typical Belvedere Saturday night.

Chapter 5
The Detour

Two weeks later Sandra waited in room 14, on the ground floor of the Flying Boat Motel. If she craned her neck to reach the windows and pushed aside the terylene curtains she could see the sweep of the river. Daddy had known the reach well. He had sailed on it, as a boy. The name of the motel would be lost on most. It was decades since the war and flying boats had put float to water here.

Sandra had inspected the room when she was shown into it. The most prominent feature was the large-size bed with a cover of green chenille. It looked uninviting but she had tested it to find it very comfortable. The floor was covered in a heavily patterned olive-and-brown floral fitted carpet. She wondered about it as she had walked barefooted across the room. There was a small refrigerator stocked with mineral water, beer, soft drinks, a packet of tired cheese, and two half-bottles of Australian sparkling white wine unapologetically labelled 'Hunter Champagne'. Mounted on a broad counter under the front window was a large television set. It could, like an invisible radio, be operated by a set of controls mounted by the headboard of the bed. Sandra tried them all. On the table there was a breakfast menu offering huge meals that would have fed a navvy for a week.

It was six thirty. She watched the news on one of the commercial channels. She hadn't brought a book. How ridiculous. Fancy bringing a book on an assignation. Lucy had told her that before her first extra-marital affair she had felt like a virgin preparing herself for an awakening. She had, she said, showered and dressed in a new negligee. Sandra had showered: and scented herself before she left home. She had checked to make sure of no surprise visits by the children and that there was no change to Jack's Tuesday night schedule. What a hell of a time, hell of a place, God, when you come to think of it, hell of a person to have an affair with.

When Simon arrived he was a flustered man in a hell of a hurry. He sneaked in like a Cold War spy under round the clock surveillance. Having flirted with her, and importuned her to be here, it was as if he were embarrassed. She wasn't wearing a negligee but her dress was new and fitted her like a glove. Beneath it she wore a new black suspender belt and pants with a black lace heart like a tart. She had thought that all of this would have excited some interest, have even perhaps occasioned some ceremony.

As soon as he was sure he hadn't been followed Simon started to undress. He didn't look at her as he carefully hung up his suit, and rolled one sock into the other. He only paused when he was naked except for his shirt. 'Aren't you going to get properly undressed?'

'I thought we might have a drink first.' Sandra went to the refrigerator and began to remove the cork from one of the bottles.

'A drink. We don't have much time you know?'

'I've got the night. I thought you told me Jessica was going out.'

'That's right. But, this is a pretty obvious place.'

Sandra had raised an objection to a motel on the edge of their suburb. 'Let's go west, south, east,' she said.' Let's be sure no one we know will see us.'

Simon disagreed. Simon was a very territorial creature. They all were, Sandra supposed. Still this was different. She could perhaps bear an encounter with an acquaintance out of the suburb in some sleazy motel, but in her old home district it would be insufferable. She had tried to impress this upon Simon. He could not be budged and insisted upon the Flying Boat Motel. His informed and persistent insistence upon it suggested to Sandra that he was no stranger to this tired, old and undoubtedly cheap, motel. But she had vowed to sleep extra-maritally and she was not going to be deterred by common sense, squalid surroundings, or even the risk of being recognized.

Sandra removed the foil and cork. She poured two drinks and handed him one. He took his reluctantly, sipped it and then placed it on the table. His hands we removing restlessly. He walked to the bed, pulled off the covers, removed his shirt and stripped under the sheet like a startled mouse. He pulled it up to his chin and asked her to get into bed.

She told herself that it might improve next time. He said, after it was over, that he was very fast, that was his reputation. His other talent, he actually used the word 'talent', was to be ready again quickly. In the meantime she lay on her back waiting. They exchanged no words. It started to rain and although the noises of the traffic on the busy airport road were dulled by the drops, there was a constant swishing of tyres. It was dark and the room was intermittently lit by the reflections of the flashing flying boat neon-sign beside the entrance to the motel.

Sandra lay on her back wondering why she was here. Adultery should be exciting and dangerous. She was neither excited nor in any danger. Perhaps committing adultery for the first time was like losing your virginity. It didn't have to be pleasurable. It was the event, the milestone that counted. For her though she knew casual coupling wouldn't be enough. It might be for some of her friends but if she was going to commit adultery it would have to be in a real affair. Simon might at least have brought some flowers.

'I wouldn't mind that drink now.' He said it in a tone that made it clear that he expected her to get out of bed to bring it to him. She threw the sheet aside and brought him his drink. It was ridiculous, she told herself, to feel shy when they had just had intercourse. She had a suspicion that he had kept his eyes closed most of the time. She couldn't decide whether he'd done so out of shyness or because he was fantasizing about some other woman.

Daddy always said that a woman should try to think of interesting things to talk about to a man. Mother agreed with that. Sandra asked Simon about his running.

'I'm doing a half marathon next Saturday. I've been training a lot, being careful with my diet.' He remembered the Australian sparkling wine in his hand and put the glass down on the bedside. 'That stuff doesn't help, not in the week before. You shouldn't have insisted. Look at it, rubbish anyway.'

'Not the quality of that Grange we had at your place.'

He was away now, expanding on the great vintages he claimed to have drunk, telling her how he and Jessica had drunk and eaten their way through Burgundy two years ago.

'But the wine, good wines are expensive in France.'

'Well that was the point, we didn't buy the expensive ones. We didn't have to. You'd be surprised at the number of vineyards, ones nobody's ever heard of. You can buy some of them for almost nothing I can tell you.' He was animated by the thought of those francs saved. 'Like the food, little cafés, fine cooking with vin ordinaries of the district.'

'Jack says they truck it in, in tankers. It's all a racket. Half of it comes from North Africa. The locals laugh at the tourists, he says.'

'Well, Jack wasn't with us and he wouldn't know. I'd back my nose and palate against his anytime.'

She reached under the sheet and touched his flaccid penis. Time to stir him up again. 'They're not the only parts of you you'd back yourself against Jack.' She tried to flatter him.

She was surprised by the way he flinched away from her.

'Now listen Sandra, we ought to get this clear. Just because we're doing this doesn't mean I'm disloyal to Jack. He's my oldest friend. We started school together, the first day. Now there's a limit to what I'd let anyone say about old Jack.'

'You're saying you're not disloyal to Jack. Then what's all of this about. If this isn't treason what is?'

'Sandra, you wanted this, more than I did. I knew Jack had been up to tricks for a long time. I thought it might be good for you, help you out, so to speak.'

Sandra received this in silence. Was it always the man who had to be put first? Sexual intercourse was something a man should have, something he was entitled to. And if he provided some incidental gratification to the woman then he was thoughtful and good. She was sure Daddy had thought that way and so had her mother. The young men she had known before marriage, except for Dan, had all thought the same way. Jack certainly did. Now Simon was taking it a step further. He had actually gone to bed with her as a favour to her. She lay silently on her back, weighing what she had just heard. Sandra was suddenly struck by a terrible thought. She was going to die one day. She had just read a book about a woman who was preoccupied with the thought of death, to the extent that she could barely live each day. Sandra lay there, her legs and arms rigid with fear. Is that what I want to leave behind me? Is this the best? She slowly, painfully relaxed her body.

Simon beside her had been concentrating on becoming erect again. All he needed was for her to fondle him. He had been trying to think of a roundabout way of asking her. It wouldn't be the same if she had to do it by direction. She was so silent. He became anxious.

'Sandra, Sandra, are you all right?'

Sandra got out of the bed without answering him. 'Sandra, what's wrong?'

She began to dress. Simon kept himself covered by the sheet. He was very firm now and wanted her back in the bed. She did not answer. He was becoming angry.

'Sandra, what the hell d'you think you're doing?'

'I'm going home.'

'You can't. I'm ready again.'

'Well, Simon, you can pick up your readiness, play with it, cut it off or do what you like with it, but you're not doing it with me again. She didn't bother putting on her stockings. She put them in her handbag, combed her hair and moved towards the door.

'By the way you don't have to worry about the bill, or being recognized. I paid in cash when I arrived. It's yours for the night.'

He sat up on the bed. 'What the hell's going on. I thought you said you could stay the night?'

'I just decided I didn't want to. It's all a mistake. You know Simon, I never liked you. I'm so ashamed of myself.'

'There's nothing to be ashamed of. People do it all the time.'

'Not for doing it, but for doing it with you.' She opened the door and walked out into the rain. She went around to the back of the motel where she had parked her car, unlocked it and drove home.

How long ago had that been, ten, twelve, twenty years? Things you wanted to put out of your mind always seemed recent. She could still see the flashing boat sign and hear the swish of the tyres on the wet road outside. She could still remember Simon after that evening, calling twice, puzzled and irritated, wanting to meet her, to console her, he said, to make things right.

Well it wasn't the worst thing she'd done in her life. It was one of the silliest. She was so ashamed she decided to tell no one, not even Lucy. That turned out to be a joke. That bastard Simon had as good as told her, probably as a reprisal for the way she had left him that night.

'How could you have done it with that little runt?' She had said when she told Sandra she knew. 'But listen Sandra, if you want something on the side let me know. A woman like you doesn't have to take a mean, stupid, desiccated little swine like Simon. He's just the sort to push a woman towards lesbianism. Rotten little bastard kiss and tell. He said that you were frigid, needed treatment. He did his best, but just crept out when you were asleep.'

Sandra told Lucy the real story. 'Not that it makes much difference Lucy. Is it better not to be married? What have I got to look forward to?'

'I'm not going to tell you you've got two beautiful children. They're not enough for consideration. Children can be problems themselves.'

'Not my children. They won't be like that.'

'In this suburb, in this decade, with their parents, they, you, haven't got a hope. They might avoid the drugs, nothing else. Jesus Sandra, look at how we all drink. You've taken me away from the point. Simon, yes, simple stupid venal Simon. Don't go with the little bastard again no matter what happens. I can find someone for you if you want.'

'No.'

'You're not thinking of doing something really silly are you, like leaving Jack?'

'No.'

'Don't do that. You're not the sort of woman to survive on her own.'

'Daddy always said most women needed a man, especially those who said they didn't.'

'Daddy? That Daddy of yours thought he was fucking Socrates and Bertrand Russell rolled into one.' Lucy noticed the look of horror that appeared on Sandra's face. The combination of rough language and a criticism of 'Daddy' were too much.

Lucy held her hands out in a placatory gesture. 'I'm sorry, I meant no harm. I apologise for daring to question Daddy's sacred memory.'

Lucy was right, of course, about Simon. But she was too hard on Daddy. Strange that. Lucy's father wasn't very different except he had spent all their money. There was certainly never going to be a reprise with that little creep Simon. Although it was wrong to speak ill of the dead there was no law against thinking ill of them. Simon had collapsed with a massive heart attack three years later, after he had proudly come twenty-third in the veterans' class of a half marathon at Surfers Paradise.

Sandra, back in the present, poured herself another glass of wine. She then very deliberately inserted the cork tightly into the neck of the bottle. She would drink no more tonight. She would take half a Mogadon and read, then she would fall asleep and sleep.

She selected a book from her bedside table, *The Middle Ground* by Margaret Drabble. Even Jack had taken to boasting about her reading. 'Sandra's into modern literature now, reads all the time, women's books, biographies, even plays.' He couldn't quite keep the patronizing tone out of his voice. Like most doctors he didn't allow himself much time for reading. Reading for pleasure didn't make you any money, and besides it was hard enough to keep up with medical science these days. In truth, he was a little scared of Sandra's middle-aged foray into a world of words and imagination.

Sandra tried to keep quiet about her reading. She didn't want to be steered towards improving works by well-intentioned, educated women, or those who obtained degrees in the otherwise suddenly arid years of departed adult children. Nor did she want to be told she should enrol in a course. For the time being the lunches and her own random approach to books suited her well enough. Indeed she was constantly surprising herself by the way in which her general knowledge was expanding. She wished that all those years ago she had been encouraged to study and graduate.

So she read her Margaret Drabble. What a strange lot of women she wrote about. There were some women of her generation like them. Lucy perhaps. Strong, effective women with robust sex lives and a network of sympathetic female friends. Educated women mostly, with good careers, detaching husbands as no longer comfortable old clothes, but with children who seemed to remain devoted. It was an unpredictable life they lived, but they seemed happy in it. Or were they? Was Lucy? These were difficult questions. She carefully marked the page she had reached and put aside the book. Margaret Drabble also made her uncomfortable. She went to bed and took up the latest Anita Brookner and tried that.

Sandra fell asleep with her bedside light still on.

Chapter 6
A Tennis Party

By middle-age, parents should not be troubled by their children. As she showered and then dressed, Sandra thought of the day ahead. She knew she had many faults. She knew that she was not clever. She had always tried to be a good mother. She would have been surprised to know that her contemporaries thought that she had succeeded.

Could it have been something to do with being the wife of an obstetrician, gynaecologist? What a silly thought. She owed her fine figure and long neck, her silk hair and good features to her genes. Her skin still glowed, she was healthy despite the wine and sleeping pills. She had conceived when they decided to have children, almost at the thought of conception. In labour, however, it was a different story. Her two confinements were long and agonizing. Jack couldn't explain why. Painful to bear, painful later. Two were enough.

In some families there is more culpability, more accusations of blame than there are in the criminal courts. When the children had their troubles, insults and accusations flew like ICBMs. 'You bloody well spoilt them, Sandra, always have.' 'It's all very well for you to say, Jack. What sort of an example have you given them? Off with your doxies every second night, never home, showing off before the first-year nurses, never asking the children about their problems. Don't you dare blame me when something goes wrong.'

With hindsight she could see that they were both at fault. Everything she said about Jack was true though. Her problem was that she had spoiled them as Jack alleged. She had treated them, even when they were very young, as elite. And of course elitism in their adolescence was worse, more excessive than it had been when she was growing up. So much had changed since her adolescence, like access to fast motor cars, drugs, easy alcohol, more pocket money, practically no public transport, luxury apartments at the beach, even earlier puberty, contraception, absence of wars. The list went on.

Sandra dressed. She had slept well. There was no doubt that a slight sleeping-pill hangover was a great deal better than an alcohol hangover. She was proud to herself. She vowed not to drink again today. She made a cup of tea.

It was early. There were still some early morning joggers about. She went to her favourite chair on the verandah to drink her tea. Inkie, excited by her rare early morning appearance, bounced up with much tail wagging and placed his paw on her knee to remind her to pat him. She should do this more often. Inkie was a different dog in the morning.

My God how innocent we were. She sometimes looked into the hollow, hopeless eyes to teenagers today and shuddered. We had our faults. We suffered our pains. But we never had to make a commitment to long-term hopelessness. No, it came with the commitment.

Sandra looked out on to the morning. She felt in control and strangely relaxed despite what was ahead of her. She returned to her adolescence.

Sandra knew from the first moment she met Dan she couldn't talk about him at home. It was necessary to postpone the battery of questions as long as possible. 'What surname did you say? Never heard that one. How did you meet him? Are there any other dancing academies? In your mother's day girls used to learn to dance at school. If the teachers couldn't teach them, dancing instructors came to the school. Parents felt safe that way. I'm not sure you should continue with those lessons. I thought only boys from our sorts of families and schools went there. A bit pricey I would have thought for a boy from that school and that kind of suburb. Does he come on his own? Surely there aren't a lot of them allowed in. The city is growing so much there seem to be people everywhere no one's ever heard of. No, I don't like the sound of any of this. Your father and I need to talk a few things over.'

It didn't matter that she would know in advance what the questions and comments would be. She could easily predict the reactions of Daddy and his network of cronies. If you mentioned a name they hadn't heard of, they'd use their connexions and influence to find out about the person, like a group of hunters chasing the last of a species previously thought extinct.

She had been attracted to Dan from the first. Attraction was one thing, succumbing to it was another.

Brisbane had a population then of perhaps four hundred thousand. The Labor government had been in power, for almost forty years. The Party consisted of a powerful alliance of public servants and lawyers, non-militant unionists, the Catholic Church in Brisbane, about half the police force, a substantial portion of the judiciary, and a team of self-seeking journeymen politicians, or so Daddy said. Daddy and his friends were, of course, strongly opposed to the unions and the Labor Party. That didn't mean they condescended to the political struggle themselves.

Daddy and his friends were inveterate clubmen. They were members of the Constitution Club. It was, simply, the Club. It seemed to Sandra on the rare occasions when she had visited to be a rather gloomy place, let the old man be welcome to it. Its smell was a distinctly male one, of cigarettes and cigars, leather and boot polish, whisky and the inferior housekeeping of a place not overseen by a woman. There they talked about wool prices, strikes by wharfies, the War in which they had served, politics, and the outrageous tax on a bottle of good Scotch.

When they had drunk quite a lot they would talk about their school days. What wonderful memories some of them had of those days. Daddy tended to be vague and forgetful about most things but if you asked him how many rugby matches St Mark's won in 1931 he could tell you not only the number but also what the winning margin was in each of them. He was less certain about the matches they lost. Nicknames were bandied about. Masters who never hesitated with the cane were spoken of with affection.

Even though their party, the Tories, as they wistfully called the barely conservative opposition, was not in power, they still managed to wield some influence. These were the last days of the great divide between the Catholics and the Masons. Each had fought the other for power for decades. However, each knew that the other could not be entirely dominated. Accordingly, by convention, a Masonic police commissioner alternated with a Catholic one. And some measure of cross-political pollination was tolerated. A Masonic labour politician might find his campaign funds increased by a contribution from a conservative Masonic businessman and a rich Catholic store owner might make large donations to a labour Catholic cabinet minister.

When Sandra was a girl these arcane matters were for the men. Her mother, who was more intelligent than her husband, nonetheless tolerated her exclusion from important affairs. Sandra thought she regretted her subservience now but it was far too late to correct that.

Jack and she didn't need to be thrown together all the time, just occasionally to remind them of each other. Also you wouldn't, Daddy said, want Jack to be tied down too young. Boys, men, have to sew their wild oats: better they do before they marry and have children. This was the way they were conditioned. It was not that there was any subtlety about it. It was just the way their sort of people did things. The children would pick it up by osmosis, although Daddy would have called it breeding.

Sandra knew all of this, although if she had been asked to talk about it or explain it she couldn't have. Jack was not unattractive. He was a good athlete and rugby player, and sure of himself. He was a prefect at school. It was supposed to be flattering to be asked to dance at the dancing academy and be taken to school dances by an older boy.

Although Sandra sensed and understood the assumptions about her future, she found herself resisting them and their inevitable conclusion. She had mixed feelings about the idea of love. It was a small word but a big concept. She doubted whether what passed between Daddy and Mother was love. She couldn't, when she dwelt upon it, think of much love between her friends' parents. But she did know that the tall, intense boy from the state high school stirred feelings in her that neither Jack nor any other boy she knew did.

Lucy was a quieter person then than she was now. She had, however, begun to strike out early in a way that her parents and their friends couldn't understand. Among all the girls, and later women, she was the only possible confidante.

Sandra drew her aside one lunch hour. They sat secluded and partly concealed beside the trunk of an old camphor laurel tree in the corner of the school grounds. The Anglican nuns disapproved strongly of earnest tête-à-têtes.

'Lucy, did you notice that high school boy at dancing classes?'

'You think I'm blind now. The tall one who never takes his eyes off you. And I think, you him. He is a high school boy. What would your father say?'

'I think I like him very much.'

'Chemistry, eh? All of the oldies think you and Jack are made for each other. There's not much you can do about that.'

'Esme says that he lives near a St Mark's boy. They sometimes play tennis together. Do you think they could have a tennis party, a mixed party? My parents wouldn't say anything if it was a St Mark's boy's place.'

'Where is this?'

'At Creekdale.'

'Creekdale? Where, I ask you, is that?'

'I'm not too sure. On the south side. You go through Woolloongabba, I think, towards Manly or Wynnum.'

'You're well informed.'

'It can't be too far away. He goes to school at the Morcam High School.'

'My father always says that if a residence isn't within walking distance of a tram line it shouldn't exist.'

Extended acreage living was not yet fashionable, before people moved out and built *Gone with the Wind* plantation mansions with swimming pools, gravel drives, stables and three garages to house the family fleet. When that did happen their set never moved and never acknowledged that different ways of life were turning them into amusing anachronisms. Creekdale, though, was not a suburb even later to be acknowledged as a suitable habitat for the nouveau riche or, indeed, anyone you would want to know.

Sandra inquired about it as discreetly as she could. No one seemed to know very much about it. Some said that a lot of migrants lived there because the land was cheap and the rates low. Besides, the local council wasn't very strict. Apparently you could build pretty well what you liked and take as long over it as you wished to do it. Many people bought army tents left over at the end of the war and erected them as long-term temporary dwellings at the back of their allotments as they laboriously saved to buy building materials to construct their three-bedroom combined sitting-and-dining room houses near their road alignments.

The event was however arranged. Esme's friend, Paul, a St Mark's boy, would have a tennis party at his parents' house on the edge of Creekdale. In addition to some St Mark's boys, he would, albeit grudgingly, invite Dan, a near resident. The girls, Esme, Lucy, Sandra and some others from Sandra's school would also be invited.

It was unthinkable that the girls would travel by public transport: tram to the city, a change of tram there, to Woolloongabba, and then a bus to Creekdale, which lay far beyond the reach of any tramline. On no account was Sandra prepared to have Daddy do the driving. It wasn't as if the fathers of any of the other girls would be less disapproving of the venue, it was because Daddy would very quickly sniff the wind about Dan and forbid any contact in the future.

Esme's father drove them down in his large silver Buick. It was the last decade of the grand American sedans. He was a successful general practitioner at Longcrest Junction and had owned an American V8 saloon car from the day that he set up a practice. Inside, the car had deep leather benches for seats and the five slim young girls had plenty of room. They were dressed in white pleated tennis skirts, sand shoes, with white socks and carried Angora cardigans in case it became cool in the late afternoon.

The journey was an adventure after they passed through the 'Fiveways'. Some of them had been to the Gabba cricket ground with their fathers so that was familiar enough. Esme's father, always the wit, said, 'We're passing into Geronimo's territory now.' Sandra cautiously looked around her. Nothing looked very different to her. There were the same sorts of rows of old timber houses with verandahs as in their street. The houses were smaller and some of the grounds not as well kept but there was nothing to suggest that this was a different place.

Esme's father continued to make comments about the areas as he drove through them. 'Some of these parts aren't too bad. Still there's only one place to live in Brisbane when the chips are down.'

What on earth was he talking about, Sandra asked herself? Behind his veneer of jollity, Esme's father was becoming concerned. He had passed through the area before on his way to the Bay, but then it was less settled, drab but inoffensive scrub, before you reached the sea at Wynnum or Cleveland.

The countryside, for they were in an area in which the houses stood apart, separated by bedraggled ti-trees and other unprepossessing, stunted bushes and scrub, was unappealing. None of the houses here was large. A number of them had poultry sheds behind, with chicken-wire enclosures for the fowls to scratch in the ground. In some places, attempts had been made to grow vegetables and strawberries. The results were unhealthy looking plants with little fruit upon them. The soil, when it was exposed, was grey and glutinous.

Sandra could see Esme's father's look of distaste as he steered the large, softly sprung sedan around the bends in the road. For a moment she thought he might insist on turning back. In the meantime he renewed his interrogation of his daughter.

'You're sure this boy goes to St Mark's?'

'Of course I am. He's in the school tennis team.'

Her father didn't regard that as a recommendation. 'Not a rugby player, eh?'

'I don't know. I don't think so.'

'What other boys are going to this tennis party?'

'Just other St Mark's boys.' Esme lied.

There was much consulting of the referdex and debate about the correct turning. Esme's father began to sulk. 'How am I going to find my way back, and at night to collect you? I can't be messing around you know. Might get a call. Then where would we be? This country all looks the same. Funny area. Funny place for a St Mark's boy to live. You wonder how people live in those sorts of houses?' He pointed generally to his left where the terrain was featureless, and raw with recently turned earth.

Lance Fullwood's house was on a block of land of two and a half acres. It was perhaps a little larger than its nearest neighbour. It had no verandahs, just a small covered porch at the front and the back. It was set on concrete posts about three feet from the ground with a brick base at the front like the courtesy panel of a desk to shield what might otherwise be exposed underneath. The house was in an L shape, in imitation of the new American ranch-style houses popular in the more prosperous less unfashionable suburbs.

Each one of these features could, if with difficulty, be accepted. What could not was the main material used for the sheeting of the building: fibro, unpainted, baring its concentration camp grey hue to all the world: fibro walls and a fibro roof, discoloured with a scale of black mould. This was the building material of other people, people who could not afford good hardwood, and bricks baked to a ripe deep terra cotta colour, people who could not afford or be bothered even to try to cover up the shame of fibro with a couple of coats of sealer and paint. As was its way, in a couple of places the brittle, thin material had cracked, and elsewhere some parts had come away leaving sharp shard-like remnants of gap teeth. Inside, the lining material would be the same, except there, perhaps, the walls and ceilings would be painted.

At the back of the house there was a rustic tennis court with an ant-bed surface. The high fence surrounding it was of chicken wire supported by trimmed local saplings that were bent in places. The lines had been painstakingly marked on the watered and rolled surface, and a brand new green net with white tape proudly stretched between the two steel posts concreted in the ground to hold it. There was beside the court an open shed with second-hand corrugated iron walls on two sides and a corrugated iron roof. Inside were a couple of old school forms and a homemade pine table with a new plastic table cloth tacked down on top of it.

Behind the court there were two sheds, also of fibro with the ubiquitous chicken-wire pens around them. There was a strong smell of wet fowl manure in the air. Disconsolate fowls scratched at vegetable scraps that littered the yards.

Sandra was ashamed that she felt embarrassed. She couldn't quite understand why she should be ashamed. She had done nothing. It wasn't her fault that these people who lived down here in this house chose to send their son to St Mark's as if he had a right to be there and to mix with other St Mark's boys and their friends.

At that thought she had become even more ashamed of herself. What sacrifices the boy's parents must be making to send their son to a private school. She actually said to herself the first lines of a prayer they said at school each morning as a penance.

Mr Fullwood was a medium-sized, over-cheerful man. He was wearing his best casual clothing, apart from the black lace-up shoes that doubled for work shoes. He was, they later learned, a claims officer for an insurance company who hoped one day to be the manager of the Brisbane branch. He sold eggs to supplement his modest salary. His wife was a large woman in a flowing dress who dominated him and was very careful about her vowels.

She knew that Esme's father was a doctor. 'Doctor,' she said, articulating each word slowly, 'the jug has just boiled, would you like a cup of tea?'

The doctor was looking anxiously around like a stranded submariner for a hidden escape hatch.

'No, I'm on call actually. I'll be back for this team at nine o'clock. Goodbye then.' He waved vaguely to the girls and to the Fullwoods, turned quickly, got into his car and accelerated away.

The boys came shyly out of the shed, all scrubbed and dressed in their best white tennis shirts, shorts, socks and sand shoes. Whites were the only acceptable garb for tennis. They were clutching their tennis rackets. One boy had not yet unscrewed the frame from the wooden stocks which kept it true.

Lance held three brand-new tennis balls in his hand as they introduced themselves. Mrs Fullwood looked on approvingly. It was an important occasion. This was one of the reasons why they scrimped and saved to send their boy to the best school. Later, when she finally left them alone, she told her husband how nice it was for Lance and his friends to meet some really good girls. She emphasized the 'good'.

'What do you mean good girls? Good by what standard?'

'You know what I mean, good families, good schools, clean girls.'

'Clean girls? What on earth are you talking about? I don't know if we should have sent Lance to St Mark's. Heaven knows it's been expensive enough. It isn't really fair to Jane either.' Jane was their daughter who had been sent, when she turned fifteen, to learn to be a stenographer. It was the old argument. He had never won it yet and he was not going to win it now so he said no more.

On the court a foursome was selected. The boys were all good players and were torn between showing off by hitting hard and placing the ball out of range, and keeping the ball in play to give the girls a chance to join in. When boy served to boy, it was a different matter though. There were much grunting and swinging of arms and the loud twang of stretched gut on ball when that occurred.

Off the court, except for Sandra and Dan, two separate groups had formed, one of the girls and other of the boys, with only perfunctory attempts to talk. The girls were asking themselves what they had in common with these boys who lived in this odd, rough-looking area. For their part, the boys were overawed by the girls in their short tennis dresses with their long, tanned legs, beautifully brushed hair, and offhand manners. They seemed different, unapproachable creatures from the girls, dressed for school in their shapeless uniforms with skirts below the knees, with whom they danced at the dancing academy on the week day afternoons.

Sandra and Dan moved away from the others. They sat on a log outside the shed under one of the few trees substantial enough to offer some shade. It was a warm afternoon and the noise of the bouncing ball against the rare conversation of the players on the court made her feel drowsy and contented. Dan sat beside her as if waiting for a command, happy simply to be in her presence.

It was not easy, however, for Sandra to think of something to say. There wouldn't be a problem with a St Mark's boy, particularly one who lived at Belvedere. There was never any need to ask anything about the background or family of a such a boy. That was one of the great advantages of living there. Daddy liked to say that the suburb was like one of those exclusive communities you find in all cities of the world; a special suburb where families live and die for generations, generally keeping to themselves, carefully allowing small quotas of the right people to join their circle. It was a bit like the

White Australia Policy, in its way, he said. It wasn't, as some thought, a matter of making enough money, buying a house and moving in. They soon learnt. It wasn't that you could live there without money, although some old families who had lost their money somehow hung on, hoping for something to turn up. Money alone would never be enough. Some people could still, as with a careful immigration programme, be admitted. Some sheep graziers came down from the country to retire. They were welcome. Then there were interstate businessmen. Provided they'd been to a school like St Mark's and owned or managed the right sort of business, they were acceptable.

Sandra asked Dan where he lived. He pointed up the road. 'Up there and around the corner.'

She could see no corner in the bland, dusty landscape but she nodded.

'What, what does your father do?' Her only interest in the answer lay in the remote possibility that his father might have some respectable position, and only lived down here out of some eccentricity.

'He's retired. He's an invalid.'

'What's wrong with him?'

'He had a stroke, five years ago. He's almost completely paralysed on his left side. He can talk but only Mum and I can understand him. We have to do most things for him. That's why it's often hard for me to get away. Mum's only a little woman. She needs me to help with lifting and things.'

Sandra received this in silence. Of course some of her friends and acquaintances had relatives who had been incapacitated by serious illnesses. And they too required the assistance of their families. She couldn't imagine them personally doing all of the onerous, distasteful tasks that were required though. Most of them would have a nurse or at least a daily to help. She knew that wouldn't be the case with Dan and his mother. She knew it was very admirable and that she should respect them for it. Somehow she felt ashamed for them.

'And what did he do before, before he became, became … ill?'

'He was a fitter and turner, a very good one.' He was proud when he said it. 'We've got things at home that he made before he had the stroke. He used to make me metal toys, beautifully smooth and polished things with wheels and other moving parts. It would be hard for him to see those things lying around the house knowing he can't, won't be able to do anything like that again. We're sure his brain's not affected. We've put those things away now where he can't see them.'

Sandra had no idea what a fitter and turner did. She knew it was only a trade, a blue-collar job. He would have been one of those men who rode the first tram or bus to work, still in the dark in winter, and who knocked off well before the bank and business managers who wore suits. He probably carried a Gladstone bag as a lot of working people did, with his lunch and a magazine in it, and perhaps some tools if fitters and turners had to use their own tools at work.

'I know what your father does.'

'How could you know that?' Sandra, startled, asked.

'Because I set out to find everything out about you that I could. I've asked everybody who might know you or your family. I went to the library and I looked you all up in the newspaper records. Your family has often been mentioned and photographed.' He said it with the intensity that both attracted and scared her.

'You had no right to do that. It's an, an …' she couldn't think of the phrase.

'An invasion of privacy. I suppose it is. I can't help it though.'

'What do you mean you can't help it?'

'I'll never know enough about you. I'll never be able to get enough of you.' It was an unconditional, irrevocable declaration.

She could remember that declaration of more than thirty years ago as if it had happened an hour before: the warm sun, the barren flat paddocks stretching away to the horizon, some distant houses and the bounce of the tennis ball upon the rolled ant-bed surface. She was, always would be, modest about her looks. Then, unbeknown to her, her fine facial features, soft hair, tall, straight legs, raspberry coloured lips, white complexion with touches of pink like faint afternoon clouds under her large eyes, and her figure, already curved and full of promise, gave her the allure that would have had the young, old and middle-aged, even the ancient, clamouring for her hand and more, and would have had her parents locking her away in a convent until she turned eighteen, if she had been living five hundred years earlier.

When she grew out of adolescence, although she was still beautiful, very beautiful, she wore her hair differently, used make-up and dressed to conform to fashion. But when she was young there was about her an ethereal virginal look, a touch-me-not look, and Dan, who read *Morte d'Arthur* and other books about mediaeval knights and maidens, saw in her then exactly what he wanted for the rest of his life.

In halting, naïve, ultimately clear terms he told her all of this. She sat on the log, listening in wonder. At school she was taught poetry and they all read romantic books. But this, this, perplexed and excited her. She knew what a great compliment she was being paid. She felt constricted. Her breathing became tight. She turned away. She couldn't look at him. He went on talking in his quiet, insistent voice. He knew, of course, that she lived a different life from his. It wouldn't always be like that. His mother said you needed something to work for, to live for. She was that.

Sandra looked at the drab house and yellowing grass, and the fowls behind their wire, still restlessly scratching in the dirt. 'You didn't say anything to her about me?' The thought that she might have been discussed at the kitchen table in one of these repellent little houses shocked her into speaking.

'No, what do you think I am? I know I'm just a boy. I don't want to be laughed at even by my mother. This is our secret.'

'We have no secret.'

'Whether you like it or not, we do. I know I would never want to be with any other woman. Whether you like it or not, you know that. And you will never forget it, never.' He said the last with a certainty that made her tremble.

She had read in the newspaper of obsessions that young men sometimes formed about girls: how they occasionally did bad things, terrible things, like killing themselves, or the girls, after raping them. She felt no fear in that regard. He was too controlled, too courtly for that.

The others finished their set. They came over to the log and picked partners for the next. The host and the best player, he chose the foursome. He would play with Sandra, and Dan with Lucy. They made their way to the court while Lance's mother brought glass jugs of sweet cordial with ice in them and put them on the table in the shed.

The game was very one-sided. Lance played to a standard far above any of the others. He restrained himself very well most of the time, but couldn't resist cleanly hitting winners past Dan every second point or so. Dan played a careful, intelligent game but his co-ordination and speed around the court fell short of Lance's.

As the afternoon passed, the stiffness between the visiting girls and the local boys lessened, although neither felt entirely comfortable with the other as darkness fell.

She asked herself now would it be any different today. They had all been dreadfully, unforgivably stand-offish. Was it wrong? Weren't people entitled to their own, to mix with people who were just like them? And that couple. Did it serve them right, with their fibro house, their fowls, their hopeless bare acres and their pretensions? It was wrong, wrong to think that way. She shuddered at how she had thought then.

Lance's father lit a barbecue that he had made himself out of the halves of a fuel tin and mounted on steel legs. The halves were filled with wood and paper which he lit and allowed to subside to a hot-red glow. Across the top was placed at one end a steel plate, and at the other, steel mesh.

The flat ground held water, and mosquitoes, bred in the ponds and swamps, began their evening patrol as the sun went down. To avoid them it was necessary to stay within a ring of smoking mosquito coils placed in a circle of tins around the fire. The fumes from the coils blended with the smoky eucalypt smell of the fire and the strong tang of cooking meat to produce an unfamiliar, not unpleasant cocktail of odours.

Mrs Fullwood had changed her clothes. She now wore a long, dark-blue skirt made of a kind of polished cotton that shone in the glow from the kerosene lanterns that were also brought out when the sun went down. She wore a necklace of jet beads and had redone her hair and make-up. Mr Fullwood had been very busy as they played the last set, arranging chairs and bringing out a camping table to add to the one in the shed. Then he had brought out the plates and glasses and cutlery and had prepared everything to enable him to start cooking.

'It's so much nicer to eat out here, in these balmy summer evenings.' Mrs Fullwood announced with satisfaction. 'We are so lucky here with our climate.'

Lucy and Sandra were at the edge of the circle of mosquito coils and barely within the light from the kerosene lanterns. Lucy spoke. 'So much nicer outside, my eye. We're here because she's ashamed of inside, probably doesn't even have a proper dining room.' She executed a mosquito that penetrated the ring of smoky defences. 'Are you sure that the mosquitoes down here don't carry malaria?'

Lucy today claimed she wasn't a snob. That was debatable. She certainly was then. What was that saying of Jack's, That somebody was so good at something he could have done it for Australia? Well, in those days, Lucy could have snobbed for Australia. Sandra told her to be quiet, because Dan was coming over to them.

Esme's father came early having safely negotiated the badlands of South Brisbane to rescue the northern suburbs flowers from the dangers of the common man. This was the way that Lucy now put it, when she recalled that afternoon. Curiously, she did often. One day Sandra would ask her why she talked about it so often.

On the way home in the big American car, none of them spoke at first. Then Esme broke the ice. 'What a funny place to live.' It was like the bursting of a dam. 'Did you see Mrs Fullwood's dress, and changing to bring out the cordial. Cordial, aargh! So sweet, cheap stuff.' 'And poor little Mr Fullwood.' Then one of the girls spoke of the lavatory. 'Plastic tiles and little crystal figures, cheap soap, paper towels and, and, deodorizers. I think they call them.' They all giggled.

Then the doctor spoke. 'Well, it's a long way from home girls. I hope you all learnt something.'

Sandra was naïve enough to ask what he meant. His ideas, he told himself, were clear enough. So were his actions. He was, in addition, annoyed that he had been asked to put into words something these girls, even at their age, but particularly with their upbringing, should understand. His silence continued as the lights of the sleek car lit up the narrow black coil of bitumen and arrogantly sped up the highway, causing the odd approaching car to be careful to stay strictly to the left of the white centre line.

At last he answered, 'I'm surprised you asked that Sandra. It's not that we're not democratic about these things. It's just that it's better that people mix with their own kind, socially, that is. In everything else it doesn't matter. Let me give you an example. We've got a very good plumber. I always have a long yarn with him when he comes to do a job at our place. I might say he's pretty sound politically too. But I wouldn't have him to a dinner party or to a cocktail party. He'd understand that. Never want it. Now the Fullwoods are different. They do want it. They want to mix with her betters socially. You see, the plumber and I have a yarn when he deals with my blocked drains, that's all right. It's not all right if he wants to be my friend, have his son mix with my daughter and her friends. Now that is over the mark.' The doctor sank back, deep into his leather seat, well pleased with his explanation.

'They were trying to be nice,' Lucy responded.

'That's the trouble, people like that do. You end up feeling sorry for them, and when you do, you're ashamed of yourself.' He had spoken spontaneously, surprising himself by his perceptiveness. It was time, however, to end this sort of unhealthy discussion. He turned a dial on the dashboard to tune the radio, of which he was rather proud. After it had warmed up, some music came on. It was a late hit parade number and after a little static they began to sing along with it.

'When you wake up in the morning on Mocking Bird Hill,
Tra la la, tra la di di, it gives me a thrill,
To wake up in the morning on Mocking Bird Hill.'

They listened to the other songs and sang along with them. And as they approached Belvedere, home territory, the tensions of that other unfamiliar place and people left them. The landmarks of their suburb beckoned them like old welcoming friends as the doctor distributed them to their houses, all within a radius of a mile of one another.

Sandra could recall it all, vividly. She went into the kitchen and made herself a cup of tea. Everything still seemed better this morning: no alcohol. Inkie too was more alert. His coat shone, and, like her, he was sharp and active. She sat in her chair on the verandah and patted him as he rolled on to his back with joy. She sipped her tea and remembered the aftermath of that afternoon.

It was all very well to join in the condemnation of the Fullwoods, to snigger at their house and their pretensions, to agree that the episode at Creekdale was closed and better not talked about. On the other hand, if you had talked and laughed with an intense, tall, young man who would literally do anything you wanted, who was ambitious and clever and, loved you, yes, loved you, could you discard him simply because he didn't live where you did? Emotions were more complicated than formulated ideas and those she had difficulty enough with. What were her emotions, her true feelings, for Dan? She hadn't taken long over that one. Like a faithful courier he was at the dancing academy next Wednesday after school. She looked around and again noticed that there were only two or three others in the same school uniform as he wore. Her father had said it was presumptuous for a state high school to have a uniform like the private schools. It still rankled with him that one mid-winter's afternoon, thirty years before, the Brisbane State High School first fifteen scored five tries to his school's one. 'Mistake to let them into the GPS,' he said.

As soon as she entered the large dance-room Dan came up to her. He didn't say anything. He took her small school case from her on to the dance floor, made perilously slippery by the 'pops', the light, dusty powder that the teachers applied liberally to it. He made her feel giddy as he executed the tight turns and twirls of the dances to the music relayed from the old electric gramophone through the public address system.

'There's a school dance, Friday night, three weeks from now.' She heard herself speak as if she were listening to someone else. 'I've got the tickets.' That wasn't true but she would make it so. 'Do you think you could come with me?' She had swept aside all the practical considerations: that she should have a partner whose father could drive them to and from the dance; that he would not know that a corsage with an orchid was an appropriate presentation to her; that her father didn't know his … She paused at that as she thought of his stroke afflicted father. Who would help his wife to put him to bed that night? How would Dan get from Creekdale to Belvedere and back again? He'd have to start at five o'clock in the afternoon, even on the assumption that the buses ran down Creekdale way. What a silly person she was. How did she think he got to school unless there was reasonable public transport? That was one problem solved. All the others mounted up. The music played. He drew her closely to his body. He was strong and assured. Unlike other male adolescents he seemed to have no smell. His uniform was neat, his tie unspotted, and his hair, shiny and clean. She wanted to go on and on dancing with him.

She smiled to herself now at that distant innocent wish. She finished her tea and knew that she should be planning her day. Not that she had anything to do. Today would be like so many others, just a long sequence of hours to be filled in somehow. She remained seated while her mind played out the end of that farcical, futile outing that she had arranged.

This time she wasn't going to have an orange dress foisted on her by her mother. But how was she to conceal from her parents who her partner was for the evening? They would never accept that she would go without a partner. If she wanted to go but had no partner they would arrange for the son of one of their friends to accompany her. How she had schemed and plotted. She spoke to Lucy about the problem. No other girl could be trusted. Lucy was also the clever one anyhow. She'd have an answer. They sat under the old camphor laurel tree away from the others.

'I think you're mad. What is this, some crazy fatal infatuation?'

Sandra looked at her questioningly.

'Don't you know what that means?' When Sandra shook her head Lucy told her. 'Temporary love, infatuation. The way you looked at him, uncontrollable lust might be nearer the mark.'

Sandra blushed. 'I just know I want to see him, to dance with him.'

'Your parents, especially your father, would kill you if they knew.'

'That's why I want your help, so they won't know.'

Lucy would think about it. She couldn't come up with an answer then.

But later, when time was short she had explained the plan with the fatalistic pessimism that would be characteristic of her as she grew older. 'It'll probably go wrong. Everything seems to, and the more complicated it is the worse it gets. You're going to have to get a St Mark's boy to pretend he's taking you. You'll have to meet your wonderful Dan there and let the St Mark's boy go. Do you know a boy who'd go along with that?'

'No. The only boys I know are from around here. They'd never help, and if they did, their parents would find out and tell mine. You know that.'

Lucy thought some more about the problem. 'What we want is a boy who'd join in for the hell of it, just to be a rebel.' Lucy slipped away regularly to see the Marlon Brando films and her mind was full of ideas for rebellions without causes. Even if she couldn't be in one she wouldn't mind stirring one up.

How harmless it all seemed now. Rebellion? A modern teenager would think it laughable that parents might exercise snob control. When she thought of her own wilful wayward, heedless daughter she marvelled at her own and her contemporaries' obedience.

If there was a potential rebel Lucy would find him or know him. Tim Keeson turned out to be the man. He was a St Mark's boy living on the boundary of the suburb. He was wild for the times. The attraction for him was that he would have a cast-iron alibi to give his parents for the evening, which he would spend at Cloudland Ballroom, an art deco monstrosity, mourned now after its demolition, that stood on Bowen Hill commanding the river and the suburbs between it and the sea. Cloudland had a sprung floor and a twelve-piece band. Public dances were held three nights during the week and almost always on Fridays and Saturdays. Girls went there to meet boys, and boys went there to meet their friends and to try to pick up willing girls. It was a place for mechanics, clerks and shop girls—that's what her father would have said. It was also a place for the making of a lot of marriages, not all of them planned. If you drove past at half-past seven you would see them walking up the hill from the bus stop towards the band pumping out foxtrots, waltzes, and livelier other dance tunes. The girls were heavily powdered and lipsticked, and they wore dresses with wide flared knee-length ballerina skirts. Tim Neeson liked the atmosphere there, he said. He claimed to have consummated a couple of sexual encounters, but even as precocious as he was no one believed that. He looked old for his age and he ran, as he put it, with a crowd from the other side of town who weren't narrow minded and stuck up like the rest of the people he knew.

Lucy was the intermediary. She arranged that Keeson would call for Sandra at her house at eight o'clock and escort her to the large hall attached to the Anglican Church where the girls were permitted to hold school dances under the ever vigilant eyes of Mother Margaret and her coterie of eagle-eyed followers. Everything important or relevant was within walking distance and so was the hall. It was quite safe to walk around the city and the suburbs at night. Her father agreed that she could walk there but he would call for her to take her home. She would explain Tim's absence later, that his father had just collected him, he had wanted to wait but they had thought it all right because there were so many other people around. In the meantime, for four hours, she would be with Dan. She tried not to think about it but couldn't help returning to it over and over.

The plans were laid. The only problem was to make sure that Dan understood what he must do. Through Lance as an intermediary she tried to meet him in the city as often as she could. That wasn't easy. There were a limited number of errands that she could do in the city as a pretext for innocent afternoon assignations.

She invented a need for cartridge paper and water colours. There was a household convention that the pallid stilted scenes she painted were pretty and that she should be encouraged. They appealed to her father because they fell so fairly within the genteel ideas and practices of his mother, who used to paint butterflies after they had been captured and mounted. Her father readily produced the money for the paper and paints and said he would meet her in the city to help her buy them. Then she could come back to his office to wait with him before he drove them home. Her father would not have imagined that she could improvise so quickly.

'Thank you Daddy, but there's a group of us going in with Mother Margaret. We have to stay together. I'll try to get permission to come to your office to go home with you rather than stay with the group to come home.' It wasn't that Daddy was really afraid of the headmistress but he had a feeling that she looked straight through him into his mind and his affectations; that she had, in short, his measure. If she didn't seek out his company he wasn't going to seek out hers.

'Well, in that case, better I don't meet you then. Pity. I thought we might have a cake and a cup of tea at Rowe's. You'd like that wouldn't you?' He spoke wistfully as if Sandra had denied herself and him a great unrepeatable treat. Sandra didn't care. Now Lance would have to tell Dan where and when to meet her.

It never crossed her mind that she was doing what young women from time immemorial had done, defied their parents, evaded and lied, and involved their friends in their deceptions. She thought herself daring and original.

They met in the Botanical Gardens near the monkey cage. There, until the RSPCA intervened, old, depressed monkeys with fur a cold tramp would turn his nose up at countered their boredom by indulging in the most shameless of practices.

The sadness of the monkeys stayed with them as they walked away hand in hand in the late afternoon sunshine, towards the river. There they sat on a seat and watched the little ferries crossing and recrossing from Kangaroo Point on the south side. Sandra explained what she had arranged. She felt a surge of excitement as she did. She squeezed his hand. He should wait just down the road from the Hall. Tim Keeson would bring her down to meet him and then go. It would be dark. No one would see them meet. Then, using the tickets she had bought—the tickets were sold for an Anglican Missionary Society—they would go in together. 'Here, I'll give you the tickets now.' She thrust them towards him.

'I can't take them.'

'What on earth do you mean?'

'Well, not without paying for them.'

She thought of those desolate Creekdate flat lands, of the desiccated trees, and the depressions that held brown brackish water, of the little grey houses, and of the father she had never seen who suffered a stroke, who couldn't work, and had to be put to bed before nightfall. It was a different world from hers but, she knew, a world of grinding poverty. There would be no talk there of flowers, paintings and pastels, and water colours and cartridge paper.

'You can't pay for them. You're my guest. There's nothing wrong with that you know.'

'It isn't right.' He stubbornly said. He looked at the tickets and was shocked that each one was ten shillings.

'It doesn't matter. It really doesn't. Because it's a dance at my school. I provide the tickets. If it was at your school you'd buy the tickets.'

'You'd never come, never be allowed to come to a dance at my school.'

She could see that it wasn't just the money that was worrying him. He was uncomfortable with the deception. Anyone who read Tennyson, of mediaeval knights and fair maids, wasn't going to be happy about telling lies, or for that matter about a society that wasn't prepared to accept a young man who literally would die for her.

They argued back and forth until he became despondent.

'It's easy for you. You just don't understand.'

She was surprised by her boldness. Now, she realized that her action was much pre-ordained. She silenced him by kissing him, hard and long on the lips. He leaned backwards shocked and excited by the suddenness of it. There was no more argument. He tucked the tickets into his shirt pocket and buttoned down the flap. They were happy now. They lingered too late as the shadows from a nearby banyan tree began to reach towards the river. He escorted her out of the park, humming at first, and then quietly singing.

'Kisses sweeter than wine,
She had kisses sweeter than wine …'

It was a tuneful, maudlin song about the circle of birth, marriage and death. Such a mournful song did not mean that he was unhappy. She knew that here would never be many jokes between them.

As she sat on the verandah she thought again of the words of that sad song:

'And then I got me a girl and married her,
And then, we soon had children knocking on the door.
Oh, Lord, she had kisses sweeter than wine.'

Yes, it had worked out to be pretty sad, just like the song except they hadn't married each other. Whose fault was that? Lucy said it was hers. Lucy might well say that with her trial and error approach it was more error than anything else. It was his fault also, that ridiculous stiff-necked pride. She was stuck up. He was stiff necked. But it wasn't too late. For somebody who read *Morte d'Arthur* it should never be too late.

Chapter 7
Dancing Days

Intelligent people, Sandra told herself, thought too much. If you thought too much you began to imagine things and usually all the bad things. After she had made her arrangements with Dan she refused to entertain the possibility that anything could go wrong. She was a little in awe of herself. It was true that Lucy had thought of much of it and had helped her with the arrangements. Still in the end she was the one who'd had the resolve to make the plan work. She was the one who was taking the risks.

She would have to have a new dress, of course. The trick would be to persuade her mother without letting her think that there was to be anything special about the dance. She was also determined she wasn't going to have something in primary colours made by the dreaded sisters Nelson. Her mother would accept that she should have a new dress. She would, however, see no reason why, when she ordered her own dresses from the Nelson ladies, Sandra would look elsewhere.

Sandra managed another excursion into the city. This time it was to buy a novel, a set book for the English course, *Pride and Prejudice* by some boring old Englishwoman of a hundred and fifty years ago. She was nonetheless grateful to her for giving her the excuse. She spent an hour with Dan walking in Queen Street looking in the windows of department stores, not seeing anything in them except the reflection of their happy faces.

That was until she suddenly stopped, dazzled by the beauty of the most elegant dresses she had ever seen. There was a small tasteful card beside them that announced that they were by Norman Hartnell, the Queen's dressmaker and especially imported for the Brisbane ball season. They were prettily shaped and sophisticated, but none more so than a silvery blue one pinched at the waist, skirt slightly flared and with a tight, suggestive powder-blue embroidered bodice. She stood in front of the window, her mouth half open willing herself to be in that dress and dancing floating waltzes to the admiration of a thousand eyes. The price was discreetly printed on an even smaller card near the left of the blue suede shoes on the lifeless mannequin with the artificial glittering black wig. It was much more money than her mother would ever dream of paying for a dress for herself.

She shamelessly targeted Daddy. As to his reputation for meanness, he would defend himself by calling it prudence. On the other hand women, wives and daughters must be given some pleasures even if they were different from those of men, and sometimes inexplicable. He asked her how much it was and blanched at the answer. 'One hundred and fifteen pounds.'

'One hundred and fifteen pounds. Do you know what the most is, young lady, that I've ever spent for a suit, tailored, and of finest material?' She didn't. 'One hundred guineas, and I wore it and I wore it and I wore it. This dress now, how many times would you wear something like that?'

'Hundreds of times, Papa.' He liked to be called Papa more than he liked even Daddy. It sounded, well, distinguished, like something out of a very literary novel, like something out of *Pride and Prejudice* in fact.

'Now Sandra,' he patted her hair. 'I know men, fathers, are supposed to be ignorant about these things. I do know, however, that no woman or girl will ever wear any outfit more than ten times. I doubt whether a woman would wear a dancing dress more than, say, three times.'

'I wouldn't wear it three times in a row Daddy. That's true. I would wear it a lot though. It could be put away.'

'You're a growing girl.' As he said it, he averted his eyes from her blossoming figure. 'You'll grow out of it.'

She laughed. 'You don't understand. A gown like that, it is a gown you know, is specially made. A cou …'—she struggled with the word and at last, with pride, uttered it, 'a couturier like Norman Hartwell knows that a dress like that is pretty special. He knows that a woman may want to make it over, wear it again, years later. It'd be made so that it could be altered to allow that.'

Sandra's father was impressed by the idea of a dress on his daughter made by the Queen's dressmaker.

Despite her mother's protests, she had her way. She could still remember how glamorous she felt as she stepped into the dress and the suave black-suited saleswoman zipped her into it. She spun around, the skirt twirling around her, and then stood still to admire herself in the mirror. Her excitement was too great to be suppressed. The saleswoman almost smiled and her mother had a momentary suspicion that something more than an adolescent's desire for a pretty gown was the reason for her daughter's persistence in begging and cajoling for this one.

It needed no alteration. The saleswoman said to her mother, as if it were a matter of some surprise, 'It fits like a glove M'dam.' She then very carefully folded the dress, each layer separated by sheets of soft tissue paper, and placed it in a large cardboard box. Sandra could see her mother becoming impatient but the saleswoman was not to be deterred. It wasn't every day she sold a Norman Hartnell, and a Norman Hartnell needed to be handled and packed—there was no alternative—in a certain way.

Her mother's suspicion communicated itself to Sandra. She realized that she would have to be very careful. When her mother had the Rover—her mother always drove a Rover—backed out of the city garage and seated herself at the wheel, she turned to Sandra, 'Now why all this fuss, just about a school dance? What's going on?'

Sandra needed time to think. 'Careful Mummy, there's a bus coming.' Her mother was an alarming driver who, after twenty five years of holding a driving licence, still sometimes confused the pedals. She brought the car to a teeth-clenching halt as the heavy City Council bus lumbered past. And then, having entered the stream of traffic, and hunched over the wheel like a pilot in deep cloud, she tried again.

'What's so special about this school dance? Going on and on at your father about a dress, and such a price: worse than a wedding dress.'

Sandra had prepared the only answer that would have credibility with her mother, and her father too, if he were to become suspicious.

'It was that orange dress, the horrible orange dress the Nelson sisters made and you insisted I wear. All of the other girls laughed at me. And besides, Esme's parents bought her an imported French dress at Starkes'. Esme was the one who was the rudest to me the last time.'

Her mother continued to concentrate on her driving but the set of her shoulders relaxed. There were no obstacles now. Sandra could daydream and fantasise until the night of the dance.

If she had been more knowing, she would have been concerned at how all of the plan seemed to fall so readily into place. Tim arrived on time. He was respectful to her father, playing his part to the brink of plausibility. His suit was pressed and his hair was short and in place. She could see the look of approval in her father's eyes. She could imagine him saying to her mother later that you couldn't beat St Mark's for turning out decent young men.

At the Hall Tim had been off like a bolter. She hardly saw him go. Dan was there, his usual grave, adoring self, this time dressed in a carefully pressed but slightly shiny, heavy navy blue suit with a faint purple stripe. It was double breasted and old fashioned in cut. It was obviously his father's, unworn for years and altered to fit. With the suit he wore a white shirt, its collar ironed as stiff as an officer's epaulette, and a new maroon tie with small blue and yellow stripes. The other boys wore their school ties. Most of them were St Mark's boys, but there were a few from other private protestant schools.

In the old clothes, he did not, as another boy might have done, look odd. His height, his dignity and gravity were of a kind with the working man's Sunday best and the toecaps of his shiny, lace-up shoes were buffed to a black enamel.

He had no words for her at first as he took in her beauty. He knew nothing of Norman Hartnell, the Queen's dressmaker, of silk or lace, of the family pearls that she wore at her throat, and the blister pearls in her ears. He knew nothing of high-heel shoes to match, or of sheer stockings, of the way a girl, a woman would lightly dab behind her ears and her breasts with a light tantalizing scent. He knew nothing of the way long hair had to be shampooed in rain water, dried and then brushed until it shone with every movement in the reflected light. He simply knew that she was indescribably beautiful and female, and he was miraculously happy.

She took his hand as he tried to take in her appearance and her scent. He lifted her hand to his mouth and kissed her fingers. It was done spontaneously, without contrivance, and the gesture made her shiver. Finally he spoke. 'I'll never see anything as beautiful again.' Other boys never said things like that: affectionate insults, jokes, or faintly risqué references to a part of a girl's clothing, this was the discourse du jour.

Dan was always going to be different. It was a question then, as it was afterwards, whether she, and her circle, would be equal to those differences.

As she recalled that evening that ran and re-ran through her mind a dozen times a month, she asked herself, again, why then, why even today, she should be bothered by what her circle thought.

That circle, 'that group of ostriches was always going to be the same, thinking that their modest fortunes could withstand the storms and tides of booms and recessions, of punishing taxes, and inherited indolence. Some only would survive. A few would grow truly wealthy. For most though, their lives would be different from what they had thought they would be. Who would ever have thought that wives would have to go out to work, not just as an interest or a hobby, but actually have to work to pay the school fees? And so many of them pretended to be playing at other activities, like giving cooking lessons, or doing embroidery, or opening a little boutique. They were really in deadly earnest notwithstanding their self-deprecating claims of not being businesswomen. 'It's the interest that counts.' That was as unconvincing as their assertions that their small Japanese cars might not be chic, but the air-conditioning worked. It was plain now, but then ...

As she and Dan had danced she was conscious of the eyes of everyone, it seemed, upon them. There were plenty of reasons for that. Dan looked like a foreign creature. And he was. He had more dignity and maturity in his little finger than those other self-satisfied boys in their dark college-grey suits and ties. The two of them were the best dancers for their age and they danced closer than any others on the floor. And Sandra knew that she was, if not the prettiest, one of the prettiest and certainly the happiest girl in the whole room.

She shuddered in humiliation now at the thought of how it ended. Had her mother's suspicions been re-enlivened? Had she detected the exhilaration with which she left the house? Had somebody told? Or was it just that her father had taken it into his head to call in early?

She noticed him first at the side door. They had just had their supper of sandwiches and cakes and tea or lemonade and cola for supper. The dance was not to end until midnight sharp. After supper the lights were dimmed and she could see him looking for her among the dancers. In a moment she and Dan would sweep past him. There was nothing she could do to prevent it.

He saw them when they were a few yards away. His suspicious mind took in the situation immediately. Another, more tactful man would have drawn them towards him. Not Daddy. He strode across the floor as they passed him, took her shoulder and said, 'Get your purse and your wrap. You're going home.'

Sandra now, thirty-four years later, could feel his long, hard fingers pressing painfully into her shoulder. Their force stopped the couple in their tracks and caused Dan to stumble and take his arms away from her. And all the while her father said nothing to him, just his dark, hard eyes boring into hers in fury. He had never struck her before. She feared he might now. He would not be defied. She scuttled off to gather her purse and shawl. Thank God the lights remained dim. She came back. He gripped her shoulder, turned on his heel and marched her to the door by which he had entered.

And all the while Dan stood there as the dancers danced around him, and the saxophonist dwelt lovingly on the high notes of 'Harbour Lights'.

Chapter 8
The Education of Sandra

You could never accuse Daddy of being a sentimentalist. He used to say that sentiment was for the Irish and other people who weren't strong enough to face the facts. Well, sometimes Daddy could be wrong. Sandra went into her room now, quaintly called the sewing room at the back of the house. It had been a maid's bedroom, just off the kitchen with its own small bathroom. Sandra never sewed there and couldn't remember how or when its name changed from maid's to sewing room. She had furnished it comfortably, on Lucy's advice, with a slightly decadent looking day bed, soft chintz covered armchairs, a small reproduction kneehole Georgian desk, a Chinese Chippendale faux bamboo chair and a blue rug from Marrakesh on the polished floor. China reading lamps stood on the side table and on the desk. In one corner there was an old radiogram that had belonged to her parents. It was the most pleasant room in the house. She had got out of the way of using it because Jack forbade Inkie the house when he was at home. On the verandah she could always have Inkie, silently sympathetic to her moods, at her feet.

Daddy or no, she was going to wallow in some sentiment now. She went over to the corner and sorted through the old long playing records until she found it, a record with the hit songs and dance tunes of her girlhood and adolescence: 'Shrimp Boats', 'Begin the Beguine', 'Top Hat', 'Easter Parade', 'Mona Lisa', 'Kisses Sweeter than Wine', 'Mocking Bird Hill', 'Goodnight Irene' and 'Harbour Lights', with banal words and soft pretty tunes she would always associate with being young. She put the record on the turntable and went out to get herself another cup of tea. She returned and was about to turn the radiogram on when she thought of something else. She called Inkie. Uncertainly, slowly and guardedly he came in, sniffing the air for a hostile presence. Assured of his safety, he dropped down contentedly on the rug, wagging his tale in gratitude before falling asleep. It was ten o'clock in the morning. Sandra was alone, no cleaning lady, no tradesman, no neighbours, just Inkie and her. She turned the radiogram on and her mind off to allow the tide of memory to flow over her.

Until the night of that dance Daddy had rarely spoken harshly to her. That night he was terrifying. It had not taken long for him to extract all the details of her, Esme's, Tim's and Lucy's machinations. When he spoke of the boy, not Dan or Daniel but, that boy, he used tones of cold contempt. She had betrayed their standards. Her mother looked on, occasionally adding her scorn, which was aggravated by her annoyance that she had been obliged to assist in buying the Hartnell gown. She didn't miss the opportunity of reminding her husband of his gullibility, which made him angrier and angrier.

Sandra was told to change and to wash her face to remove every particle of makeup. There was not time to bathe so that when she presented herself like a heretic at an inquisition, wan and child-like in her bulky towelling dressing gown and slippers, there was still about her the faint trace of the scent she had worn. She kept her eyes down like a false penitent but her parents weren't deceived. Indeed they regarded themselves as justifiably provoked by her non-repentance.

'You don't understand these kinds of people. I know little of that boy and I'm not anxious to know more. But he must have known this side, this dance, was no place for him. He would exploit you. At whatever place he frequents …'

'He's at school, Daddy, he's …'

He silenced her with his palm held high and flat like a policeman on point duty. 'Don't tell me about him. It's unnecessary. Don't interrupt me while I tell you about him and something about life. He would, as I said, exploit you. For God's sake don't you understand anything about society? With all your advantages …'

'But Papa,' she interrupted but he shouted, 'Silence.' His face was red and his tone was of the parade ground.

'I will not be interrupted. People like him want what they can't have. It's not just our money and our houses and cars. Nor is it just our good name, our connexions, our influence. It's much more than that. It's our assurance, our knowledge that we are here by right and will remain so. We'll give out the invitations. No unsolicited visitors. This suburb is like a good club. And in any club you shouldn't be called upon to mix with other than your own kind. I wouldn't want to go to his father's club.'

This excursion into social philosophy calmed him down for a minute. His wife's intervention stirred him again though. 'To think that you should want, and your father should be so silly as to buy you, a Norman Hartnell dress to wear with a boy from, where is it, I'd never heard of it before, Creekdale.'

They hammered away at her until the tears began to run. In the past, tears would have stopped her father but not this time. It was one o'clock before she was released. No sentence had been imposed. None was necessary. She knew that any further association with Dan was forbidden, and that if she were caught even talking to him she would be dealt with, probably by despatch to a boarding school in Melbourne.

In her bedroom she dried her tears and soaked a washer in hot water. She held it to her eyes to soothe the soreness. She switched out the bedroom light and shut her door. She took a torch from her little school desk and shone it into her wardrobe where the silver and blue gown was suspended from its foam coated hanger. She played the light down its length, turned off the torch to slip into bed and a truncated sleepless night.

Would any young woman, today, as old as Shakespeare's Juliet, have accepted a parents' decree so absolutely? There might still be a few in Belvedere, and in the Catholic community. There wouldn't be many though. And all that other stuff about money and position and power. What a joke that was.

Nat King Cole was singing 'Mona Lisa' now. That might, she reflected, have been the way Dan thought about her after that night.

'Mona Lisa, Mona Lisa, are you warm, are you real,
Or are you just a cold and lonely, lovely work of art?'

Where was she? Yes, all that stuff about power and money. What they had today was so little compared with what the real powerbrokers had: rich, tough men with yachts and mines and houses and even jet aeroplanes. Daddy used to boast how, when his grandfather was a Cabinet Minister, Cabinet would sometimes meet in the ornate gilded boardroom of the Queensland Pastoral Bank because most of the Cabinet were either directors or customers of the Bank. The venue saved them the trouble of walking all the way down George Street to either the Land's Office building or Parliament House where the actual Cabinet rooms were. Nowadays, of course, no respectable family would want to be in politics, although Jack said the doctors would have to get organized to stop the politicians and the bureaucrats from socializing them.

Her parents became more restrictive than they had been. If she wanted something in the city then her mother or father would get it. Otherwise, she could drive in with her mother, after school, or meet Daddy at the bus stop, as if she were one of those unaccompanied children on a long flight who had to be sent off and met at each end by a flight attendant.

She had not been a wilful child, or adult either, more the pity. She had bowed to the new rules and never given a hint of resistance. Her father resented the intrusion upon his own routine: four thirty, never later than five o'clock in those leisurely days when Sir Robert Menzies was Prime Minister and God was in his Heaven, would find him at the Club with his cronies in the ginger breaded old pseudo-Gothic, pseudo-Federation building on Wickham Hill above the city. What on earth induced them to keep the same company, telling the same stories, afternoon after interminable afternoon?

After a few months her parents' vigilance relaxed. Sandra had been far too scared to try to make contact with Dan although cryptic messages had been passed to her via Esme. She interpreted them to mean that he was waiting, Daniel, he called himself, would continue to wait. All they did was make her feel hopeless.

It was next winter before she went to town again on her own. Winter was for Brisbane, a misnomer usually. That day was different.

She wore a silk and woollen spencer and the thick dark-blue school sweater over her blouse. The sweater was shapeless and she pulled it below her waist against the chill of the windy overcast afternoon. She was thankful for the thick stockings as she hurried to complete the tasks that had brought her to the city.

It was not coincidence. He couldn't be there every afternoon, but on most of them he waited around the city bus stop at about the time she used to arrive from school when she did come to town.

She had wanted to see him again so much but she felt unaccountably shy. For a moment she turned away from him. He looked as grave as ever. They spoke together. He stopped.

'I'm sorry,' she said. 'I felt so, so …'

'Desolate.' He finished the sentence for her.

'They've forbidden us to meet, to write, talk to each other, everything. I can't, can't go against them.'

They started to walk, unthinkingly, down towards the Botanic Gardens. She stopped, and looked around to make sure he father was not in view.

'You can you know. You must. I'll help you.'

'You don't understand how strong they are. Besides …' She considered whether she should say it, 'they may be right. We come from different backgrounds and we're very young. Daddy said he meant you no harm. It's just that you'd be happier with someone, of your own, own class.'

A look of not only gravity but also of disbelief crossed his face. 'That word, "class" — people in Australia just don't use that word, unless they're talking about a result at school or a railway compartment. People don't belong to classes, here, today.'

'Daddy says they do. Whether people like it or not they're born into a certain class and not too many make it out of it. There have to be distinctions, he said. Otherwise how would you be able to meet only the people you want to, at your club, and make sure that the private schools function? Daddy knows a lot about the world and people.'

'Sandra don't let them do it to you.'

'Do what?'

'Make you live a narrow, blinkered life, mixing only with boring, mindless, conceited people who never take a chance, never take a risk, just do the same pre-ordained things all their years.' He was speaking again with that urgency that so excited and disturbed her. 'Don't think that my background is going to hold me back, I've got plans. I'm going to be very rich one day.'

'Daddy says it isn't just a question of money, its breeding.'

He stopped and looked down at her. He seemed to have grown taller in the time since they last met.

'We're people you know, not stud animals.' He was deeply distressed by the gap that was opening between him and this beautiful, simple creature. He had to do something to persuade her that life wasn't just a matter of being born, living and dying in Belvedere. Even the name, for God's sake, Belvedere. What pretension. He knew that if breeding were important, that if life were a matter of inheriting exactly the same qualities as your parents, something bizarre must have happened in his case. He was ambitious regardless of what his father and mother may have been. How could she know about them anyway. Depression children. No opportunities. 'Poor people have clever children. Plain parents produce beauties. If only you would understand. Even by Australian standards Belvedere is nothing. In the overall scale of things that little snobbish enclave is irrelevant. It's just a place where ideas, and change, and happiness are stifled.'

'Why do you think you know so much?' She was conditioned to react to any criticism of her set and suburb. 'I should think there are a lot more dreams and hopes there than in Creekdale.' She knew that she sounded cruel when she said it. She watched his face and saw the hope and joy fade out of it.

They had almost reached the Gardens. They stood looking at each other on the footpath. 'I'm sorry,' he said. 'I don't want you to get into any trouble. I'm sorry I live in Creekdale. But I'm more sorry for you. I can see your life. Do you want to be like your parents? Do you want to crush all spirit or sense of adventure in your children just like your parents are doing to you?

She could feel herself trembling from the sense of loss. She could not bring herself to call him back although she ached to do it. He turned after a few paces. 'It's not supposed to happen at my age, and if it does, they say you get over it. Some day you may be truly sorry yourself. Some day you might even think you need me. You'll know where to find me for the next three years, at Creekdale. After that, who knows?'

He walked away from her as quickly as he could. She stood and watched him as he became as one with the crowds of workers coming out of the office buildings. The cold wind dulled her as she stood alone and still. And then she hurried to Daddy's office three streets away to ask him to drive her home.

The music stopped. She tossed up whether to play it again. The old songs didn't make her happy now, but then they didn't make her unhappy either. They brought a strange kind of familiar aching and regret. Lucy said the Germans had a word for it, for hearing them again and associating them with the times when she first heard them. And that hadn't been without resistance from her parents, notably Daddy, who was as tone deaf as Inkie but insisted that she learn to play the piano, and the classical music that was expected of a girl at that time. Last month one of Esme's daughters, who played the guitar, had gone off to India to learn the sitar. Her own children were tone deaf and played hard rock.

Sandra stood up and turned the radiogram off. It was a machine that in its day had been the height of fashion and efficiency. Veneered walnut on severe deco lines, a beautifully fitted folding lid that closed over the turntable as if to conceal something unpleasant, automatic change with an arm that drew it away when a record was to be replaced, and short-wave radio when required. Jack had wanted to throw it out, or give it to the opportunity shop when Daddy died.

She would have to leave. She locked the doors after putting Inkie out and went down to the car. There was a time when its polished dashboard, black-leather upholstery and illuminated bright-green instrument lights gave her pleasure.

She drove into the city. The garage where her parents always parked had long since been demolished. It was replaced by an hotel run by an international chain linked to a shopping mall. Two of the floors were reserved for parking. The impersonality of the entry barrier that only rose when you extracted a ticket from the robot ticket machine was rudely different from the friendly young apprentice mechanic, who used to leer at her, as he brought one of the family cars to the front of the old garage and left it so that even her mother had a fifty-fifty chance of safely negotiating her way into the traffic. To Sandra the tight turns in the internal ramps that led to the new parking floors were far more perilous.

She had not been looking forward to this. Was her attitude unmotherly? Was there such a word? A mother was expected to want to meet her daughter. God, she, Sandra's life wasn't as tidy as it might have been. There were many decisions she'd make differently now. She could make some excuses for herself: her upbringing, her friends, her school, her conditioning, as she now knew to be the fashionable word to describe all of that, and her gullibility. Her daughter had had the same schooling, lessons in the right standards, but, oh, hadn't she had the freedom? To think that Daddy had feared for her, Sandra's virtue. He'd turn in his grave at the thought of his granddaughter and what she was doing.

They met at a modern coffee house, fashionably finished bistro style, of the kind that had sprung up all over the city. The menu was the usual, bagels with smoked salmon, onions and cream cheese or avocado with vinaigrette. All the breads and rolls had poppy seed on them, and a cup of cappuccino with more foam than in a shaving canister and cost an astronomical five dollars.

Her daughter was as thin as the Princess of Wales and looked more neurotic. There was no doubt that except for an excessive slimness she was very beautiful with the best features of her parents and her grandparents. She had been a favourite with Daddy just as Sandra had been his pet when she wasn't in disgrace. As soon as her daughter sat down she looked agitatedly around for an ash tray.

On these occasions Sandra tried to remember what her mother would have said or done so that she could do the opposite. The trouble was, as she frankly acknowledged, she was not an original person and she tended to adopt the language and style of her mother's friends, who in truth just used different words to convey the same insensitivity as her mother was famous for.

Nicola was twenty eight now. She had not married. There was a time when Sandra envied her freedom. But how she had squandered it. She had started a law degree. It was strange, Jack said, how all our children—he meant of the medical profession—do law now, whereas when he was a medical student it was the lawyers' children who were studying to be doctors. He made the mistake of saying it in front of Lucy who had sharply retorted, 'Empirical evidence of the objective truth that law and medicine are the greediest professions.' He fulminated but had no answer.

After Nicola found the discipline of law too rigorous she cast around for other careers. Sandra naïvely suggested nursing. That had been pretty quickly dismissed as bedpans and drudgery. Besides, Jack who knew better than most what happened to pretty nurses, was strongly against it. It never occurred to any of them that Nicola shouldn't work, shouldn't have a career of some kind. There had even been a suggestion that she might do a typing course, but on that Sandra and Jack were united in opposition.

To their embarrassment she had gone to work for a travel agent. She wanted, she said, to travel. They told her they would have given her a trip anyway. Sandra still thought in terms of the grand tour she had taken when she left school.

'That's not what I want Mummy,' she said, 'a subsidized trip on an ocean liner, if they have those things nowadays, with a couple of other genteel girls to see the Eiffel Tower, London Bridge and the Changing of the Guard. How out of date can you be? I want to go to the East, to Bangkok and Beijing, Hong Kong and Bali.'

'You haven't got a drug problem have you dear?' Sandra knew after she asked it that it wasn't a very intelligent question.

It had provoked a great outburst. Sandra was accused of being 'sublimely stupid'. She in turn had responded, not unintelligently, as she thought of the time, by saying, 'I'm not the one who failed law.'

'You couldn't even pass physiotherapy when it was just a course in social etiquette and massage.'

Well, that was rather cruel, but children could be cruel to their parents. Sandra knew.

Thinking of the conversation now did remind Sandra of her time at the university. There had been a family discussion about that too. Daddy wasn't, as he said, a university man himself. That didn't mean, he lied, that he was against it. However, apart from the doctors at the club, most of his friends were not university men. Even most of the barristers and solicitors he knew had qualified by passing examinations set by their professional organizations. The same was true of those few accountants who had been admitted to the Club. Generally though, the membership consisted of doctors, judges, graziers, company directors, a smattering of very senior bankers, admittedly a couple of university professors, and solid businessmen. The point was that most of those men hadn't needed a university education. Why was it necessary for a young woman to go to university?

To her father the university was also a place of dangerous political ferment and immorality. That, together with the fact that he was not a man to indulge in reading books or abstract thinking, further disinclined him against university education, especially for a girl.

Unfortunately for Sandra the choice of courses was not large. Physiotherapy was one of the few in which she had matriculated. That was another respect in which much had changed. Today, there was such a demand for places in the physiotherapy faculty that the matriculation standard had been raised to vertiginous heights.

It was then a soft course. It was no myth that it was a course for young women who wanted to marry a doctor. Most of the lectures, particularly in the later years, were given at the General Hospital, and the students were constantly thrown into the company of medical trainees. When Sandra started, there were no male students at all in her faculty. The physiotherapist she went to herself now was a man and the degree was as eagerly sought by men as women.

Her mother impressively favoured a physiotherapy course at the university. She was well aware of the opportunities for propinquity between the medical and physiotherapy students. She thought, as did many of her friends, that the wife of a doctor was about as good a life choice as any young woman could make in those days of high taxation. It also might make Jack focus a little bit more on Sandra. Her mother hadn't been in any doubt for years that Sandra and Jack were a suitable couple and the sooner he became a doctor and married

Sandra the better. Settled and married, that should happen to any young woman. She told Sandra this in veiled language. British girls—yes, she used the word British—should not be like savages of some primitive country, where girls were married off as soon as they could conceive. She was against the American trend towards full careers for women, whether they married or not.

So Sandra went off to university to learn to be a physiotherapist. Daddy did notice that some of the daughters of his friends were going to university to take arts degrees or to learn to be teachers. A few were even studying medicine. They were regarded as blue stockings. He was glad there had been no question of that sort of course for his daughter.

Enrolment at the university brought other complications. For the first year at least there would be many lectures at St Lucia, at the main campus. Sandra couldn't be expected to take the bus. That would take far too long. Anyway, adults of Daddy's family didn't use public transport unless they had to, not in the city anyway. They bought her a Morris Minor, only slightly used: a fine piece of English machinery, Daddy said; with rounded mudguards, and a nice soft curved look rather like a chubby baby. Inside, its fawn leather upholstery was still in good condition and the carpets on the floor were barely worn.

Sandra's mother taught her to drive. From the beginning she instilled in Sandra her own sense of absolute fearlessness in traffic and utter disregard for other road users. The dangers were compounded by her mother's short-sightedness, inherited by Sandra. Both refused to acknowledge their disability by wearing glasses in public. Driving a car on a public road, her mother said, was being in public.

Sandra needed a student's wardrobe: not then shorts and singlets and sandshoes, or sneakers as they called them now, for university. She would wear proper clothes, smart cotton dresses in summer with stockings, or skirts and shirts, with high heeled shoes. In the brief Brisbane winter she and her contemporaries would go to their cupboards, mothballed for summer, and get out their pleated woollen skirts, twin sets and light woollen checked dresses, and an overcoat on rare cold days. All of this had to be chosen and paid for. The Nelson sisters, to Sandra's relief, had retired, to live on their earnings and their mistresses' allowances and to collect and wax the fine furniture and porcelain with which they surrounded themselves. Daddy's objections to the expense was ritualistic rather than heartfelt. He duly paid up when the time for payment came.

Lucy was to attend university too, having effortlessly matriculated in every faculty but was pressed into psychology. Her own choice would have been architecture. Her parents thought that unsuitable, for some inexplicable reason. Lucy speculated that perhaps her parents thought she might be brought into contact with rough building types. A latent irreverence for what she described as the 'Belvedere way of life' was beginning to manifest itself.

The government of Australia introduced Commonwealth Scholarships. Practically everyone who passed the Senior Public Examination was able to matriculate. A scholarship provided all university fees, and for students whose parents could satisfy the authorities that their income was a little below an average income, a modest living allowance. The Universities were ceasing to be the preserve of the few, the very studious or the rich. The numbers were expanding rapidly, and already the park-like grounds and the recent but elegant sandstone buildings were beginning to be desecrated by ugly additions and asphalt.

Until the first day of orientation week Sandra had never been on the campus. She was glad that Lucy travelled with her in her car. The university seemed a large and forbidding but enticing place. She found the familiarity of the older male students disturbing. Most of the activities of orientation week, except for those of the Women's Club or the Newman Society, were organized by bold male students of predatory inclination.

'I'm going to like this place,' Lucy said, 'quite a lot I think.'

Sandra looked around. Nowhere could she see a boy from St Mark's, or even a boy from the dancing academy. There seemed to be a variety of students. The law students were immediately recognizable, not just by their coats and ties, and the suits the more pretentious of them wore, but also by their pompous manners. The engineers affected a rough and ready heartiness that they carried on to the Rugby field. Architectural students wore their hair on the long side, and their shirts were open necked and in bright colours to declare their affinity with the modern. The physiotherapy students were much like Sandra, elegant, well dressed, conservative and stand-offish. The least distinguishable were the arts and science students. Unless they were very brilliant and could go on to be university lecturers or professors, they would end up as school teachers, and that was not thought by Sandra's set to be a good career.

Sandra certainly couldn't imagine herself married to a schoolteacher.

'That's what will probably happen to you, you'll end up marrying a school teacher or you'll be one yourself. If you're not careful you'll end up a crotchety old spinster like some of these.' She told Lucy as she pointed to some of the students.

'Well, let me tell you something,' Lucy replied. 'Perhaps I might end up being a schoolteacher but I certainly won't be a nun or an old virgin spinster like any of those who taught us. I won't be.'

In the semi-circular courtyard in Orientation Week there were stalls and demonstrations, set up by clubs competing for new members. Sandra did not quite know how to manage this sudden freedom. This was a new world. Her parents knew nothing of it. Although they feared its loose morality, but, as unlearned and superficial as they might have been, they still had a sneaking, unspoken respect for what it represented.

Sandra tried the fencing club, submitting to the unnecessary touching and prodding as an eager young man helped her to put on the padding and mask, and showed her how to take up the epee. She was attracted to the Drama Club and the Revue Club but decided that neither of these was for her. She had seen the posters and the photographs for last year's show. Her parents would insist on coming to see anything that she was in and she could imagine their horror at the bawdy humour and skimpy costumes. They would probably withdraw her from university immediately.

On the Friday of Orientation Week there was a dance in the refectory. Alcohol was banned but the ban was ignored. It wasn't that she was unused to the sight of men drinking. Daddy's friends, and, yes, it had to be admitted, Daddy himself, were often the worse for wear. They always remained gentlemen though. Daddy had strong views about men who couldn't hold their drink. She had once overheard him talking about a young officer during the war, to some of his friends, 'Bloody pansy, couldn't drink, couldn't hold it, bloody gutless, pissed every night before the balloon went up. In our day if you couldn't hold it, you weren't allowed to drink at all.' None of that had prepared Sandra for the obscenity of drunken young men going outside to vomit and returning, expecting girls to dance with them as they prepared to start drinking again. There was no one in control. She would almost have welcomed a vigilant nun and a flock of parents swooping down on the disgusting young men, to, yes, to hose them down and send them away to learn some manners. She said to Lucy that if Orientation Week was typical, she could do without a university degree.

As the weeks went on she began to adapt. She liked wearing and ringing the changes in her new clothes, driving her little car, without teachers and parents supervising everything she did.

One Saturday evening each month there was a dance at the Medical Students' Refectory near the Royal Brisbane Hospital, the Vic Park Refectory as it was called, a large, former temporary military building placed near the hospital and on the edge of the Victoria Park public golf links. The refectory was frequented during the day by medical and physiotherapy students, and on Saturday evenings, when the dances were on, by nurses, other students and all the young world of Brisbane as had social aspirations. Whether it was because of their nonchalant manners, or their daily familiarity with the human body, all nurses were regarded by the students as potentially loose women. Some of them worked hard to foster the image, a glass of beer in one hand and that other symbol of female licentiousness, a cigarette, in the other. On dance nights the place was crowded and noisy. There was little other entertainment, no night clubs or pub music, just picture theatres, Cloudland Ballroom, and the Blind Institute Dances. The Blind Institute, a dance hall in the Blind School, had a worse reputation for fights and casual violence than Cloudland.

'Where else could a maiden go?' Lucy said to Sandra. 'I don't fancy a medical student much myself but thank God it's not just medical students who haunt the Refec.'

With some misgivings, Sandra's parents did not try to stop her going to a Refectory Dance with Lucy. There were injunctions about whom she might talk to, and when she should get home, but nothing else. Her mother had made inquiries about the place and knew that the medical students frequented it. Daddy had reservations about her mother's unqualified embrace of the medical profession. There had been a time, he told her, when doctors, although they were received in society, were not really part of its inner circle. Just because you needed a dentist from time to time didn't mean you had to mix with them socially. Everyone needed a plumber or a carpenter too, he would portentously say. Even so, he conceded, they did seem to make a lot of money.

Jack was at the dance. At the time he was concentrating upon a couple of bold and big-bosomed nurses but was aware that he had a duty to perform towards Sandra. He should by rights have been in the fourth year of his medical course. The distractions of the nurses, the rowing club and card games in the students' common room, allied with an intelligence only a little above average, had been retardants. There was never any suggestion that he should be refused permission to finish his course, even though he had had one particularly bad failure. There were several students who had done worse and had been allowed to continue. It was no impediment to his halting progress that the Professor of Surgery had been nominated as a member of the Club by Jack's father.

Jack had decided that he would work a little harder now. The fact was that he was tiring of being a student. He would apply himself and finish in three years. He wasn't anxious to marry, but the time would come, sooner rather than later, so he had begun to keep his eyes open, taking a long-term view as he had told himself, and later insensitively confided to Sandra. to her his fixed intention in the meantime, and later, as it turned out, to seduce and sleep with as many moderately attractive young women as possible.

So Jack danced with Sandra for the first time since those afternoons at the dancing academy. Until Dan had come along she had been rather flattered to be paid attention by this older boy, well known as an oarsman, with strong muscles, confidence and physical strength, and who was of social world in which they both moved. It was the same at this dance. The other, silly, first-year physiotherapy students fluttered around, shamelessly vying with the nurses for the affections, even momentary attention, of the medical students. And they weren't the only ones. Lucy recognized a number of girls from the Arts faculty. When she pointed them out to her, Sandra felt a strong resentment at their presence. She even felt a little angry that Lucy was there. The Arts faculty, and the others at St Lucia, could have their own dances. This really wasn't the place for them. If it came to that, if it weren't for the medical students, this would hardly be the place for her either. There wasn't much refinement about the venue. Its grey external fibro walls for an instant took her back to Creekdale. This was no time to be thinking of that. She concentrated on her dancing. The music of the four-piece band could hardly be heard over the hubbub of the crowd and the dance floor was small and congested, made bearable only because few of those there were interested in any kind of conventional dancing.

After the dance Jack offered to drive her home. She told him she had her own car. It was parked it on the roughly gravelled drive that lead to the Refectory. He said he would see her to it then. She looked around to find Lucy. She had been dancing with a young man Sandra had not seen before. She wasn't in sight. It was not her fault that Lucy wasn't anywhere to be seen. Sandra said, yes, she would like Jack to escort her to her car.

At that time Jack had no particular sexual designs on Sandra. Still, honour had to be satisfied.

As Sandra fumbled for her car key, he took her in his arms and kissed her. The action didn't surprise her. She was rather disappointed, however, by his predictability and lack of subtlety. She allowed herself to be kissed again and then drew back. She found the key and opened the front driving-side door of her car. Jack leaned across her and opened the back door. Somewhat more roughly than she had expected, he pushed her into the back, at the same time pulling the front door closed.

He had not intended to go far with Sandra but somehow, something about her, something unyielding pushed him beyond what he had intended. For a moment he thought of Norma, the qualified obstetric nurse, two years older than he was, willingly waiting for him at the dance, and hoping, perhaps even believing, that he might marry her. He put her out of his mind, kissed Sandra, and began to run his hand up her stockinged leg. She wasn't ready for that. She took his hand away and placed it firmly on the back of the front seat.

Sandra marvelled now at her innocence and virtue. That's what they called it then, 'virtue'. It wasn't virtue, repression more like. She thought of her daughter. Neither virtue nor repression there, more's the pity. Untidy life. Still, who was she to say? Pretty messy herself, at least half drunk half the nights, a husband with the intelligence and morals of a buck rabbit and, she, dreading meeting her daughter for an hour at lunchtime.

She reverted to the past. With all of its agonies perhaps it was better than the present. Still, the future … She had that. Nobody else knew, not even Lucy. Likely, unlikely, a dream, a delusion. 'Not at all, it won't be long now.' She thought of travelling overseas, to Europe and coming home, one stop only, in a long silver canister with wings, flying inexorably onwards, unstoppable and safe, through the day, through the night, storms sometimes, the clouds, but always true and certain to reach the destination. The imagery of the skies seemed particularly appropriate. That's the way he would come. There was no reason now why she wouldn't go back with him: whatever he wanted.

Still the past had to be faced and then exorcised. Jack had taken his right hand from the back of the front seat and, as his left hand fiddled with the clasp of her bra, he had inserted it into the right cup. There wasn't enough room for that large, heavy hand against the tension of the elastic, and she recoiled from the clumsiness of it. When she told Lucy about it later, Lucy said she thought Jack as erotic as a cup of cold black tea without any sugar in it. Sandra had let his hand stay there for a few seconds. All of the girls at school used to say that was all right. They had numbers for each of the progressions on the sexual ladder but Sandra could never remember them. Whatever happened that night, a two, a four or a six, perhaps, it certainly wasn't a ten, which Sandra did remember. Jack sheepishly got out of the car and helped her into the front seat.

She started the car and turned the lights on so that he would walk away while she composed herself, straightened her clothes and combed her hair. She could hear the music as if it were a long way away and the muffled sound of raised voices, competing against the contrapuntal. That was the first time that a man had put a hand on her bare breast. She didn't, she decided, think much of it.

Today, she assumed some women became lesbians because of experiences like that. Lucy had tried it. Well that was Lucy. It certainly wasn't because some man may have handled her clumsily. 'Not worth the effort,' she declared.

Sandra continued to go to the dances and diligently attended lectures. She tried hard to understand the configuration of the human body. The more she tried the more ridiculous it seemed, with its hard and soft places, and different parts to carry out its innumerable and complicated functions. She would look around in class and watch the serious expressions on the other faces. She would listen to the lecturer as he spoke of muscles and veins, cartilages, hamstrings and joints and bones, and organs that she had never heard of and of which she wished to hear nothing further.

It was becoming apparent that physiotherapy wasn't for her. If it wasn't physiotherapy, then it couldn't be anything else at the university. The pleasures of the campus also begun to dull. So many of the students took themselves so seriously. She went along to the Revue Club without telling her parents. She had been full of excitement. The old, permanent it seemed, student in charge called himself the President of the Revue Club. The members, men and women, dressed in black, tight polo-necked sweaters or T-shirts and black trousers. They ran around doing the President's bidding, smoking and swearing and lovingly calling him Komissar behind his back. He acted like a combination of Fellini and Robert Helpmann, sometimes shouting, sometimes feline, always despotic. His principal occupation was to write, it seemed to Sandra, filthy skits.

She was little interested in sport but she had taken up tennis again. For a time she was a member of the tennis club. There was little social about that club. They acted as if they were waiting to be spotted by the Davis Cup selectors, and hit the ball, at your body usually, as in a war and not a game.

After that she didn't know what to join. There were various literary clubs and a chess club, a stamp club, a club for anything and everything. Sandra in club land, she used to say to herself. Even Daddy with his incurable penchant for club life might have found it rather tiresome.

She decided not to return to university next year. That was a decision to keep to herself until the last moment, after the anguish her enrolment had caused. Besides, she didn't know what she wanted to do. She couldn't possibly stay at home. She thought of her mother's round of morning and afternoon teas, of lunches and bridge, of dress fittings and hairdressers. That was a great irony, Sandra reflected. Where precisely was she herself now? 'God, I can't let history repeat itself forever.'

The difference, she now reflected was that she'd dispensed with the tea and bridge and concentrated on the wine.

August was supposed to be a high point. It was the ball season. It coincided with the Royal National and Agricultural Sow at the Exhibition ground, called by the Press and everyone else, the Exhibition. Graziers brought their thoroughbred stock to Brisbane to be exhibited, judged and sold for large amounts of money. Daddy said the prices were exaggerated. It was in the interests of everyone, he said, the buyers, the sellers and the agents, to talk of the fabulous sums paid for fat, docile Herefords and shy Merinos with deep curly coats and nervous, darting eyes.

Daddy enjoyed Exhibition time. The Club became very lively and the accommodation section full. It was an opportunity to catch up with old friends, from schooldays and the war years. It didn't matter what the hour was, there could always be found at the bar sunburnt men in tweed-checked coats whose hats on the hat rack seemed a yard in diameter. All the Clubs held an 'At Home' during the Exhibition week but no 'At Home' was as important or as well attended as the one at Daddy's Club. Daddy was a member of the organizing committee and all the family were expected to attend. It was held on the first Sunday of the Exhibition. Thereafter there would be the Agricultural

Ball, the Bushwhackers' Ball—that was another high point and the Commemoration Ball that most of the students attended. There were also the Angus Ball, the Brahmin Ball, the Hereford Ball and balls in honour of every other breed of cattle known to man. Bull and balls, Sandra smiled to herself at the thought.

For the week the tradesmen and clerks and shop assistants were banished from Cloudland so that its famous sprung floor and the alcoves around its circumference could be taken over by young men who wore dinner suits or tails, and women in long ball gowns and with real jewels.

Her mother began to talk of Exhibition week long before August. She said there was something special about country people, 'so honest'. She was impressed by their wealth and the reverence in which the social columnists held them. She couldn't understand why Sandra was unaffected. 'I can't understand you. In my day we loved balls. We looked forward to Show week—all year. You could wear your Hartnell dress.' It was the first time since that dreadful night that her mother had mentioned that dress.

In the end she had gone to the Bushwhackers' Ball and the Commemoration Ball with Jack. They went to the first in a party with Jack's relatives from the country. It was one of the few balls not held at Cloudland. The neo-classical City Hall, with its tower that dwarfed most of the city and its elegant stone-and-bronze reliefs by the sculptor Daphne Mayo, was the background for the tableau vivant of male drunkenness and bad taste. For this ball dinner suits were unacceptable. Old sets of tails were borrowed, found, or cut down and worn with white tie. Most of the men carried supplies of alcohol into the Hall in overnight bags, and some even in suitcases. Alcohol was said to have been outlawed at dances because the daughter of a Premier of the State had been molested by an intoxicated youth at a dance during the War. For this week though the Licensing Branch declared an unspoken amnesty. The young men still acted as if, by carrying in twice as much alcohol as they could drink, they were doing something wicked and dangerous.

Sandra did not think of herself as witty, but it did seem to her that the people in Jack's party were duller than most. Their conduct veered between extremes. There was one tall, heavily freckled cousin whose name she didn't catch who sat morosely drinking beer for the first three hours, never dancing with the pretty girl who had come with him and helped him open the bottles. After three hours, he got up with great deliberation. Sandra thought he was finally going to ask his partner to dance. He ignored her and walked to the steps from the dance floor to the stage at the back of the auditorium where the band was playing. He carefully mounted the stairs and walked across to the percussion section where he took aim and kicked a hole in the side of the big drum. The band stopped and its leader began to remonstrate with him. The band leader was booed and the vandal cheered. His action was regarded as a great triumph. One in a faux English accent, 'What a rag!' 'Good old —', again she didn't catch the name. She looked sympathetically at his partner, who turned her eyes away, her face expressionless.

Jack was drunk as planned. He had arranged for a taxi to take them home. He lolled beside her in the back seat too drunk even to make a perfunctory fumble at her clothing. She knew that she was supposed to be pleased by the attentions of this handsome medical student. If this were a courtship, then what would a divorce be like.

The last Ball of the week was the Commemoration Ball. The poorest of the university students saved up for this one. In the daytime there had been a university procession with floats generally regarded by the community as a boorish display of bad manners by too many over-privileged students. In this view her father was for once united with those in the city whom he would neither meet nor wish to meet, those whom he regarded as his social inferiors. The next day he would be heard tut-tutting over his breakfast as he read newspaper accounts of bawdy undergraduate humour, and the waste of policemen, whose task it was to censor the most offensive of the floats.

Taking little joy in it Sandra got out the Norman Hartnell dress for the Ball, unworn for years, yet still fine and new looking, if smelling of mothballs. Her mother hung it in the sun to rid it of the smell and to let the creases fall out. She also engaged the local successor to the Nelson sisters to enlarge the bodice.

She had never put Dan out of her mind. She heard what he

was doing from time to time. Brisbane was not an easy place to be anonymous. She knew that he continued to play tennis and had been made deputy school captain of his High School. Not that that would have impressed her father. For him there were only the GPS schools. He was, she believed, well on the way to being a qualified accountant now. She never spoke of him to anyone.

Four years of unremitting snobbery, however, had had their effect. Daniel was not, she had come to accept, for her. In due course, as an untainted, wholesome package, schooled in the arts of Belvedere manners and style, she would be delivered up to Jack, a male of her own kind.

Introspection came late to Sandra. She seemed to do little else these days. Then, she had not analysed her feelings for Jack. He was certainly handsome, assured, usually, superficially well-natured, virile enough, perhaps too much for her. How things changed. At forty-nine years of age she oughtn't to be frustrated as she was, most of the time.

Her daughter would come soon to distract her from these morbid memories. She pushed aside the water the waitress had brought, and ordered a glass of chardonnay, chilled for too long. She was reminded of the vulgar advertisement for a brand of beer that showed a strongly biceped young man in a singlet, tight shorts and boots and socks, sipping a bottle of frosted beer, and turning to the unseen audience, wiping his brow and then sighing, 'That's better.'

So Jack had called for her in a taxi to take her to the Commemoration Ball. She couldn't recall, even then, that he had asked her to go with him. She was sure that no invitation had come from her. It just seemed to be assumed by their parents by now that they would go to these kinds of functions together. Sandra didn't know then of his regular nocturnal visits to one of the drive-in picture theatres that had become popular in the city. For any young couple with access to a motor car, these theatres were the perfect antidote to chastity, abstinence and parental control. The best car was a station wagon with back seats that could be folded down. Surprisingly, it was Esme who told them first about station wagons and some young men who kept inflatable mattresses in the back. Jack didn't have a station wagon, just the use of his mother's small car. It was later, long after they married, that Sandra overheard one of his friends laughingly repeating one of Jack's stories of how difficult it was to avoid the gear shift, and how the first step was to persuade the girl to get into the back seat.

They went first to a pre-ball party so as to arrive at the Ball about ten o'clock nicely primed, as the boys said. The police applied themselves only randomly and casually to the apprehension of drink drivers.

The pre-ball party was at the Carlton Hotel. It has gone now but then was a venue for society functions and Western graziers.

After the party they piled into taxis and the few cars that some parents had lent them for the evening. Jack had spent the night so far talking to a dyed-blond-haired final-year physiotherapy student with an exaggerated reputation for fastness. Her escort had already passed out once, and was revived by wafting a singed feather under his nose. He was on his feet again temporarily, but in no condition to dance.

She contrasted those days with what she saw around her now. Physical intimacy between unmarried young men and women had not been just discouraged: as many obstacles as possible were put in its way, more often than not fairly effectively, by parents on both sides. At the same time, most young women, certainly those in Sandra's set were brought up to understand that their main role was to please their husbands. 'Western Geishas in marriage,' Lucy called it. With all its faults the present system had a lot going for it, she thought. Sandra remembered the way her mother used to advise her and supervise her dressing. Paradoxically, she bought her sheer underwear and black suspender belts that would have been acceptable in a Belle Époque Parisian bordello. It was almost as if her mother were saying, 'You'd better wear these, just in case he gets lucky tonight despite all our best endeavours.' Sandra didn't need a padded bra, but the mothers of the other, smaller-chested girls went out and bought them for their daughters. The notion of a parade in a slave market was not farfetched by much, Sandra thought, as she submitted to a foam bath, perfume hair sets, and high heels that would have failed any workplace health and safety test. Sandra was reminded of the very popular sheep dog trials at the Exhibition. A good, well-trained sheep dog will automatically teach its progeny, by example, to herd sheep. Sandra's generation of mothers was like that, passing on in unspoken ways the rules to govern the relations between the sexes, and the expectations that each could have of the other. Nicola, the drama devotee, had spoken of Ibsen's women as the first women. Well, precious little good that had done her with that vain little would-be tomcat she'd briefly had for a husband.

Sandra's thoughts were interrupted by the arrival, finally, of Nicola. She had only a short time before been thinking approvingly of the honest and free approach that her daughter and her contemporaries had to life. Now, when she looked at her, she questioned the advantages of that honesty and freedom. They, Sandra and her friends, had believed themselves well equipped for motherhood. No matter what was said then about increasing opportunities for women, and the trend towards working wives, few of her generation believed that any of that would apply to them. They didn't want those opportunities. They would rear and teach their children in the same way as their mothers had reared and taught them.

Sandra noticed with pain her daughter's taut, neurotic expression that she saw on the faces of so many of the girls Nicola knew. It didn't make any difference whether they were married or not. They seemed to Sandra to drift between domestic and work crises like ferries with disabled motors. Sandra was still uncertain how, even if she had really understood what was happening, she could have prepared her daughter for the bright new world of sexual, no, she remembered they'd changed that, gender equality.

Nicola was preoccupied with something else and Sandra guessed that she would leave as soon as she half-decently could.

'There's nothing wrong?' Sandra asked, trying to keep the hereditary inflection out of her voice that her mother would have used to convey a criticism of a daughter in an otherwise apparently sympathetic question.

'Nothing.' It was sat flatly. 'I'm afraid I don't have long.' Her daughter picked up the menu. She had long, elegant fingers like her mother, although Sandra noticed that she had been biting her fingernails again and had gone to painstaking lengths with an emery board and pearl nail-varnish to conceal the uneven, broken edges. Sandra anguished for her but there was a chasm between them. She believed everything was against her in her relations with her daughter, her ignorance of so many things, her own unhappiness, her inability to resolve her own life, and the times, the bloody times, how they had changed and made her unsure of so much she had been brought up to believe.

She offered Nicola a glass of wine. It was refused. She saw a flicker of disapproval in her daughter's eyes as she ordered another for herself. Who the hell was she to disapprove of her mother, with her own shattered relationships, a failed marriage, an abortion, an incomplete university course, and a nervy, distraught manner that made all her close relations uneasy in her company? She answered her own question: her mother's daughter.

'How's the job?' Sandra tried to sound conciliatory.

'The usual, backpackers trying to cut a hundred dollars off a nine hundred dollar fare to Bangkok to join the great hippy trail.'

For a moment she sounded like Daddy at his most scornful. A glimmer of insight touched Sandra. Would they, in two generations, still be speaking this way, as their money ran out and those prolific Asians whom Daddy had fought and still despised bought and settled the country, and turned Sandra's children and grandchildren into an anachronistic tribe of bewildered spectators?

'Dear, would you like to try something different?'

Early lines of discontent in Nicola's pretty face deepened. 'Like what?'

'Well, perhaps you could try the university again. It wasn't that you couldn't do it, it was just that …' She broke off unable to find any neutral words that would not insult her daughter.

'Back to university, with the kids with their dirty lank hair and their bicycles or clapped out old Datsuns, or the born agains, your friends from the chardonnay set, getting a bit of belated education, and something on the side from senior tutors with too much time and too little healthy exercise. At least you spared me that Mother.'

She said it all so definitively and angrily. That boy, man, who'd stolen her late adolescence had something to answer for. It wasn't her fault, or Jack's either for that matter. Nicola couldn't wait to be seduced by, and then married to, the tall urbane young merchant banker, as he called himself, she met the first time she had gone to a disco after she finished school. It was not, she had told her mother, just any old disco. It was the disco, the one in the financial district of the city, near the river where an astute developer had demolished a picturesque old warehouse and replaced it with mirrored and masonry towers to which the accountants, solicitors and stockbrokers had migrated like lemmings to pay the high rents, and in the case of many wipe themselves out, as the excesses of the eighties boomed and bust.

Sandra wondered whether a disco could be any worse than the alcohol-fuelled pre-ball and post-ball parties she had attended. These days, as a parent, you had no real say anyway. She couldn't imagine Jack turning up at some function, like Daddy, to exert his authority and drag a daughter away from unacceptable company. Slight chance. It was a long time since Jack had been in any position to exert any moral authority over any member of his family anyway.

Sandra had had to admit that at first Michael seemed all right. He spoke and dressed well. His manners were good. He talked of his work, only a little boastfully, about how that day he had arranged for a hundred thousand BHP shares to be crossed, and how he was working on a Part B statement to defend a takeover of a local pharmaceutical company. You could expect a young man to be talkative if he was doing well. At the time Sandra had only two doubts. He tried a little too hard and was a little too aware of how handsome he was.

She had made Jack confront him when Nicola fell pregnant. Fortunately he had no knowledge of Jack's frequent infidelities and Nicola was, by now, far too embarrassed to confide anything of her family to Michael. Not that Nicola would have known the details: she was far too self-absorbed for that. The ensuing marriage had been almost as clandestine as it was ill-advised.

After the marriage Michael's bravado soon evaporated. It all came out eventually. He was just a clerk living in a bedsitter at Stone's Corner. Stone's Corner. That had rung a bell. All the claims were false. He had taken out a personal loan to buy the very clothes he stood up in, and the second-hand sports car was on hire purchase, payments due long in arrears and repossession imminent. The marriage lasted only a few months. Nicola said she wanted to keep the baby. Jack was against it. Sandra was not so sure. She couldn't bring herself to think of a baby, a granddaughter being lost to her. She talked to her friends. Lucy said it didn't matter a damn these days, it was happening everywhere.

'Abortion, surely not,' Sandra said.

'That too, but I'm not talking about that. I'm talking about keeping the child. You remember the Booths? When their daughter got married the three-year-old child of an earlier misalliance was the flower girl. Charming, everyone said. Look how progressive and tolerant we all are. If the girl really wants to have the child, let her. It'll mean that you'll have to bring her up of course. Still that might be good for you. You've got bloody precious little to do now.'

Full of resolve Sandra went home to tell them that the child must be born. She was too late. Jack had arranged for a colleague to do the abortion that afternoon. There was much that she had brought herself to forgive in more than thirty years of knowing Jack, but this she could not forgive. She didn't have the words or the anger to tell him what she thought, just a deep encompassing sorrow that put her on the verge of clinical depression.

What made it so much worse was that Nicola blamed her now. She should have stood up for her, against Jack. Nicola couldn't do it on her own. 'I needed you, I needed your support. And where were you? Out with a bunch of silly women who've never grown up, eating lunch and getting sloshed,' she had cried with great globules of tears running down her pretty, distraught face.

The pain had, in a fashion, passed. The family resentments subsided and submerged, to surface in rare fits of recrimination. Sandra and Nicola were never, however, to be completely comfortable with each other again.

Nicola ordered a green salad. She did little more with it than rearrange the lettuce leaves. She had a fear of bulimia. Sandra wanted to reach out for her, to her. She feared to be rebuffed. She tried to make light talk of her daughter's forthcoming holidays. When next was she coming home to dinner? As to that, Nicola gave the usual non-committal response. She only came when it was unlikely that her father would be home. She treated him with a kind of restrained but obvious contempt. 'What else would you expect of a man?' Mothers were supposed to be better.

After Nicola left, Sandra ordered coffee. She admitted to herself that she was relieved that duty was done for a fortnight. The office workers had returned to their offices and Sandra was one of a few remaining at the tables.

When Sandra was a girl the picture theatres showed two feature films per session and the sessions continued with brief intervals from ten o'clock in the morning until eleven o'clock in the evening. Her mother was an unpunctual woman. They would often arrive when the first film had been running for half an hour. They would then have to wait until the point at which they entered was reached again. Her mother always said the same thing as they raced to leave. 'Time to go, this is where we came in.'

Sandra was reminded of this as her thoughts returned to that Commemoration Ball, the only one she ever went to.

It had never occurred to Sandra that Dan might be at the Ball. As a day student, she never gave a thought to the multitude of evening students whose earnest campus it became after darkness. She couldn't even imagine the campus at night, a place no doubt of great seriousness, the preserve of students whose courses would take double the time of the day students: students who had worked hard during the day, and would sit down to a reheated meal at ten o'clock before trying to read notes of the material that a lecturer, disgruntled at having to return in the evening, had just rushed through. But they were bona fide students just as entitled to go to the Commem Ball as the day students. Some did labour under a sense of inferiority. By mingling with the splendid creatures of the daytime, their status as students might be legitimized. Sandra hadn't understood that. Indeed, it would not have occurred to her that the university was supposed to be a democratic place, a melting pot of ideas, backgrounds, aspirations, people and opinions. They no doubt talked about that sort of thing in the Arts faculty, sometimes in Law also. She never bothered to listen to any of it when Lucy or others regurgitated it. The Physiotherapy faculty, whatever it may have since become, could not then be accused of being a place for abstraction or originality of thought.

Jack, at the Ball, was still intent on the older physiotherapy student. Sandra paused in her mental narrative. Why, oh why, had she ever married him? Any rational assessment at any time before she found herself in bed with him on the honeymoon night would have told her what a mistake it was. How could the wasted years be redeemed, even if ...?

She was dancing with one of Jack's friends in their party when she saw him. How like him it was that he should be dancing with a girl so much like himself in appearance, who was, as she found out, a first cousin who was at the Teachers' Training College and studying one university subject part time in the evening. He had changed little except to grow, if anything, more solemn, disciplined, actually ascetic looking. Her first sight of him arrested her. Her partner, stopping too, asked what was wrong. She said nothing and resumed dancing, wanting Dan not to notice her, and yet to notice her.

She felt a tap on her shoulder. She stopped again and turned around. Behind him she could see his cousin standing alone on the edge of the dance floor as couples glided past. Dan moved immediately in front of her when she turned and stood several inches taller than her partner, who was vainly trying to make a point of looking him up and down. There was something about his evening suit, the way it was pulled in unnaturally at the waist, and its shininess that told her that it was hired for the night. On anyone else it might have looked comical. His grave demeanour turned whatever he touched into a matter of seriousness.

Sandra dismissed her partner with a nod and began to dance with Dan. The years fell away as she followed his sure steps. He knew everything about her.

'I don't think physiotherapy is for you.'

Then she told him of her lack of interest in the course, of how bored she was, and uncertain what she might do next year.

'Marry me,' he had said. 'Your parents would try to forbid it until you're twenty one, but if you insist they couldn't stop you.'

'You must be crazy.'

'No, just certain. I've told you, I know exactly what I'm doing and where I'm going.'

His assurance disturbed her as it had before. In Daddy's tones she said, 'You're an accountant's clerk and in four years you'll still be only a qualified bookkeeper.'

'I'll be much more than that.'

'I'm sorry, that was hurtful. I shouldn't have said that.'

'You can't help it. Usually it's the presently wealthy one who says, "I'll take you away from all of this". I will be wealthy. That's not the point. You told me that. Do you have any idea what your life is like, what it's going to be like if you marry that medical student they all want you to marry? Your life will be … endless disappointment.' He spoke with urgency and conviction. She did not know how to deflect him. She resorted again to her most cutting voice, hating herself for doing it. But he presumed too much.

'You're still a boy. You have nothing. Our upbringings are so different. I won't marry anyone for years. How can you claim to know anything about Jack?'

He ignored the question. 'A vain hope. They'll have you married before you know it. You speak of different upbringings.' As he said this the tempo of the music quickened and the volume increased. He spoke louder to be heard. He was emphatic and right.

'We're two young people living in unimportant suburbs in a little city thousands of miles from anywhere or anything that counts and I love you. That's what we have in common. What divides us is a ridiculous misunderstanding by your parents and their friends about who they are and what they mean, here, or anywhere else. That illogical, dying, anachronistic, unforgiveable social snobbery should divide us now, in the most egalitarian country in the western world, will be scoffed at in a few years.'

The sound of the long words and the meanings within them made her feel faint. She contemplated a life with him. He would exhaust her, if he were to think and talk this way all the time. He must have sensed this.

‘Sandra, don’t let them do it to you. There’s so much happening in the world. Belvedere’s just a little place with a few people in it who don’t understand, who’ve lost the capacity to understand, the world around them. They’ll even lose their money in the end. I don’t read only accountancy. I read history. The money’s not going to stay locked in little social enclaves. It’s going to come to the enterprising, new people.’

Sandra knew that one. ‘The nouveau riche as Daddy says.’

‘Everyone in this country is nouveau. That’s the whole point. Even in the old world, ancient places, the famous families are losing their importance and influence. To impart that sort of idea and to try to apply it to people here makes us laughing stocks.’

Enough was enough. ‘I don’t know why we’re having this conversation. The whole idea is, is —’ she thought of the word her father used when he was faced with a new concept, ‘preposterous’, she finished, rather proud of herself. But still they danced on.

Sandra never knew what happened to the cousin. They returned neither to his nor her alcove party. Although he knew so much about her he was insatiable in seeking more. The sum of it wasn’t very much, she realized in hindsight. She also realized how incurious she must have seemed about him, and how he had not been troubled by that. He was so unlike other young men she knew, boys really, who were bursting to tell her how smart they were, or how many tries they had scored, or winners they had hit, or worse, how much beer they could drink.

At about midnight she saw, out of the corner of her eye, Jack carefully measuring his pace across the dance floor. The older physiotherapy student was dancing with the man who had brought her to the Ball. She had a reputation as a tease. Anyway, Jack didn’t look happy. Sandra wasn’t prepared for a row. ‘I must go.’ She disentangled herself.

‘You can’t, not again, not like that.’

‘I’m not going to have another incident, not here.’

‘He doesn’t own you. I do know about him.’

‘You wouldn’t know anything about him.’ Jack was quickly closing on them. The earlier drinks and a few nips from a concealed flask, and perhaps a rejection by the faculty tease, had made him belligerent.

She could see it in his red face and his bulging eyes. 'I'm going now.'

'You, I shouldn't go. I went before, I'm not going this time.' He held his ground waiting for Jack to arrive. Sandra didn't know whether to go or stay. She waited.

Jack sounded morose and dangerous. 'Where have you been, Sandra, I've been looking everywhere.' He lied. Then, in a slurred voice, he spoke as if Daniel were not worth addressing personally, 'Who's this? Haven't I seen it before?'

'Daniel, you've met before, a long time ago,' Sandra replied.

'I remember now, the Creekdale boy. I've heard about you. Out of your league here aren't you?'

Although he was younger by four years, Dan was inches taller than Jack and cold sober—deadly cold sober, Sandra amended after it was all over.

He must have learnt how to fight somewhere. Sandra supposed if you lived at Creekdale, went to that High School, and were good at your schoolwork, you might also need to know how to look after yourself. There was no nonsense about a punch on the point of the chin. With statacco precision Dan landed three punches, a left over the heart that sent Jack reeling back in shock, a short hammer jab with the right to the stomach and then another left to same place on the heart. There was nothing left to punch. Jack was on the floor, unconscious with a light stream of foam draining out of the left side of his mouth.

When she recovered from the shock of it, Sandra knelt beside Jack and cradled his head in the lap of the Norman Hartnell dress. Which Dan had said of, as they danced, 'You must have had a premonition we'd meet. I remember it so well.' Now the foam mixed with bile from Jack's throat was discolouring the silver blue silk with a stain that would never wash out. She looked up at Dan. 'I never want to see you again.' She said it with a thoughtless vehemence that left no room for argument. For a moment he looked down on her and then turned on his heel to pass through the crowd gathering around the prostrate man. Only the nearest had seen what had happened, and they were doubtful that what they thought they had seen had actually happened. It was all over in thirty seconds.

Jack started to recover. Sandra, relieved now, was anxious to go. 'Please stand clear, it was the heat, and perhaps a little too much to drink. He was accidentally bumped.'

It was late, and a great deal of alcohol had been taken. People had slipped on the floor already. Jack was going to be all right. It wouldn't do his reputation much good if the story got around. There was a silent consensus to treat the whole thing as an accident.

Jack's male friends took him to his home. They sent Sandra home alone in a taxi. She examined her feelings as the taxi drove across the bridge over Breakfast Creek and turned right on to the wide road beside the river. The rawness and the brutality of it had stunned her, and then, when she had recovered, thrilled her. The events were beginning to take on a rather grand aura. To be fought over was something of a compliment. To be a person for whom someone would take such a risk was much more. There had been nothing of the larrikin about Dan. He was a young man deeply concerned to live respectably and usefully. It would have been anathema for him to be arrested and charged with assault. She didn't know what happened to aspiring chartered accountants if they were found guilty of fighting, but she imagined that such a conservative profession would view physical violence with abhorrence. He had probably risked his future for her. Still it was for the best. She had sent him away once before. The second time would be the last. There was no reason why their paths should cross again. But still she wondered, doubted … longed. No, the last must be suppressed.

As the cab came around a curve in the road the broad flat river glowed like a swatch of purple velvet, its surface dotted with gold points of reflection. Among the cargo ships tied up to the wharves there was a beautiful white passenger liner with all of its lights illuminated, dwarfing two tugs standing ready to push her out to the ocean on top of the outgoing tide. Despite the hour, there were people lining the decks for a last sight of the city. The ship seemed so clean, so pure and so uncomplicated. She heard the blasts of her whistle and the sound of a bell as she began to move. Sandra told the driver to stop and wait. She crossed the road and leant on a railing to watch the elegant ship make its way down river towards the sea. She watched the phosphorescent wake wash up on the rocks below her, as the ship followed a bend in the river and finally disappeared from sight. How she wished, wished now, today, she was on that beautiful ship.

Sandra called for the bill, left money on the table and got up to leave. She walked to the car park, collected her car and drove home extra carefully because of the wine.

Chapter 9
Grand Tour

Sandra sat on the verandah that evening remembering the 'trip'. Her father again had been torn. He was pleased she had finished with the university but irritated at the amount of money he had wasted to send her there. On balance, he thought it perhaps worth the price even though there was to be a further cost, of a grand tour.

Nowadays everyone seemed to be able to travel overseas, just as Nicola had said, backpackers, business people and the superannuated. You could see them haunting the duty free shops that had sprung up all over the city. And the young and arrogant in their black T-shirts, with the logos of Hard Rock Cafes in London, Delhi, Bangkok, Hong Kong, New York and Budapest, saved up to go again on any creaking third world airline that would carry them for their pocket money.

Sandra's set, however, would only travel on a gleaming white P&O liner like the one she'd watched head down river on the night of the Commemoration Ball.

Parents took comfort in numbers. A girl would rarely be permitted to travel on her own. It was better if she shared a two- or a four-berth cabin, preferably the latter. Parents deluded themselves that if their daughters travelled in company, their virtue would remain intact.

And curiously, despite the best efforts of the young women, for the first time unsupervised, in one of the most romantic settings imaginable, the parents were right. There were simply too few young men to go around. Young men were expected to be studying, or to be going into business, starting a real career. Such expectations kept most of them on shore.

The deficit did though encourage the girls shamelessly to launch themselves at the young and not so young officers who accepted or discouraged their advances, according to their moods and degree of satiation, with world-weary, sea-weary indifference.

Sandra was disappointed by her cabin. It was sold as a two-berth deck cabin but it had only one window, and that was small and in a corner. She thought she could detect a smell of mildew competing with the body odour, in the close quarters, of the rather camp steward who showed them to their cabin. When he left, Lucy, who had scraped up the fare somehow to travel with her, turned to Sandra and nodded at the door. 'He'd get pretty short shift on a route like this.'

'What do you mean?'

'Don't pretend to be so naïve. He's one of those, queer as a March hare.'

'Oh, that. I expect he's got boyfriends in the crew.'

'Did you see how many young women, about our age, coming on board? If you wanted to get laid you'd have to queue up.'

Sandra was uncomfortable at the coarseness of Lucy's language. She needn't involve Sandra in all of life's experiences that she was, as she said, thirsting for. Well, it was to be hoped she got some of them. She'd had to stoop to so many deceptions to make the trip.

Lucy's parents, although, as they said, were 'old Belvedere', were almost bankrupt. As Lucy cheerfully accepted, it's all right to be lazy if you're clever and rich. Her father was neither rich, nor clever, nor industrious. He now held a grace-and-favour position as a sales consultant, really a salesman, with a whisky importer whom he had known at school. He treated short working days as his divine right. Although his wife held some brewery shares that paid a good dividend, and he had his modest commissions, they didn't provide enough for his Club dues, whisky and green fees.

Lucy had won a Commonwealth Scholarship which funded her university fees. She would also have been able to qualify for a small means-tested living allowance but her father, who was as opposed as Sandra's father to tertiary education for women, was unwilling to expose the extent of his impecuniosity in an application. It was an aunt of Lucy who intervened to secure her this trip by paying the fare and giving her two hundred pounds to tide her over until she could find a job in London. The plan was that the two girls would spend a year overseas, Lucy working some of the time and then returning to perhaps finish her university course. Sandra, well, as for Sandra, it was expected that when she came home she would 'settle down'.

The liners left from Sydney. They travelled there by train, a party of Lucy and Sandra and her parents. They were all booked into the Founders Club, the best in Sydney.

Sandra paused in her thoughts. She was rather pleased with the way she had taken herself in hand. Since lunch she had drunk only one glass of wine. And it was not, as her daughter said, chardonnay. It was a sauvignon blanc. Was that the same? It didn't taste like a chardonnay, but then the more alcohol you drank, the less your palate could distinguish. She called for a half bottle and measured out half a glass of the wine and then carefully took only a mouthful.

They had sleepers of course on the train trip to Sydney. God, what a terrible journey that was, almost twenty hours to travel six hundred miles. Her father boringly reminded them every half hour how worse it had been during the war when the trains were pulled by obsolete, patched steam-engines, and they were constantly shunted to sidings to let trainloads of material more vital than troops roll past. She recalled the first-class apartment in which she travelled with its antimacassars on the back of the seats, like those on a Balkan President's chair, and the polished cabinet work above, with the different Australian timbers neatly fitted and joined to make a symmetrical pattern of polished woods. Fitted above the seats were photographs, fading to sepia tones, of old bullock wagons in pre-1914 Pitt Street in Sydney, and Coolangatta and Tweed Heads. She had looked at those old photographs as the train laboriously made its way to Sydney until at night her bunk was made up and she gratefully closed her eyes to sleep. The trip was, no, should have been, a watershed.

Unthinkingly Sandra drank the wine. Unthinkingly she poured herself another glass. She looked around for Inkie. He was not here tonight. Perhaps he too had sniffed a different breeze, had had a second wind, and was off prowling the neighbourhood as he officiously used to do when his nose was infallible and his step jaunty and provocative. She would call him soon.

Sandra tried to stay in the present. Somewhere, down there, were some real thoughts and real emotions. So much of her life she had denied them. She wasn't the only one who did, and not just at Belvedere. Everyone was repressed in this bloody city All over the town, the state, the country, England, America too, it could be assumed, all over the world except in Asia and black Africa, people were living the superficialities, drinking but not tasting the chardonnay, outwardly urbane and polite, and inwardly living and feeling nothing.

Sandra again felt on the edge of a great truth. That was presumptuous. Great ideas, great truths were not for her. A life that had been sustained by frocks and gowns and German cars, and parties and wine and brunches, a little golf, and only latterly a little literature, a life that had, except for Nicola's drama, avoided pain or hard decisions, wasn't likely to produce any great insights.

Sandra felt the wetness on her cheeks. She was crying. Drunk. There were a few times in the past that she had cried. She wasn't really drunk now. She willed herself to stop crying. She couldn't stop. The tears continued to flow. She went inside and returned with a box of paper tissues.

After she expelled Dan, a second time, she had more than half expected him to make early contact with her. Over and over her mind replayed the scene that had left her sitting on the floor in her stained Norman Hartnell gown nursing the head of her designated fiancée, and boring, cowering and embarrassed, all at once. Out of the corner of her eye, she could see Dan leaving. What an extraordinary man he was. Passion and control were at war, and passion had had a rare triumph. His life was laid out in an implausible plan. He would fix up inefficient businesses. He would be a company doctor and an investor. Some of the businesses he would gradually acquire himself. He would move on. Eventually he would target two or perhaps three areas of business activity and concentrate on these. There wasn't the slightest doubt he would become wealthy, probably very wealthy.

They talked as they danced. 'You don't understand Dan, it's not wealth that will do things for you,' she said. She had spoken of connexions and clubs and families and addresses, clothes, and even brands of motor cars.

'No, Sandra, you don't understand. The world's changing, it already has. You're saying money can't buy those things. It's the other way around. Those sorts of things once begot money. They don't anymore. The Cabinet of Queensland will never meet again in the boardroom of the National Bank. The bar at the Club won't hear who the new Minister for Finance is, before Parliament and the media are told. Money will buy anything, club memberships, the right address, the lot.'

'You can't buy a family.' She thought herself very clever when she said that.

'Families won't matter. There'll be a new kind of elite. Not attractive? I agree. But that's how it'll be. In any event, there's not much attractive about the old order.'

It was at about that point that she had seen Jack heading bellicosely across the floor, and when that's when she had silenced him.

She could recall the actual words Dan used. She had heard them, been impressed by their sincerity and conviction, but in the end had dismissed them and him. Might it have been different if he had spoken to her, even tried to speak to her before she boarded that ship?

Sandra and Lucy travelled on the *Oriana* to England what turned out to be the end of the era of sea travel to Britain. In a few years P&O ceased altogether to ply the route that they had sailed for decades: Sydney, Melbourne, Perth, Colombo, Port Said, Gibraltar and Southampton. If you travelled first class, as they did, you still had a ship's case, like a small wardrobe, with your name and the words 'cabin luggage' neatly stencilled on it. Your other luggage was labelled 'Not required on voyage' and was stowed in the hold.

Not being in grand cabins there was no maid to unpack and iron their clothing. That service was for the few on the top deck. The women still though packed evening dresses, and those who travelled with their jewellery deposited it in the ship's safes, from which it could be taken out for a dance or a party.

The girls familiarized themselves with the distractions of the voyage—films, gambling, entertainers, deck games, shops and bands and lecherous young and not so young officers, who waited languidly for the advances that would surely come, especially as the ship approached the Equator.

Some of the young women, a few hours out of Perth, began to flirt with the stewards. It was bad enough, thought Sandra, when the girls in second class did it, and utterly, incomprehensibly bad form when a few in first class acted in the same way.

They had an horrendous crossing of the Great Australian Bight. A freezing gale blew uninterrupted from Antarctica to challenge a stream of Roaring Forties air, which caused the ship to heave in a thick mist as the cocktail of winds and water swirled around them. Sandra stayed in her cabin, racked with nausea and self-doubt about why she had chosen to make this journey. Lucy spent her time playing cards and drinking whisky with the Purser and two of his staff. She was for the rest of the cruise their favourite, for whom nothing was too much trouble.

At Melbourne they had been joined by a Second Australian Cricket Team who were travelling to Colombo, and then to India for a series of matches. Most of the young women and a few of the unattached older ones welcomed their arrival on board. The officers were less enthusiastic. Still there remained plenty of women to go around.

After Perth, a day out into the Indian Ocean, the world took on a happier hue. There was no more mist, no more wind, just a gentle breeze and sea and sky. The finest cruisewear was taken out and ironed, and make up applied. There was much promenading on the deck and saluting by young officers.

Only a week ago Sandra had read in the newspapers of a conversation between a cricketer of the fifties and sixties and a contemporary player. The elder had asked the current player how many suits, counting evening suits of course, did a player need to take to England these days, now that the tours were shorter and they travelled by air. The modern player was puzzled by the question, 'Suits, suits, you mean track suits, don't you?'

Not all of the team on the *Oriana* had been gentlemen either. 'Second at cricket, second eleven socially,' Lucy ruled.

Other passengers were not prepared to dismiss them so lightly. Apart from some three or four of the most handsome of the young deck officers, the ship's Captain who was rarely seen, and a third engineer who was said to look like Errol Flynn, the cricketers became the most sought after males.

The times really were quaint, Sandra reflected. The team used to be closeted for an hour or so every morning in a large room that opened off one of the salons. At first no one was quite certain what went on there. The idea, in those days of gifted amateurs, that tactics might be subject of long discussion, was fairly quickly dismissed.

The truth was even stranger. The players were being taught etiquette and manners, how not to offend Muslims and Hindus and to keep their mouths shut about the White Australia Policy. Some of them were being schooled in such elementary matters as the correct way to hold a knife and fork, which pieces to use for which course, not to speak with their mouth full, and always to wear a tie and jacket, preferably a suit when they went out.

It was interesting to watch these young men who had so much confidence—even though they were seconds—in their athleticism, come to grips with a way of life that was new and strange to many of them. At the beginning they looked uncomfortable as course followed course, often having unwittingly eaten three on the first round. There were some labourers among them who looked so ill at ease in their suits that it would have been a mercy to tell them they needn't bother eating in one of the dining rooms. It was incongruous that two of the most uncomfortable looked entirely different on deck, batting gracefully and fluently at the improvised nets that had been rigged up in the largest clear space available. There they practised, not very seriously, more to give the bored passengers another entertainment than to improve their game.

It was unfair of Lucy to dismiss them as mere seconds. They were not all destined to play second fiddle. In fact a number of them did go on to play for Australia, some with much distinction.

Len Steer was not one of these. On the rebound, Sandra selected him for the predictable banal, de rigueur shipboard romance she had to have. Thirty years on, she had trouble in calling to mind any physical attribute or feature about him except one. He had for most of the cruise insisted on affecting a particularly unattractive designer stubble, years ahead of its time. Not very convincingly he defended his position with the team manager by claiming, as did current players, that his skin was very fair and needed the protection of a few days' boycott of the razor.

Lucy had said the name 'Len', as if discussing a distasteful insect. 'You can't possibly have anything to do with someone called Len. Len! And it isn't just his name. Look at him. What does he do in real life anyway?'

'He's, he says, he's in timber.'

'Have you looked at his hands and fingernails? They'll tell you. In timber! I bet he's a carpenter's apprentice.'

'I never asked for details.'

Lucy was bored. 'Sandra, talk about snakes and ladders, first an apprentice accountant, and now an apprentice carpenter.'

Lucy was mocking what she would now readily describe as her pretensions, as if she were one to talk, with her rag-bag of would-be student radicals, drop-outs as they'd call them today, and young academics battening on to female students.

'It doesn't worry me, but it would your parents, and as surely as night follows day it will worry you if anything looks like coming of it.' Lucy persisted.

They had had a silly argument then. Sandra criticized Lucy for her immodesty, her clothes and her forwardness. 'You didn't come back to our cabin until 3 this morning. Which one of the deck officers were you with? Do you have to queue up for long, with the other girls, I mean?'

'Sandra, you don't know how lucky you are to have me around. Even with me, I think you're going to muck it up. You don't know what you're on about. You know what you should do? When this floating fucking great gin palace gets to Colombo, you should get off and catch the first boat back to Australia.'

Sandra remembered that. It was the first time she could recall Lucy use 'fucking' with all the easy familiarity of a man. It had been the forerunner of many such occasions.

'You should drop the bearded boy wonder, travel home, steerage if need be, get back to Brisbane, tell your stupid, ignorant, toffee-nosed parents to get fucked, and then elope with the bloody humourless but rather lethal apprentice accountant of yours. You might even take the opportunity before you do that, on the way to Colombo, to get laid, learn how to do it so you can wrestle a sigh of appreciation, if not a laugh, out of that youth. I'm serious Sandra. Don't continue this cruise. If you do this grand tour I can see exactly what your life will be. I don't think there's going to be much joy in it.'

'You're a fine one to talk. What's your life going to be like if what you're doing here's the pattern, your future? If you don't catch a disease, you'll get pregnant. If he, whoever he is, marries you it'll be a disaster; if he doesn't you'll be disgraced. When I say marry you, I'm assuming you'd know who the father is.'

Lucy glared at her for a moment. Sandra thought she might even slap her in the face. But Lucy was a strong woman. She didn't. They used to say women couldn't make good friends. Never trust another woman, that was the rule. All women were bitches and even dull women knew that instinctively. The rhetoric of the sisterhood today contradicted that, but then Sandra thought their conduct more often than not contradicted the rhetoric.

The female students in Arts had taken up some French woman, Simone, with a difficult surname. She was the fashionable author of the moment. Lucy said she agreed with every word she wrote: Marriage was a compromise, those who survived may have escaped torment, but they couldn't escape boredom. Marriage was not a career. Women had been consigned to meaninglessness other than for their bodies. Women would control their own sexuality. Lucy said she was well in charge of hers.

Lucy had taken the book on the ship and shown it to Sandra saying, 'This is not just a book, it's an education. Every woman capable of reading should read it.'

Sandra tried. It hadn't taken her long to lose patience and fall out of sympathy with its author. She had never read such nonsense, she told Lucy. 'The first chapter's just about queer men wanting to sit down to urinate and women in envy of the penis wanting to stand up to do it. She lost me by page fifteen.'

Lucy accused her of superficiality. She was lazy. 'Let's face it Sandra, you're my oldest friend, but Christ you're not smart.' It was not the first time anyone had told her that. It had taken Sandra decades to realize that she could read and think and reason, often with insight and sometimes a degree of originality.

'At a guess I could say I lost my virginity at about 14 degrees latitude. I cannot, I confess, tell you the longitude or the time. I could give you the date though.' Lucy told Sandra about it a day later. She was crying as she did so. 'You thought I'd dispensed with it a long time ago, didn't you?' She supplied her own answer. 'That was just talk. I did try, half-heartedly perhaps, a few times. It can be surprisingly hard to lose your virginity when you're really trying. Why am I crying? Except in novels when the maiden is taken when she's hot and enraptured, by an almost parfait knight, the first time is a kind of rape. You were right. After it he wanted to bundle me out of his cabin, muttering something about the company's rules in relation to women. He was rough and inconsiderate although not surprised, I think, that I was a virgin. 'Rules,' I said. 'The rules are that you're supposed to do whatever the passengers want, and it's a happy result for you and the company that what you've just done coincides with what cruising women want. Well let me tell you something, you didn't do anything for me.' That incensed him. He pushed me out the door. There wasn't a queue outside, not then, but I suspect that I wasn't the only silly one that night.'

Sandra offered to get her a drink but she refused.

'In a way, it was probably for the best. It's behind me now. It might even be the best way, the impersonal way. No complications, Sandra, can you understand our parents?' She was cheerful now and her eyes were dry. 'They watch us, they warn us, they tell us it's our most precious possession and then they send us, send you, let me, go on a trip like this, when every novel and magazine and fundamental commonsense tells them we're likely to lose it on the way. Can you explain that?'

'Daddy doesn't read novels or magazines except *Australian Business* and the *Thoroughbred Breeders' Magazine*. He wouldn't expect that to happen and with me and it won't.'

'Let's leave that Victorian throwback—sorry, sorry, let's leave Daddy out of this. What about your mother, what would she be thinking? Don't tell me she wouldn't know what this is all about.'

Sandra mused on what Lucy had said. She had never really understood her mother's attitudes to her, sometimes vain, sometimes fond, sometimes protective, sometimes cold. Was there an element of jealousy in her? How had she and Daddy really felt about each other? Intimacies between her parents were not to be thought about.

Had she touched upon it then? Sandra asked herself as she finished her glass of wine. At Lucy's words spoken in that little cabin, against the insistent throb of the ship's engines, had Sandra then had a presentment that unless she did something her life would be like theirs. It was not as if their voices were often raised against each other. Instead there were long sullen silences, the only human intercourse being that absolutely required for the performance of domestic necessities, arranging for clean shirts, obligatory attendance at functions and the preparation and serving of meals. What did they have in common? Had she thought about what she and Jack would have if, when, they married? Friends, backgrounds, schools, parties, the past. Robert Menzies, the wool boom, Nat King Cole crooning in the background, MGM musicals and the Vietnam War.

Sandra stopped remembering at that point to apply herself to the pressing needs of the present. She went to the refrigerator and emptied some ice cubes into another glass of wine. She had been told that the ancient Romans diluted their wine. She sat back in the wicker chair. A mosquito droned around her. That was one problem about this exclusive bloody suburb. The mosquitoes bred in profusion and were as angry as they were persistent. With a slight headache from the lunchtime wine not yet obliterated by the evening dosage, she rose and brought back a mosquito coil which she lit and placed in a metal dish downwind of her chair. Inkie back at her feet, looked up, sniffed the acrid smoke in distaste and moved to the other side of the chair.

Before she could return to the past Sandra needed to decide whether she would prepare a meal. Jack was still away. He rarely ate with her in the evening now unless they went out to friends' houses, or infrequently, a restaurant together.

For a time, Sandra had, with some reservations, taken up good health. There were varying degrees of good health. She had not gone for the ultimate which was as complicated and exacting as an obscure oriental religion. It involved first all the engagement of a dietician. In Brisbane there was only one you'd go to, all the girls said so, Charles N. Bergin, he of the sharp eyes, a narrow, wise face, long scrupulously clean black hair that he wore in a ponytail, a manner that invited the most private of confidences, and a fifty per cent interest in the factory that manufactured the vitamin pills that he sold his clients. Almost exclusively they were the wives of successful professionals and businessmen. He worked in tandem with a sympathetic doctor who rubber stamped his recommendations. It would have been risky not to have a doctor on board. Some of his clients were married to doctors. To a man the doctors disapproved of the vitamin regime, but were convinced that although it was not therapeutic it was harmless, apart from the expense.

The next degree of dedication to the cause required regular attendance at one of the health camps in the vicinity of the city. The most fashionable was situated off a barely accessible road to the north east in a particularly unprepossessing landscape of boulders, a few valiant sprouts of grass, and a great deal of mud when it rained, as it rarely did, and dry and dusty, when it didn't. This was the cheapest land available; real dry gulch country without the long horns. The location, the owners said, was selected for its isolation and detachment from the distractions of the city. The bedrooms had polished timber floors, iron beds, and a wash basin with water rationed during the days when the area was plagued by regular droughts.

There was a gymnasium and swimming pool, and were some rough walking tracks and a cliff for inmates to abseil down, hand over hand, pushing off with their feet from time to time. There was also a line rigged across a small gorge. The braver clients, fitted to a safety harness suspended on wire which slid along the line, were congratulated when they traversed the chasm.

The camp was popular with large companies who sent their executives there to meditate, gain confidence and bond.

That was the way the day began, with a bonding and relaxation session in the communal dining room. There an amateur psychologist muttered imprecations and advice that he had picked up in California in the late sixties, and encouraged people to stroke and touch each other, and for long periods look into the eyes of a partner, selected by lot.

After that exercise there was breakfast which consisted largely of ground up wholegrains and whatever fruit some local profiteering fruiterer had remaindered last week. One glass of fruit juice was allowed as was unlimited dry wholegrain bread, subject to dietary advice by the director.

Walking, jumping, jogging and a meditation session filled out the morning. Lunch was made up of copious quantities of grated carrot, beetroot, tomatoes, cucumbers and enough lettuce to feed vast colonies of rabbits.

The afternoons tended to be drawn out. They were supposed to be devoted to private exercises and thought, although you could if you wished, for a small extra fee, engage one of the staff to help you in the gymnasium or accompany you on walks, a useful precaution Sandra had thought in view of the large red bellied black snake that had crossed the rough track a few yards ahead of her on the only day she had availed herself of the service.

Yes, Sandra had taken 'the cure' there once, and once only, that is, if you could call three days of a seven-day booking, 'the cure'. By dinner time on the first night she was telling herself what she had said a long time ago of her marriage, 'there has to be something more'.

For dinner there was some cooked food, small anaemic portions of steamed chicken or fish, and bucket loads of broccoli, with iced water or vegetable juice. In the evening, afterwards, you might be permitted to look at a workout video on the television so long as you were in bed by nine thirty. They said it wasn't compulsory that lights were out by ten o'clock but it couldn't have been an accident that the hot water ran out and the electric supply became intermittent thereafter.

For this stalag experience of a lifetime Sandra had paid two thousand dollars in advance. Jack refused to pay, on conscientious grounds. For once he was absolutely right. On the third night, as she said, she went over the wall.

The bloody staff had had the cheek to try to stop her going. She had cracked when it was her turn to do the abseiling. 'That's what the whole experience is about,' the muscular young instructor lectured her as she declined to take her place at the top of the cliff. 'It's to give you confidence, to stretch you, to teach you, you can.'

'Can what?'

'Can overcome your fears, control your life, be your own master.'

'Bullshit,' she had said, thinking that Lucy would have been proud of her.

She dropped the rope, and strode off in her designer joggers and Gucci shorts. Behind her some of the other inmates were calling, 'Sandra, don't be like that.' Everyone had to be on first-name terms. That was a rule. One corpulent businessman who, she thought, might have had designs on her, was more vociferous than the others and called out, 'Don't go Sandy, you can do it. We all know you can do it. Do it, Sandy, do it.'

The instructor had hurried after her. He was probably underpaid and would be blamed for the defection. 'Serve the little bastard right,' she had thought. They were all Nazis. 'He's part of the plot. Got what he deserves.' They were equally difficult when she told them at the office she was leaving. 'We never give refunds,' one of the bloody conspirators had said. 'We can't understand what's wrong with you.'

Sandra wasn't prepared to argue. She valued her freedom too much. She could disappear here, lost up some dry gully or be poisoned by a vicious snake. Who was to say anyway that they wouldn't drug her, and hold her against her will. She told herself not to be hysterical. What sort of a place was this anyway? There was a locked gate across the entrance. She had better be careful she didn't offend them so much that they wouldn't let her out.

She had been unable to resist one retaliatory gesture however. As she drove past the gulag keeper she depressed the window button on her door, put out her head and screamed out, 'You're just a team of fucking charlatans.' All the way down the winding road, she alternately congratulated herself on her escape, chuckled with relief, and marvelled at her language.

Years before, when Jack had attended a medical conference in a doctors' paradise outside Essen, a spa called Bad Kirkoff, Sandra had taken a legitimate cure there: spas, pine baths, aromatic pine walks, gentle exercises, serious multi-qualified doctors with blue eyes and perfect manners, instruments that could guide you to the moon, weighings, measurings, blood tests, injections, rest, suitably cooked and elegantly presented meals, beauty treatments, mud baths, concerts, massages and saunas. Now that was a cure. She was not sure what Jack had got out of it. He spent most of his time there talking to his Australian colleagues about the fees the German doctors charged.

She finished her wine. How time passed when you were remembering. Now how did all of this start? She had been about to make a decision whether to prepare herself a meal. That had lead her to thoughts of her own body and how she had not always pampered it the way some of her obsessive friends did. Would she cook or not? No. She would finish the bottle first, then, if she were hungry, she might make herself a sandwich.

Food was like sex. She was getting less of each these days. How long was it since Jack … She put that question aside. Unlike her mother, who had employed a maid who sometimes cooked, she had become a competent cook herself. That too had been a fad among her friends for a time: they seemed to spend their whole life searching for perfect beans, and soufflés that would rise as punctually as the sun.

Thank God wine was a natural food, she rationalized. Bound to be a lot of vitamins there. She poured herself another half glass and opened a packet of dry biscuits, slimming biscuits they claimed, not because she was hungry. She thought she should eat something.

The same women were still searching for an elusive fitness. They did step, aerobics, water aerobics, swimming, and, the marginally certifiable, jogging. It was difficult to resist telling them, I told you so, as they tore hamstrings and their knees were reconstructed.

Lucy said, 'It's a conspiracy of silence by the doctors, just like the tourism industry that prevents publication of the statistics on shark attacks on Jap tourists.'

'But why would the doctors want to keep it secret?' Sandra asked.

Lucy's reply made perfect logic. 'Because most of the doctors are joggers. Look at that husband of yours. Spaced out most of the time. It's something to do with oxygen deprivation.'

Sandra had very rarely jogged. Lucy was right. They were all so damned self-satisfied about it, condescending to those who didn't. It was like Daddy's Masonic membership, only much more pernicious and dangerous.

Sandra did do some swimming. It might be all right to look like Jane Fonda, but if you weren't careful you might end up sounding like her.

Sandra sipped her wine and put health and food out of her mind. She was back with Lucy and her anti-climactic shipboard revelation of the loss of her virginity. Sandra vaguely flirted with the cricketing carpenter, as Lucy called him behind his back. On the last night before they berthed at Colombo, there had been a moment, a moment that could have gone on, but he had paused for a few seconds too long to admire his well-set-up self in a mirror, and the moment passed, Sandra held on to her virginity.

They watched the cricketers disembark. The others waiting to disembark gave them a cheer and wished them luck. Sandra looked on without joining in. 'They are only the second eleven after all,' Lucy pointed out.

They had one day ashore for the day themselves where they had seen the elephants working and fed them bananas in the stifling heat, shocked by their first Asian landfall and its powerful odours.

For the rest of the passage, Lucy and Sandra applied themselves to cruise life, as best they could as if it were 1937. They wore the evening dresses that they had bought for the voyage and the little halter sun suits that were the rage at the time. They went ashore and were entertained by at Port Said. They spent hours on deck as they passed through the Suez Canal. They went ashore to see the pyramids, and stopped briefly at Gibraltar where they were lectured by the first officer about the might of the British navy, and told that Gibraltar would always belong to Britain. Daddy would have thoroughly agreed with those sentiments, but would have been angered by an Australian who taunted the officer about the Suez fiasco.

Excitement overtook the passengers in the heavy swells of the Bay of Biscay. There were farewell parties and a final ball after which some of the really desperate tried, but still failed, to lose their 'most precious possession'. Lucy had the pleasure of snubbing the third engineer, who had assumed that she would willingly fall into his arms for the last dance. The women on board exchanged addresses and vowed to meet in England, somehow in the immeasurable future, and in Australia when they returned. Most never saw one another again. There was much packing and repacking, and passengers asked the crew what the weather would be like when they arrived.

Neither then, nor now, in retrospect, had Sandra enjoyed the voyage. Today people compared air travel unfavourably with an ocean passage. They were doing it from books and films and not direct experience. Sandra was not sorry to leave the cabin of that already anachronistic liner, with its faint but still pervasive smell of mould. Nor was she displeased to leave all that enforced company and unspoken insistence that she join in. It may have been a long way better than a Health Camp, but it was a great deal worse than twenty four hours in the front compartment of a 747.

They had taken the train, still called the boat train, up to London, where, bewildered by the early darkness, the fog, the roar of traffic and the cold, they had tried to get their bearings. Sandra brightened momentarily at the sight of a red London double-decker bus. Somehow that was reassuring. Daddy still called England home although his forbears hadn't lived there for more than a hundred years. He would still have described the bus and anything else characteristically English as a symbol of Empire.

Cook's had booked them into the Strand Place. 'You'll feel at home there,' the agent said. 'Queensland House is practically next door and Australia House is just down the road. You can walk to the theatre district and there's lots of cheap restaurants nearby.'

The hotel had many rooms and specialized in tour groups. When they arrived in the foyer they had had to wait for a second wave of Japanese who had just flown in and pre-empted everyone else at the check-in counter. About that Daddy would have had a great deal to say.

They spent a week in the hotel while they tried to find a flat in London. Lucy still spoke of that week as one of the most depressing of her life. The flats all seemed to be in basements with a watery glassed window at eye-level. The washing facilities were as primitive as those of a bush camp, and hot water a valuable commodity to be bought on time payment through a gas meter.

Daddy had, in the end, relented to some extent about expenses and allowances. It was just as well. They took the first liveable flat above ground they could find. It was just behind the Bayswater Road and, although it had no view of it, was within walking distance of the Hyde Park. The agent told them that in England you had to pay for an address. He dwelt upon the first syllable of address. It was Sandra's first experience of a need to economise. Lucy couldn't pay anything like her half so Sandra made up the difference. In the beginning Sandra was so lonely she would have paid Lucy to stay with her if she'd had to.

It hadn't taken Lucy long to find a job. When she got it she had been critical of her co-workers. There had been times during the last year when Sandra had wondered about Lucy's politics. Daddy had queried them himself. 'Lucy, that friend of yours, seems to have gone a bit bolshie.'

'Oh, I don't think so Daddy.'

'She says some pretty wild things. Well you know my views about the university. That's the sort of thing they teach there.'

Lucy's job was as a secretary. Sandra pointed out that she couldn't type.

'Not much, but I'll learn. Most of the girls I've seen here read by pointing at each of the letters of a word, and count on their fingers. I could write the letters in calligraphy quicker than most of them could type.' It did not take very long to find a job.

The work was bearable and not exacting. The position was with a commodities broker in the city, near the Corn Exchange. 'Can you imagine, they still call the place the Corn Exchange. Most of them would never have seen a real commodity in their lives,' she exaggerated. She did like the late starting hour and the long lunches that her employers regularly took, which lead to an unhurried afternoon tempo. She told Sandra she should take a job. 'It won't tax you, I promise you that.' She had left unsaid that even Sandra's limited talents would not be a disqualification.

So Sandra found a position. She became receptionist at the firm for which Lucy worked. All that were required were a polite manner, a moderate punctuality, good looks and tidiness. The job had been, Sandra now realized, as if destined, made for her. She had not told her parents what she had done until after she had been working for six weeks. Daddy would be impressed by a commodities broker but she doubted whether he would accept that his daughter had become a mere receptionist. Lucy told her to tell him that she was a personal assistant to the manager and she did. She received a surprised but still warm letter of congratulations from her father, and a tentative inquiry whether she would still need all of the allowance that he was making her. She never answered that inquiry.

One late February evening she had come home chilled and a little homesick. In the letter box was an envelope addressed in a hand that was familiar but yet unfamiliar. It had an Australian stamp. She unlocked the door, turned on all the lights and the heater as high as it would go. She then took off her overcoat and sat at the little table in the tiny sitting room which served as dining room as well. She tore open the envelope and began to read. As she remembered, she felt the need to see it, hold it, to have it in tangible form in front of her.

Sandra got up. From the bottom drawer of her chest of drawers in the bedroom she extracted a thin leather briefcase. She stopped at the refrigerator to pour another glass of wine and returned to the verandah. She turned on one of the lights above her chair. She lit another mosquito coil to replace the one that had burnt out. She sat down and sorted through the brief case. It was a lady's case of soft leather but it held many thin pages, almost all of them of airmail paper. She took out the first of them. The flimsy blue paper had faded to a mottled grey and yellow and was brittle with the years. She began to read the careful stilted sentences.

'It was not easy to find your address. However, as you see, I was finally able to do so. I got an acquaintance to ask Esme. The acquaintance was a male. I tell you this because I want you to know that I will never look seriously at another woman while you are alive. I know you will think when you read this that no one could make such a promise knowing that everything and everyone are against him so far as any life with you is concerned. You must understand however that I am a person who means what he says. I do not change. I know what I want and I will work to make sure I achieve it. You must know that I love you. I loved you from the first time I saw you at dancing classes. You do not know how often, unseen by you, I have watched you. I will cherish you all my life, no matter what.'

The words enthralled Sandra now, perhaps even more than they had then.

'I apologise for upsetting you at the Commemoration Ball. I am sorry that your beautiful dress was ruined. It was, I think, as much that you had worn it go with him, as his insults to me, that made me react as I did. I am not an impulsive person usually. I can be deliberate and careful about anything except you. It will always be that way.

'You must know that I want to marry you, now, in five years time, in twenty, however long it may take.

'I know that I could never persuade your parents of my suitability. I will not upset you by insulting them. I simply say this, that their world, which will if you are not careful become yours, is a make-believe world. I do not think it ever existed in Australia. I am quite confident that it did not in reality ever exist in Brisbane. Your father is no doubt a good man but how could he delude himself into thinking that a suburb, a mere place, some inherited money, and the membership of a men's club could justify his condescension and snobbery.

'We are beyond the verge of a totally different world. I do not know how much better it will be. I know that it will be very different. Inherited wealth, conservatively invested, is going to be of much less financial relevance. You see I have found out that I really do have a gift or business and money. Please do not think that I am boasting when I tell you that I could easily afford, already, to buy you a house, at Belvedere cost, but not at Belvedere. Belvedere will never be the place for you and me.

'I have studied you see, the stock market. I managed to anticipate a takeover of a major insurance company in Australia. I had a courageous bank manager who was prepared to back my judgment by lending me money to buy a large parcel of shares, and to buy some for himself. It was a solid company so there was always little risk of loss. A bidding war between two companies fighting for the prize eventuated. I made enough money to buy a house and a new car.

'I will make more and more money. I will be richer than your family ever was. Marry me now before that happens. I think you really do love me. It is only different when all the snobbish and unhappy things your upbringing has taught you intrude.'

He was right of course. Sandra set aside the letter for the moment and sought to recapture her feelings when she read it for the first time. Now she was a middle-aged woman, more than middle-aged, who drank too much, drinking on her verandah as twilight shaded into night with only a dog for company. She began to cry in self-pity and then stopped to finish the letter.

'If you think about it you will realize that already I am better established financially than any of the men you might marry. The money I have is my own money, earned already by my own skills. That medical student whom I had to punch will never be able to give you what I will.

'You know then how I feel, as if you could ever have doubted it. I know that in some ways I am different from most people. I am accused by the other students of taking myself and the world too seriously. I cannot help that.

'As well as taking my chartered accountancy examinations, I am continuing to study at night to take a commerce degree at the university. I will, therefore, soon be a graduate as well as a chartered accountant.

'I am not surprised that you became fed up with physiotherapy. I do not think that you are cut out to be a masseuse or whatever the work of a physiotherapist is. Your role in life should be to do interesting things and meet interesting people, and to do that with a husband and children who adore you.

'In my reading the other day I learnt that it was the practice of the Emperors of China to refuse to receive unwelcome letters. I hope that my letters to you are not unwelcome. I said 'letters', because I intend to continue to write to you, at least a few times a year, forever, until you marry me. I will not, I vow, ever marry anyone else.

'This may not be much of a love letter. It is the best that I can do. I am neither a poet nor a person prone to exaggeration.

'Please keep well, please come home soon.

'With undying love, Daniel.'

She had read the letter then with mixed feelings. It was impossible not to be flattered by it. Not too many women of twenty were accustomed to reading such unqualified declarations of lifelong love. The angular formal language lent the letter a special antique charm that was both thrilling and, in a way, rather frightening. She had been shocked by the repeated reference to money. That too was of the eighteenth or nineteenth century. There was an implication that she could be bought, as could anything else for which she and her kind stood.

There were other letters. Not as frequent though as promised.

'Another year without you has passed. You must make your decision soon. To dislocate a family with young children would normally be a very bad thing to do. It is excusable here on these grounds.' He could not help writing as an accountant.

'First, your husband does not really care for the children as children. They are simply people whose name he has and of whom he will be proud only if they perpetuate his standards and attitudes.

'Secondly, I would cherish and love any child of yours more than your husband ever would.

'Thirdly, I can show and give you and them a way of life that would enrich us all in every way, morally, intellectually and financially, although I sense that you may misunderstand me when I talk about the necessity for money and the freedom it brings.'

Over the years, he sometimes expressed himself in different words but the message remained unmistakable, 'I will marry you under any circumstances, anytime, anywhere.'

Jack either never noticed or was indifferent to any letters Sandra received. Indeed as the years passed he showed little curiosity about what she thought or did. It was as if Dan were a hard, silent, distant taskmaster, always watching over her, always waiting, but never actually criticising or coming close. She was fearful, God knows why, that he may have found out about Simon.

In other non-personal respects the tone of the letters changed, or so perhaps she imagined. He became more sophisticated as the years passed. There came a time when any reference to money disappeared. He wrote with more understanding as if he were there, with her, in sympathy with her faded hopes and approaching middle age. He wrote as if it were the most natural thing in the world that he should do so and that she need not reply, except of course when she came to say 'Yes', which he seemed to believe to be always imminent. He offered assistance 'of any kind'. He seemed to be well acquainted with the illnesses, concerns and angst of her generation of women. He warned her about these. She must make sure that her calcium intake was sufficient and balanced. Did she exercise regularly? It was essential that she do. How often did she have a check up? His language was the language of an affectionate and anxious husband who had long lived happily and familiarly with his wife.

Sandra returned the letter to the case and leant back in the chair. No one knew of the correspondence. She made a decision not to finish the bottle this night.

When she was in England Jack had written once a month. Those letters were awkward, almost as if they had been written under the dictation of someone else. He wrote of his course, and his desire now to finish as quickly as he could. The only endearment was at the end when he signed himself somewhat tentatively, 'Love Jack'.

She and Lucy had done all the conventional things on that trip. They worked for four months and then resigned. They bought a second-hand car to tour England and the Continent. To tell the truth the trip was a disappointment, an anticlimax. On her return she became engaged to Jack. It seemed to please both sets of parents a great deal. Nicola was born a year after. Sandra was happy as a mother.

When the boy was born, she was pleased, but she could not say she was happy. The child's conception had not been planned.

In bed, alone, Sandra tossed and turned. Eight days, she thought to herself: decision day. She began to think of the arrangements she must make. But then Dan would take care of everything. Obstacles would fall away in front of him. She had no need to feel guilty. She had truly tried. The children were adults now. Jack would be hurt or rather his pride would be, but he would soon recover.

Those letters, some typed, but most in longhand, those letters, were they real, were they truly from him? What an absurd question. There they were, in as her children would say, hard copy. Hard copy? What a strange way to describe flimsy pieces of paper, torn at the edges. Still, sometimes in the night she would wake, wondering, considering, whether she had imagined them.

Chapter 10
Daddy's Last Race

Jack returned from Cairns late without apologies or explanations. They had since eaten together, twice, discussed Sandra's lunch with their daughter, talked about how Inkie was ageing, debated whether Jack should trade his Mercedes in for a new one, and slept chastely in the same bed. As Jack gathered his wallet and car keys, Sandra told him she would be meeting George for lunch today. 'Would you like to come?'

'Far too busy.'

If he hadn't been busy he would still have contrived a reason not to go. George remained a profound disappointment to Jack. At school he had been uninterested in sport, and reluctantly played the minimum compellable of it, which was still rather a lot. Some of the masters who had taught Jack were there still. What would they think of a son of his who wouldn't play sport? It was very embarrassing.

George redeemed himself in his final year by scoring a matriculation pass high enough for him to study medicine. To Jack it was unthinkable that anyone would pass up an opportunity to be a doctor. Jack had treated George well, even warmly during the month between the results and the announcement. He named the lecturers, and identified the traps medical students should avoid. He talked of specialties, even entertaining the possibility that after he graduated Jack might not choose obstetrics and gynecology.

George confided to his mother what he wanted to do. He was surprised by her understanding and sympathy. Yes, she accepted, that you could make a good career there: all the varied fields that they could work in nowadays, and yes, she was aware that the training was very good for a business career. His mother thought she knew quite a lot about the profession.

He made his announcement to his father at nine o'clock when he was about to begin eating a late dinner after finishing his rounds at the hospital.

'You want to be a what?'

'You heard him Jack, he wants to be an accountant.'

'A bloody little bookkeeper with a red pencil and a plastic briefcase.'

'That's not the way it is, not now, if it ever was.' Sandra shocked Jack with her intervention.

'And what would you know about it, what would you know about anything? You couldn't even finish a course in physiotherapy when you could pass if you could spell cat.'

Jack fumed to his son, 'Has she been filling your mind with these silly ideas. She's always resented my career. God knows why. It's one hell of a lot more useful to the community than being a businessman.'

It was an unspoken aspect of their relationship that although her father had sponsored the match, Jack had come to resent him. In their later arguments he sneeringly mocked her 'Daddy', the businessman, scion of 'The Club' and the Jockey Club. 'What did he ever do? Did he ever pass anything?' The invective was fuelled by a resentment that Sandra's father had left Sandra enough money to leave her financially independent. His next words surprised her. He had not mentioned Dan in more than twenty years.

'I suppose it's because of that fellow who chased you before we were married, that High School boy. Pretty high and mighty he thinks he is now.'

It was better to ignore the taunt. 'It's his own idea entirely. He just doesn't want to be a doctor. He wants to do something in business. Can't you understand some people just don't want to be doctors?'

'She's right Dad, it's not the life for me. I just couldn't do it.'

'To turn down this opportunity. I can't believe it. You know how few qualify to do it. There are people who'd give anything to be allowed to do medicine.'

'That's the point,' Sandra had never opposed Jack on a matter of this kind before. She astonished herself by her language. 'They're the ones who should do it, not just the privileged children of parents who are doctors, a lot of whom have had intensive coaching anyway.'

'Well,' Jack was stunned by her response, 'you're a great one to talk about privilege. You're qualified to speak aren't you. Hot house flower of an indulgent household, doting father, never stretched mentally, either of you. The only difference between him and you was that he at least fought in the War and put in an appearance at work for forty years. What was it you did, had a token job as a receptionist in London for a few months?'

As the argument became uglier, the lines of distress on George's face deepened. He knew, however, that any words from him would prolong the quarrel.

'That's a fine way to talk about my father, talk about service to the community. Unlike some people I know he did his duty.' Although this was a shaft that Sandra had levelled before, it had lost none of its potency. Sandra's reference was to the contrast between her father's military service during the war and Jack's repeated deferral and eventual escape from compulsory National Military Service when he was a student. He had used many strategies to secure deferrals, and in the end had persuaded a friendly Medical Board of a defect in the feet on which he now jogged every morning.

'And, if you remember,' Sandra turned another screw, 'it wasn't all plain sailing for you in your medical course. There might have been a bit of privilege there too, in letting you repeat. You wouldn't be allowed to do that today.'

'Yes, and who never looked back after that, in Brisbane, and then in Scotland?'

Not long after the marriage he had worked and eventually taken his post-graduate course in obstetrics and gynaecology in Scotland. It was true, as he claimed, that he had applied himself very diligently there. Still, she was not ready to acknowledge that. She was fighting for her son's future.

'You did exactly what you wanted to do. And so will George.'

'I won't support him, financially that is, if he insists on this apology for a profession.'

'He'll be supporting himself pretty soon and until he does I will.'

'Would you stop it, both of you, please?' George cried out in frustration. 'It's not a matter of money. I can work while I'm studying. I'll be paid, if I can get into a firm. And with my results I should be able to get a job with one of the good firms.'

'This is between your mother and me.'

'It's not. This time it's about me, not you two. Don't make me ruin my life too.'

His father rounded on him.' And what do you mean by that?'

George was blushing with embarrassment. He had his mother's pale skin and when the blood rushed to his cheeks, as with her, his distress was obvious. 'Nothing. What I meant was …' He was unable to finish the sentence.

The argument continued, each saying increasingly hurtful things about the other. George stopped his ears with his hands and left the room. Like a fire that had burnt too high and too brightly, their anger cooled, leaving in its place barely smouldering embers.

Later Sandra consoled George. 'He can't make you do medicine and he can't stop you from being an accountant. I'll make sure of it. And I want you to go to university first to take a degree. I wish I had. No one is going to look down on my son.'

It was a rare domestic triumph. George went to university, took his degree, worked with a large and reputable firm and became a qualified accountant, just like, she told herself, Dan.

The year after they returned from Scotland had not been a good one. And yet it had started so well. Jack had been accepted as an assistant to the second most fashionable obstetrician and gynaecologist in the city. What that initially meant was that if your baby couldn't be induced, and was to be born in the early hours of the morning, or on Saturdays when the sun was shining and the golf course beckoning, you got Jack instead of his mentor. That didn't matter though. What was important was that he got a good start. Soon he'd be the one on the golf course, he told Sandra.

They moved into the first house they were to own. Daddy had put up the deposit and the bank fell over itself to lend the balance to this rising young medical star. Sandra had to provide a guarantee of the loan of the balance.

Lucy was at that time a long way away from being in business as a decorator, but even then she had taste and knowledge. Sandra asked her to help. They had many happy hours selecting curtains and colours and all the other practical and decorative paraphernalia. In Jack's view, this was a woman's affair, was entirely appropriate.

She learnt that she was pregnant for the second time a week before Daddy died. How thrilled he would have been had he survived, to see a grandson.

Although people said Daddy had died just the way he would have wanted to, Sandra wasn't too sure about that.

Mr Rentle's membership of the jockey club, and subsequently of its governing committee, was one of the high points of his life. The 'Long Paddock Jockey Club' was, as Daddy would proudly tell anyone, interested or not, the third oldest racing club in Australia.

Becoming an ordinary member of the Jockey Club was a reasonably simple matter. It was accepted that you couldn't run a jockey club in quite the same way as 'The Club'. For a start, you needed many members, and that meant you had to lower your standards, set the bar a couple of notches lower, as Daddy used to say. That didn't mean anyone could join of course. You needed to have several referees and to behave yourself once you got in. Daddy used to say the race course was a great melting pot, a democratic place. The ordinary public were welcome and all classes rubbed shoulders; 'class' that recurrent word in Daddy's vocabulary. In the last couple of years Sandra had strived to avoid it, speaking instead of a group, or a circle. She had also tried to discard 'set' and 'type'.

The racetrack was Mr Rentle's gesture to classlessness, his exercise of *noblesse oblige*, to stroll through the crowd acknowledging the greetings and respect of all and sundry, including the jockeys and trainers whose malefactions, whether actual and suspected, were resisted with unforgiving vengeance by the Committee, whether the stewards had the evidence or not.

'Racing must be kept clean at any cost. The sport is bigger than the individual.' That's what the Committee said.

It never seemed much like a sport to Sandra. More like money and rivalry and furtive dealings, and overdressed women asking themselves what they were doing there every Saturday afternoon. The Committee men had their own private bar, presided over by a drinks' steward who had held the position for forty years. Entry to the bar was by invitation of a Committeeman only, and he was bound to make sure that any guest left the bar when he did. Sometimes the owner of a horse that won the main or last race was invited into the sanctum, provided, of course, the owner was a man. As a special concession if the horse were owned by a woman, she might be given a drink in an anteroom.

For some people the racetrack was their Wednesday, Thursday and Saturday occupation and sanctuary. There was usually a midweek race meeting on Wednesdays, a Committee meeting on Thursdays and then, on most Saturdays, the major race meeting of the week. On the Thursdays, the Committee, most of whom were retired and with a great deal of spare time, talked the same matters over, again and again. It was extraordinary how long they could spend on the wrong positioning of the running rail last Wednesday, whether the back stretch was yet ready to be top-dressed, or whether jockey Jones should have been outed for six months or twelve months for not showing enough vigour with the whip. 'Insufficient vigour' was regarded as the best charge to bring because it was too vague to be defendable.

With somewhat less style, but with as many rules and conventions as a Japanese tea ceremony, the Committee gave lunch and afternoon teas in the Committee dining room to their guests on race days. The Chairman, almost always until recent times a knight, so honoured for his services to racing, stood with his wife at the entrance to the dining room, which was located at the end of a long corridor beneath the main grandstand and offered no view of the track. Inside, suspended from the ceiling, were two large television screens on which the races were shown as they took place. It was a common sight for guests to be huddled round the sets, eyes fixed on the screens and unseeingly and unthinkingly shovelling food into their mouths.

Except on days in which a wine shipper sponsored a race, the

Committee served Australian sparkling wine, and indifferent indigenous still whites and reds. The food menu never varied, limp salads, large bright red prawns, crumbed cutlets and crumbed fish, a baked ham, port wine trifle, apple pie, ice cream, mint chocolates still in their silver wrappings, and coffee.

You weren't encouraged to linger in the luncheon room. After all, there was afternoon tea to come and the real business of the day was the racing and not the food. Afternoon tea reminded Sandra of those traditional afternoon teas served at Rowes Restaurant. The fare never varied in the Long Paddock afternoon tea-room either: thin sandwiches, cucumber and cheese and tomato, sponge cakes, dainty iced small cakes, fruit cake and tea or coffee. There was a small bar in the corner but you were not encouraged to use it. The afternoon tea-room was the domain of the Committee wives over whom the Chairman's wife cast an imperious eye to ensure that the other wives did their share of hostessing.

None of the Committeemen wanted any change, ever. Sandra's father had without consultation and in a rare and revolutionary stroke once told the caterers to place Chinese hot spring rolls on the afternoon tea menu. He had made a surprisingly happy acquaintance with exotic food during a stopover in Hong Kong on his way to England the year before, and thought it might be interesting and enlightened to allow others to share in his discovery.

This unprecedented departure from tradition provoked the most dreadful wrath on the part of the Chairman and two other members of the Committee. It had even been rumoured that Daddy's action had for a time jeopardized his prospects for the next Chairmanship.

When Daddy had begun the long climb to Committeeman, the club had been wracked by sectarianism. The Irish and their Australian Catholic descendants had always had an affinity with the turf but the successful breeders tended to be Protestants who held their entitlement to govern the club as one of inalienable right. 'The trouble was,' a former Chairman said, 'if you look at their ancestors and knowing what we do today about the Irish, you couldn't trust them not to get drunk before the first race.'

Unfortunately for him the other faction had come to have the numbers, in consequence of which he had had to make a rapprochement that ensured that a representative of each religious faction held one of the important offices of Treasurer or Chief Honorary Steward.

Daddy was not a good judge of horseflesh. His friends told him that he couldn't expect to win races unless he bought good stock. He was not prepared to outlay more than a few thousand for a yearling, a practice he defended by pointing to some of the famous winners of the past that had been bought for a song. Until near the end, few of his turned out to be winners.

And then he had a great stroke of luck. He bought a yearling by an unknown sire out of a dam that had won three minor metropolitan races before breaking down with a torn ligament. Anyone else in the business, or as Daddy preferred to say, sport, except the impoverished and optimistic trainer who owned her, would have had her put down. Instead the breeder had put an old, unsuccessful stallion over her and produced a wall-eyed, foul-natured, dragon-breathed, ill-conformed chestnut filly that he sold for eleven hundred dollars to Daddy after she had been passed in at the yearling sales. She could, as it turned out, run like the wind over six furlongs.

Daddy's own trainer had been reluctant to take her. It was only because of the owner's position as a Committeeman, and the knowledge that any trainer could be brought before the Committee on a conduct charge, that induced him to do so. At first he was unwilling to take the filly seriously, educating her in a rudimentary way only, and leaving her until last of the new batch of yearlings to be broken. When the time came for her to be given track-work, he had put his daughter up, because there weren't enough jockeys available for the good horses. He refused to believe his daughter when she predicted wins for the filly. 'She's a bitch,' he said, 'a wall-eyed mongrel that only that tight-arse would buy. If he wasn't who he is, I wouldn't let her near my stables. You be careful of her my girl, foul-tempered bitch, if you don't keep out of her way, she'll kick the bejesus out of you.'

The trainer continued to refuse to believe his daughter's claims. He wasn't even willing to put the stopwatch on her. To take the owner's money to stable and train her was one thing. To enter her in a race as her trainer was another altogether. When it was unavoidable, he consoled himself with the thought that no one would pay much attention to her first race, which was little more than a picnic meeting at Esk, a small town about fifty miles north-west of Brisbane. He sent his overseer up with two other horses and engaged a young apprentice to ride them all. He certainly didn't back her.

The filly, now named Centuria, with Daddy's silks of white stars on the background of his regimental colours, won the eleven hundred metres race by eight lengths pulling up. She had started at forty to one, paying her owner for his one hundred dollar bet far more than the winner's prize money. The trainer said it must have been a fix, the other horses were pulled. Indeed there was an inquiry, but it went nowhere because the filly's superior speed was verified by the outstanding time she ran for the race. 'Must have been using a two bob watch,' the trainer stubbornly insisted.

She continued to win, at Toowoomba and at Southport, at diminishing odds as the word got around. 'The old fool's finally got a useful horse,' the knowledgeable grudgingly admitted.

Sandra had been at the track for the filly's first metropolitan meeting. Practically the whole of whatever extended family her parents possessed was there. By then the odds had shortened and she was to start at three to two. The trainer had even come around to believing that he didn't have a bad horse on his hands.

What excitement there had been that day. Jack had come with her to the races. They had all gone round to Centuria's box to admire her before the race. Characteristically the admiration was not reciprocated. The filly had lashed out at Jack and had almost succeeded in biting an aunt of his who had attached herself to their party. The only person who could confidently handle her was the trainer's daughter, and as a reward for these shows of spirit, the young woman had nuzzled her with her nose and told her what a clever girl she was.

Daddy was flushed with pleasure as the mare was paraded after the race. Daddy had never known a prouder moment since he had been mentioned in despatches during the war. After all these years, and without going overboard financially, he had shown them all. The filly won by a head.

He had congratulated the trainer and the jockey, accepted the gold cup on the lawn in front of the main stand and proudly made his speech of acceptance. He then took Sandra and Jack and his wife into the anteroom to the Bar. He poured them a glass of Australian sparkling wine, held his glass aloft to toast Centuria, and fell over, dead of a massive heart attack.

Sandra stared at him lying on the floor, his best navy-blue pinstripe trousers damp from the spilled wine and his face set in an expression of astonishment.

Sandra remembered little of the rest of that day. There was vaguely in her mind a recollection of doctors kneeling beside him, of Jack, a gynaecologist helplessly looking on, of other Committeemen wiping their brows and arguing about whether the rest of the meeting should be cancelled.

'Only two races to go. Can't call it off now.'

'A mark of respect. I think we should. Committeeman, a chair and all that.'

'No, he'd want the races to go on. You know that. He was a soldier, don't forget that,' the train said. 'Can't call it off. All bets would have to be returned. The whole racing programme for the eastern sea board would be disrupted. Besides, there's our contract with the television racing channel. Can't break that.'

The others murmured their agreement.

The last sound Sandra heard as she left the course was the caller excitedly calling a photo finish for the sixth. She had never returned to that or any other course.

Forever, it seemed, her father had dominated her life. So many of her actions and decisions had depended upon the answer to the question she posed herself. 'What would Daddy think about this?' The question was not usually a hard one to answer. Daddy was a man of clear opinions upon most matters. He had also been one of the few people able to exercise any control over his wife.

The funeral had been both a nightmare and a social event. Strangers kept on coming up to Sandra and offering their condolences. Her mother complained about their presumption when she had come afterwards to Jack's and Sandra's house to spend the night. She had already begun to exercise her new found assertiveness.

The months had limped on towards her confinement. She had felt out of sorts the whole time and found herself weeping without warning in the late afternoons before Jack came home. In those days he did sometimes come home to dine with her. She became short with her friends, some of whom ceased to visit her, or to ask her out, as the birth approached. Lucy remained loyal.

She did have to give her that. Right from schooldays, up to now, she was reliable. It was a pity that she hadn't taken her advice more often: not of course about that Gold Coast spiv—really, Lucy's standards had slipped since then—but about other matters, people to watch and not to trust, and how to survive when you were betrayed. It hadn't helped Lucy much. She, Sandra, still had a future.

Sandra had expected that it would be a long, grinding confinement and it was. Throughout its twelve hours Jack managed to look in a few times, in total perhaps for half an hour. Her mother had stayed for a while but it was Lucy who spent the whole time with her. Jack's main contribution were 'Push, come on push,' and to Lucy, 'I told her she could have a Caesar if she wanted.'

George, when he arrived, made up for it. He was a regularly featured baby, although a nervous one. After he was born Jack actually put in a full hour with them, watching Sandra feed him and nursing him himself. He assumed that the child would be named for him. There was a strong flavour of proud primogeniture abroad. Sandra was immoveable in her insistence that he be named for her father, and so named he was.

Lucy visited her the night before she was to be discharged from hospital. She seemed preoccupied and angry. Sandra asked her what was wrong. In detail she described the latest crimes against matrimony her husband had committed. To Sandra it sounded like more of the same: drinking, unreliability, suspected adultery, suspected only at that stage, and idleness. It was the last that aroused Lucy's fury most.

'Lazy bastard,' her language was by then unrestrained as any man's. 'The so-called best school, best connections, and he can't even hold down a sinecure. I don't know where he can go from here.'

By now Lucy had one daughter herself. Her husband, who had been at St Mark's with Jack, had not matriculated. As soon as he could, had taken a position with the Landscape Pastoral and Stock Company. Unfortunately for him the grand days of the pastoral companies were passing. There was a worldwide glut of wool and commodity prices were falling everywhere. The wealthy, old-established families were doing their own shearing, and the holidays at Surfers Paradise were either curtailed or finished. The good old days when the pastoral companies acted in all capacities short of procuring for their country clients had gone. The companies themselves were struggling. The time had ended when managers allowed their staff to spend long hours in the bar with a favoured client, or if a cadet went off for a few days with the son of a valued client did not to sack him. No more would Lucy's husband patrol the bars in the two squares between Adelaide, Queen, Creek and Wharf Streets, dressed in his traditional outfit of tweed jacket, summer or winter, woollen tie, check shirt, flannel trousers and highly polished tan elastic-sided riding boots. All he could manage now was a job, on commission only, as a real estate salesman.

'He's drinking more than ever. The savings we had have just about gone. I don't know what we'll do.'

'I can give you something to tide you over.'

'I hate it Sandra. Why did I marry him? Of all people, I should have known. It's not the money. It's the attitude, the stupidity, the lack of insight that these people, we people, yes we people, had, still do, into the vacuous silly, lives we lead. And we seem to do it from generation to generation. Well my daughter's not going to. Don't you let him,' she pointed to the baby, 'fall into the trap. That reminds me, you wouldn't have seen this.' She reached into her handbag and took a folded page of the Telegraph, the afternoon tabloid. She flattened it out and handed it to Sandra.

There was a photograph of Dan at the top of the page from the business section of the newspaper. He was dressed in his signature black suit, white shirt and self-patterned, sombre tie. The caption under the photograph read, 'Daniel Bencham, an accountant working with Stone & Stokes, winner of the Young Accountant of the Year Award.' She read the story beside the photograph. 'Daniel Bencham was announced as the winner of the Australian Young Accountant of the Year Award last night at a special dinner to inaugurate the award, given by the Australian Governing Body of Chartered Accountants, in Brisbane. This city was chosen for the presentation because it is the winner's home town.

'In announcing the winner the Chairman stated that although the standard of the candidates was very high, the judges had been unanimous in selecting the Brisbane man. He was obviously the outstanding candidate. He demonstrated a versatility in doing all phases of an accountant's work.

'The Telegraph asked Mr Bencham how he felt about winning the award, 'Naturally I'm very honoured. I hope that I can go on to improve myself further.' He was asked what his special interest in the profession was. 'I'd like to become a professional business advisor. I want to learn as much as I can about as many businesses as I can so that I can understand the mechanics of business and develop ideas and systems for the flow of work and the saving of money. There's a lot of that sort of thing going on overseas now, already.'

Sandra could hear in her mind the words being spoken. He would have said them with that undeflectable, messianic enthusiasm that made even dull business sound exciting. She continued to read.

'The competition is funded by the Chartered Accountants' Society of Australasia. The prize is a return air fare to England or the United States together with a subsidy for living expenses for a year. The winner, who must be under 30 years of age, will be expected to work with accounting firms or other business organizations to which he will be introduced.

'Mr Bencham who is a single man, said he intended to spend additional time in both New York and London, meeting any further expenses himself.'

Sandra put down the paper. 'Why did you show me this?'

'Why did you read it so closely if you weren't interested?'

They looked at each other for a time and then Lucy reached out and put her hand on Sandra's. 'Neither of us has done too well, no one as badly as me perhaps. Don't worry Sandra, I don't know whether you're carrying a torch for him or not. Your secret's safe with me. One thing is certain though, he'll be carrying one for you.'

Sandra didn't reply. She wanted to discuss, she said, how she might help Lucy out. She could give her some money, but what was the long-term solution: was there one?

'The long-term solution, my dear, is to divorce the bastard, get access to the small trust that he's got an interest in and can't so far spend, not to see him ever again with any luck, get a job and look around.'

'And Jaqueline?' Sandra asked about her daughter.

'For a while it'll be child-minding centres and my parents. Everyone will have to make sacrifices. They're the ones who brought me up to be so dumb as to marry him. We're the last you know,' she added.

'The last of what?'

'The last generation who'll believe what our parents told us was true.'

'Children of all generations have doubted what their parents have believed and told them.'

'You don't understand what I'm saying. The next generation will overthrow ours. It'll be a full-scale revolt. It's started already. You only have to listen to the music. It's their Internationale. They'll think and say that what we were taught, and the circumscribed way we lived, are absurd and repressive. They'll tear it all down.'

Then Lucy said something odd. 'Madam Bovary, have you heard of her?'

'No,' said Sandra. 'Who's she?'

'A creature of fiction. Famous. A woman with problems. Daydreams are problems. Don't be a Madam Bovary.'

And now Sandra was going to lunch with her gentle, accountant son, who had never torn anything down and was unlikely to be Young Accountant of the Year. Not that he wasn't able. He had given Sandra some advice about her holdings that had increased her income. He had also achieved what she had thought unachievable, the disentanglement of Jack's failed tax schemes. Until they had failed she had sometimes wondered whether Jack was a gynaecologist or a businessman. He was always on his telephone, the number of which was in the teledexes of accountants, solicitors, business associates, and several tax entrepreneurs. The last had to do it the hard way, by contacting his receptionist. Sandra couldn't keep up with them. Over the years there had been an avocado plantation, 'rent a bull programme', a share in a blueberry farm, a caravan park—that had been the worst of them all—a joint venture in a shopping-centre development, and latterly the refurbishment of decaying suburban banking buildings. It was just as well that Jack was as energetic as he was, and had the earning capacity he did, for none of the schemes were successful except the shopping-centre, which might yet support him in his retirement. George was now trying to convince him to invest in blue chip stocks. Jack resisted. They lacked the excitement and hope of a tax-free fortune that the other investments promised and never delivered. He and his colleagues seemed to be engaged in an interminable contest to see who could become the richest, and in the most original of ways. Their conversations were full of references to bull or bear markets, p/e ratios, yields, franking credits, capital gain taxes, margins and cap. rates. They talked at length about retirement, a retirement which few of them were likely to enjoy. The statistics were against them. Whether that was because doctors died young, or couldn't bring themselves to retire, Sandra didn't know. But on they talked and boasted, as they scrubbed up, waited for the anaesthetic to take, cut and stitched, showered and dressed.

He always asserted that he wasn't going to hang on, he just wanted to be sure he had enough to maintain the same standard of living as he had when working. Standard of living, that was a joke, a frenetic driving from hospital to hospital, consultations in his rooms by the dozens, medical conferences, memberships of the Council of Gynaecologists and Obstetricians, his time-consuming ambitious business deals, his obsession with jogging and his inability to abstain from making a pass at any nubile young female doctor or nurse who crossed his path, didn't sound like much of a lifestyle to her. How would he translate that into retirement? Well, that was not going to be her concern anymore.

Unlike her daughter, George was already at the table when she arrived. He had chosen the place, again a contrast, with the smart brasserie where Sandra usually met Nicola for lunch. The restaurant was plain and served plain food. You could have a cappuccino but the management would have preferred that you stuck to filtered coffee. The décor and fittings were in keeping. Once when they had gone there *en famille*, Jack had looked around, sniffed, and pronounced, 'Accountants' Café'. Nowadays he was much less critical of his son although he adhered to his position that George had chosen a merely useful craft when he could have practiced the high art of medicine.

Sandra kissed George as he held her chair for her and made sure she was comfortable. 'You're looking so well, mother.' He said it with a surprised sincerity.

Sandra knew that she looked fairly well, if a little drawn. She had dressed with special care for this outing. Of all the parts in her marriage, this, her son, was the one of which she could be truly proud. She studied him to make sure that he was well. He wore a very dark suit, and a blue silk tie with foulards of deep maroon with a white shirt. His hair was short and neatly brushed. His shoes gleamed from their daily polish. He was slim and fine boned like his mother. He had enough of her good features to be handsome without being effeminate. Thank God, the only one of his father's traits that he had was a concern with physical fitness. Though George had never been a sportsman, since he had left school he had applied himself to a strict regime of regular exercise and running.

To be companionable, the young man ordered a glass of white wine which she knew he could sip but not finish. He was very conscientious about his work and would not take the least risk of befuddlement. Sandra took nothing. She was resolved, nothing before ...

Of all the people she would not wish to hurt George was the most vulnerable. She sensed that he saw in her qualities she doubted she had. That stemmed from her tireless defences of him against Jack's tyrannies and caprices. He was the only one in her family to place her on a pedestal.

She chatted with him about his work. He accepted that it might not be of any interest to her, so considerately he spoke in terms of office personalities and incidents, telling engaging little anecdotes that might amuse her, a few of which were self-deprecating. Then he spoke of some of their grander clients, only rarely naming names she might know. The truth was that few of them rang a bell. This was a new age, an age of entrepreneurialism; as Daddy would have said, of a wave of vulgar nouveau riche who rose without a trace. The memory reminded her that Daddy had always claimed the phrase as his own. Lucy had told her that it was Whistler who had first used it, but that Sandra could be assured that it wasn't conscious plagiarism because her father was unlikely to have read a book to plagiarize, other than the Stud Book, and Who's Who. So much of what Lucy said was hurtful, but so true you couldn't do much about it.

Sandra asked herself whether she should begin to prepare him for what she was about to do. It would be pointless to ask Lucy's advice because Lucy would tell her not to be silly. 'They adapt you know. It's happened with so many of their friends' parents. He's unlikely to be surprised. Children notice these things. Don't you think your children would be aware of how their father's been playing around all these years? Grow up Sandra, grow up.' She could hear Lucy saying it but she wouldn't accept that the sensitive young man sitting opposite her would understand, even if he might forgive.

She would have liked to have seen him settled or, if not married, at least in, as they said now, in a settled relationship. She and Lucy had attempted a mild piece of matchmaking between him and Jacqueline. It had come to nothing. Lucy said that Jackie's problem was battle fatigue. She had been both non-combatant and combatant in too many wars between Lucy, her two husbands and various lovers.

'She's a girl with a lively intelligence. But she's too weary, worldly and knowing for your son. Pity. If they'd made a go of it she would have had, with your money and George's decency and industry, a much easier life than I've had. A little boring perhaps, but you can't have everything.'

That criticism had been a call to arms. 'He's not boring, he's just shy, and, and sensitive. I think he's had a lucky let off.'

Lucy did not return the anger. 'You're probably right. What a sorry mess, we've made of things.'

Sandra ordered a salad which she picked at to make sure that she ate nothing of substance. It was if she were going into training. This is ridiculous, she told herself, I've always been able to eat what I like without becoming fat. Nonetheless she pushed her plate aside leaving everything but some lettuce and cucumber that she carefully chewed before swallowing.

George asked politely about his father. A little pathetically he said, 'You know I think Dad's pretty pleased with me the way I've sorted out some of his tax problems.'

'Pretty pleased? Pleased, he's proud of you, and he damned well ought to be. Those other high-priced accountants were hopeless. He talks about you to his friends all the time,' she exaggerated, 'tells them they should sack their present advisors and consult you.' Jack had said it, but only a couple of times, and then incredulously because he'd remained unsure whether to be proud or ashamed of having a son as an accountant. What a preposterous person her husband was. 'Serve him right.'

Sandra wondered how things between them would be. Would Jack and George make an unlikely alliance in condemnation of wife and mother? Perhaps there would be a tripartite union of son, daughter and husband to revile and hound her. Sandra involuntarily shuddered.

'What's wrong Mother? Is something wrong?' He was all concern. 'You ate nothing. And you've said nothing. Tell me, Mother. Is something worrying you?'

She turned aside the question by interrogating him about his diet, his health, his friends and, in particular, any girlfriends. She wanted him to be happy but knew that she would still find it hard to reconcile herself to a permanent woman in his life.

Later that night after picking at a small evening meal she had prepared, with Jack, before he left the house to check on his patients, and, she guessed, to meet his mistress, she reflected on the day and her future. She determinedly took a cup of tea rather than a glass of wine onto the verandah.

Thoughts were whirling around her mind. She feared for what her children might come to think of her, but not her friends, or her associates at her clubs. She could imagine them down at the Club sniggering about what she had done. 'Dark horse, dark mare, more like, that one.' There would be jokes and innuendos. How would Jack cope? Well he would, as she had, just have to learn to live with it. There would never before have been a person so put upon and betrayed. Jack had about as much sense of fitness and justice as a randy monkey. He wouldn't suffer any sexual deprivation. The money might be a different matter. She had heard some horror stories of women whose independent fortunes had been stripped away by orders of the Family Court in favour of less wealthy husbands. Surely Jack wouldn't try that. Not that it would matter in view of where she was going. Still, as Daddy always said, it was important that any daughter of his have some financial independence. He had left half of his estate to Sandra outright and the other half similarly, to be relaxed on the death of her mother, who could enjoy the income for life.

Then there were all the other practical details to be sorted out, the packing, notes to everyone, arranging for Mrs Simpson to come more often. She paused. It never occurred to her that the domestic arrangements would cease to be her responsibility. And what about the house? Whose house would it be? Inkie presciently reminded her of his presence by snuffling. You couldn't say much about a marriage if it was easier to leave your husband than your dog. George would look after Inkie.

But who knew? With him so many things were possible. He was a magician. What had that article said about him? She went back to the bottom drawer and extracted the 'Review Magazine' in which it appeared five years before.

This time there were several photographs: of Dan, from the paparazzo's long-distance lens, in front of his house in the Cotswalds; a blurred image through the windshield snapped from the tarmac of him at the controls of his Lear jet; a photograph of the Botticelli drawing sold at Sothebys to an anonymous bidder, later to be established by a leak from the former owner, to be Daniel Bencham; an even more grainy photograph of him attending a premiere of a revival of a John Osborne play at the Haymarket in London with a famous blonde actress and, a blurred old black-and-white of a young couple dancing, him and her. The last photograph was of Dan as a solemn, young accounting man in a dark suit. This was his world and life as laid out in a tabloid.

She reread the text. It was, as they say, an in-depth profile, but without the benefit of an interview with its subject. It was written in the breathless, revelatory, style of highly inventive, investigative journalism. The introduction was set out in caps.

'The Informer has conducted an investigation into the wealth and affairs of one of Australia's richest and most reclusive businessmen. Nancy Craven and Luther Kick travelled the world and interviewed many people to produce this account. Despite repeated requests, most of which were not even acknowledged, the subject Bencham was always unavailable to be interviewed or for comment.

'Bencham's shyness is matched by an equally strong aversion to being photographed. We combed most of the press files of Australia, and many in England and the United States, for photographs. We were obliged to use the few that this evasive billionaire did not manage to avoid being taken.'

The article itself began with a series of questions.

'Who is Daniel Bencham? What does he own? Where are his residences? Where does he really live? What is he worth? Why has he never married? What are his ambitions? How often does he return to Australia? What political influence does he have in this country of birth? Who are his associates? Who are his business partners? Everything about a person so rich must be a matter of public interest. In short, what makes Daniel Bencham run? What is he hiding?The Informer set out to find the answers to these questions.

'The Informer met many obstructions in their search for the truth about this mysterious but powerful figure who controls the lives and destinies of so many people.

'We started with a cutting from the *Telegraph*, a new defunct Brisbane afternoon daily. An early article describes Bencham as Young Accountant of the Year. It contains the only interview recorded anywhere as being given by him. He told his interviewer his ambition was to go into business. He certainly fulfilled that ambition.

'We chased down Mr Andrew Reston, the former senior partner in the firm of accountants in which Bencham was then working. Now long retired he had this to say about his former pupil, 'It's hard to remember him very well. He was tall, quiet, reliable—he had no sense of humour. I remember that. A very intense young man but undoubtedly very reliable. I wouldn't have thought him very outstanding myself, meticulous, polite yes, but not a big personality. I was surprised in a way that he was selected as Young Accountant. Oh, yes, we must have nominated him. I think we had a policy of nominating two students in the firm who got the best examination results. The practice then was for the judges to consult the clients with whom the nominees dealt, and the examiners. They must have all given him a very good reference.

'The word "intense" pops up all the time in any discussions about Bencham. Practically everyone we interviewed, those who knew him only slightly and those who knew him well, used it when they were asked what stood out in their minds about him.

'We tried then to locate some of his contemporaries, to discover how they remembered him and whether there had ever been any later contacts. We could have been searching for the invisible man. No one had personally heard from him in years.

' "Not surprising," said Mark Fete, now a partner in a leading firm of accountants, and then a student with Bencham. "He wasn't one of the boys, ever. No one ever knew what he was really thinking. He was at the other end of the spectrum from me, always studying, very ambitious."

'What else could he bring to mind? "There was a girl somewhere. Not that I ever saw him with a girl. But others—don't ask me who after all this time—spoke about some great unrequited passion. There was an incident, I think, something at a ball one night, a fight. You know I haven't thought about that for years."

'We began to wonder whether this businessman with a reputation for calculated ruthlessness was really a romantic at heart.

'We followed up the rumour of the dance hall brawl but could uncover nothing further. We got one lead which suggested that Bencham had taken boxing lessons when he was a student.

'Yes, Bencham did take boxing lessons. We found this out at Bullet Murphy's gym which has been operating at the same address at Elizabeth Street in Brisbane since 1945. Its founder, Bullet, was so named because he survived a rifle shot in the chest in 1942, by an assailant never arrested or named. The bullet was never taken out, hence Bullet's nickname, but that is another story.

'A former middleweight who'd taken his share of uppercuts, Bullet struggled to bring back memories, and when he did he told us Bencham said he wanted a fine mind in a healthy body. He didn't put it quite that way but it was clearly what he meant.

'We dug deeper. We obtained a copy of Bencham's birth certificate. It showed his mother's occupation as home duties, and his father's as a boilermaker. They were married at the Baptist Tabernacle in Edward Street, Brisbane in 1937, a typical depression couple.

'We found his old family house, now much transformed by its present owners, Mr and Mrs Blocker. "No, we had no idea that Daniel Bencham ever lived here. Sure, of course we've heard of him. Wealthiest man in Australia isn't he? That is, if he really is an Australian now. Who'd have thought he would have lived here. Not that he'd recognize the old place if he saw it now."

'The Blockers showed us round the property. It was easy to visualize the humble Bencham residence as it must have been when the young Daniel was growing up there. It had started as a two-bedroom cottage, kitchen, bathroom and a combined living and dining room, in total about 80 square metres. There would have been at this time an outside earth closet and a lean-to laundry with an old wood-fired copper for washing. Outside, a clothesline, not even a Hills rotary hoist. The land around is flat and featureless. Attempts to pretty up this rather dismal area have had mixed success.

'Bencham's family probably came to Creekdale not long after the War. Daniel was enrolled as a pupil at the local three-teacher state school. No one knows where the family lived before then. They never owned, just rented, the cottage at Creekdale.

'Bencham's father, although unemployed during the depression, was a boilermaker, a worker much in demand in wartime. His trade was a reserved occupation so he never served in the Armed Forces but worked throughout the war years at the dry dock at South Brisbane. He continued working there until 1950 when he was struck down by a massive stroke that left him bedridden, speechless and totally dependent for all of his daily needs. Those were met by his wife and

Daniel, an only child. His father was, by all reports, a big man and his mother a slight woman. Mr Bencham senior had to be turned over at regular intervals, his back rubbed and oiled, his soiled bed made and remade, fed, taken for outings in a wheelchair—who knows where, in that suburb of dirt roads and pitted footpaths. The Bencham day started before daylight. Dinner, tea as he would have called it, was at five o'clock so that Bencham senior could be settled for the first half of the evening.

'Pleasures in such a household were few. It was a lonely life for a young man growing up at a time, which was, for others, and should have been for him, a period of opportunity and leisure.

'Just how the young Bencham coped with all of this, how it moulded and inspired him can only be a matter of speculation. It was during these years that the desperate resolve never to be poor again, never to be looked down upon, never to have to ask a favour, must have been forged.

'No one has been able to find a photograph of the young primary school student whose results were good enough to secure him a place at a selective State High School, which took the best students unable to attend the crème de la crème of private G.P.S. schools.'

Sandra almost knew the article by heart. It was Lucy who had drawn her attention to it, but she would herself have eventually come upon it, at the hairdresser's, or on one of her periodical visits to her husband's rooms to collect some papers for her to sign—these days after checking—connected with one of his tax avoidance schemes.

The story brought back to her the flatness and clay and damp of Creekdale. It saddened her again as she read about it, but the sadness was a sadness for herself and Dan. Dan had merely told her that his father was an invalid, and he sometimes helped his mother care for him. But then Dan never complained about anything, except her timidity. Dan was tough, Dan was independent. Dan never needed anyone. He had proved that. Wanting and needing were different.

Lucy and she had discussed the article as they did most things. 'Don't believe everything, don't believe most things you read in a newspaper, less in a weekly magazine,' Lucy said.

'But it all sounds so true. The journalist's got the landscape right. Why wouldn't the rest of it be true?'

'Read it Sandra, just read it, pure tabloid stuff. You can tell straight away most of it's made up. All that bullshit about digging deeper, people not knowing anything or not wanting to talk, wanting their names suppressed. Jesus, Sandra, sometimes I wonder where you live, what you think about, what you read. I thought you read books these days.'

'I have read quite enough Lucy for my purposes.'

'Well, whether you read anything or not you shouldn't get carried away by that article. What does it matter at any rate whether that part of it, any of it, is true? Christ, the man ought to be decorated when you look around at the bunch of silver spoon eunuchs we were forced to mix with, Jack excepted. Silver spoon yes, eunuch no.'

Lucy had a license to talk on any topic except Jack unless Sandra brought his name up. She suffered from a moral schizophrenia when it came to Jack. Sometimes she supported and praised her husband. At others, she spoke the truth about his insensitivity and mocked him. She was the sole arbiter of when and in what respects he might be discussed. She frowned at Lucy and the topic was dropped.

She picked up the article and continued to read on, the words familiar but ever interesting.

'We did, however, find one early photograph of Daniel Bencham as a secondary school student dancing with a beautifully dressed young girl in a gown which our fashion editor is certain is a Norman Hartnell of the period. Her face is turned away from the camera instinctively, as a reaction to the flash, so it has been impossible to make an identification. Such a dress at the time would have cost the equivalent, in today's money, two or three thousand dollars and her dancing sandals are of equal style and quality.'

Sandra looked at the black-and-white reproduction of the photograph of the two of them at the dance. It had been taken only ten minutes before her father had arrived to expel Daniel from her life. She could remember the photographer. It had always been the same one at the school dances. He had been another unexpected success, a society photographer in London now, who sometimes for huge fees photographed the Masai in Kenya, a glacier in Alaska, or a beautiful model in the souk at Marrakesh, for *Vogue* or *Harpers* or *Vanity Fair* or some other glossy magazine. She would have liked a photograph of the two of them but the events of the evening prevented that.

'We have been unable to find out when and where Bencham worked in the early years. There is anecdotal evidence that he took the first holiday of his life, at Nice, staying at a small pensione two streets back from the Promenade des Anglais. What he thought then of the city's Belle Époque gambling houses, the decadent faded luxury and fashionable existentialism of the Riviera, no one knows. It's a long way from Creekdale to the Riviera.

'After he returned from overseas some matters had to appear on the public record.'

The journalist wrote as if Bencham, by having done things as privately as he could, had deprived them of some valuable rights.

'On his return he immediately set up his own accountancy practice. A bold and not quite proper course to take at the time. He had no family, no commercial connexions and, as far as anyone could tell, no friends. Just his wits. He took a room above Pennys, a cheap department store in competition with Woolworths, with street frontages to Queen and Adelaide Streets and now long gone. Then its upper floors were occupied by a number of firms of solicitors and accountants and the occasional dentist. For a bumptious, unknown ambitious young acountant to take a room there was the height of presumption.'

Sandra baulked at that word in particular. You could apply a lot of adjectives to Dan. You could never call him bumptious.

'Against all the odds he succeeded. For the accountancy profession it was a time of transition. Local firms were just beginning to ask themselves whether they should link up with interstate and international firms in the huge, exclusive multi-national groupings that now dominate the profession. He must have had overtures from a number of those firms later as he ate into their client bases in the special areas in which he practised. In the beginning he employed a secretary/bookkeeper part time, a woman who had previously worked for his old firm and had retired only to come to him a few weeks later.

'We were able to interview Mr Larrimin Allen who at the time was the owner of a small brass foundry. "I'll never forget him. I just took his name out of the pink pages. Why him? I think because there was only one name, nothing flash, and I had to go to town that day to buy a pair of boots. There was a boot shop across the road from his office. My business was in real trouble. I had lots of orders but I never seemed to be able to make a decent profit. I was working ten hours, six days a week and getting less than I was paying any of the three men who worked for me. I'd never had much use for accountants or lawyers before but I was desperate, ready to throw the towel in and go back to working for wages. I thought for once I'd get some advice, probably be no good but all I had to lose was the cost of one appointment.

'"He had an old girl, a real old girl at a typewriter in a corner of the room that he'd partitioned off with plywood as a reception area, and two hard wooden chairs. Somehow though everything was neat and tidy. When I got to know him better he told me he'd done the partitioning himself. Pretty good with his hands as well as his mind. All the joints were mitre cut and everything properly sanded and stained and varnished. There was no carpet on the floor, just boards waxed and polished. I think I must have been one of his first clients.

'"He had a plain office desk, a sheet of plate-glass on top of it as they used to in those days, a pad, pen and pencil, a kind of an ornamental ink-well and nothing else. I told him what I was there for, the advice everyone wants, how to make a whacking great profit. I showed him my tax returns for the current year and for the last year. He was quick. He was soon talking my figures as if he'd been sitting in my foundry for months.

'"He said my trouble was I was not making a sufficient run of products to get the turnover. Look at this, he'd point to some figures he'd underlined in pencil in my accounts. Look what you've spent on moulds. You must be making about thirty different products. What you need is to get some component contracts that'll give you a full return for all your setting-up costs. We'd then discussed likely buyers and he came up with the names of some bathroom fittings manufacturer.

He seemed to know a lot about other people's businesses. He told me to go to them with a proposal to make some of their components. You've got to have a business plan. He was right. I did everything he told me. I soon made some pretty good profits. His fees? Didn't want any. A ten percent share of my business if I made a profit in the first two years after he advised me. Somebody told me he shouldn't have done that. Unethical. I don't know. I heard lots of similar stories about other professionals getting a hold of their client's business and not doing anything to improve profits. I didn't mind I can tell you. Later, when I was ready to retire he bought me out, paid a very fair price. I've no complaints."

'It was the same story when we contacted any of his former clients, same modus operandi, take a share, improve the profitability, buy them out later if they were willing. No one was prepared to say he put pressure on them to sell. The general picture was of a satisfied customers.

'Daniel Bencham never took a partner, or even an associate. He employed young accountants but they knew that they would never be given an opportunity to become partners in the practice. He came to employ more than ten people, including secretarial staff in the end. 'Had a mind like a computer', one former employee said. He didn't know how he kept track of everything.

'After ten years his fortune was estimated at five million dollars. His accountancy became secondary to his business interests. His office became his personal counting house. He was taking no new clients and encouraging his own clients to move to the best of the young accountants whom he had employed and who had left when he frankly told them he wouldn't be taking any partners. By now his business interests extended to Sydney and Melbourne. They were all small businesses, of many kinds.

'After 15 years he sold out everything in Australia. He did so on the wave of economic euphoria that accompanied the advent of a new government. No one knows for sure how much the sales realized. Figures of as much as twenty million dollars have been estimated.

'He disappeared from the Australian scene. He had sold up not just his business interests, but the modest house he lived in at St Lucia near the university, his car, his furniture, his practice, the lease of his offices, the lot.

'Australia lost sight of Daniel Bencham. Occasionally in the broking houses and the merchant bankers' offices his name would be mentioned. But no one really knew what he was doing. There were no yachts or ostentatious appearances at Sothebys to bid for Impressionist paintings, or great takeover battles for overpriced companies. Everything he did was done as anonymously as a spectator at a crowded sporting event. except for the occasional appearance at a charity function with a beautiful actress or a widowed aristocrat, but never the same one twice.'

That had given Sandra pause but only for a moment. If he made repeated appearances with the same woman, she would have been more concerned. He had to be seen with women. Otherwise people would whisper and innuendo flourish. But anyway he couldn't be expected to live a monkish existence.

'He had his weaknesses, however. Renaissance drawings and Louis XIV furniture. He was reputed to be an expert on them.

'It is said that his grave, tall, stooped figure in a black or midnight-blue suit and dark glasses was often to be seen at the flea markets in Paris, or in the St Elmo district in Buenos Aires, discriminatingly separating the authentic from the "made yesterday". He was also a regular visitor to Florence and Vienna to review the great Renaissance pictures there although it has never been suggested that he acquired anything other than drawings. It is somehow befitting that this shadowy figure should concern himself with pencil and black-and-white chalk only, the shadowy mist and dusk.'

Lucy had asked how they could write such 'bullshit'. 'They make him sound like a cross between a member of the Mafiosi and a fifth columnist. Look what you missed out on Sandra. Might have been a lot more fun than the medical mechanic you married, though I'm not too keen on that undertaker's suit and the black shades.' Sandra had not been concerned. Even Lucy didn't know about the irrevocable promise.

'Questions are repeatedly asked why he has not married despite the actresses and the aristocrats. Is there a hint of ambiguity about his sexuality?

'We contacted Sandy Simes, the well-known Australian expatriate freelance photographer who has specialized in photographing, usually unaware, and often in compromising circumstances, leading society figures including the Princess of Wales on whom he is an expert. Had she ever snapped Daniel Bencham with a woman during a dirty weekend at Cannes or Venice? The answer was "no". For a time he had had one of his followers keep watch outside a residence that he rented at Westbourne Grove, but to no avail. Are the beauties a blind? Why has he never married?

'The other question that everyone asks is How much is Daniel Bencham really worth? The same secrecy as envelops his private life equally obscures matters that should be thrown open to scrutiny. Informed estimates can only be made. *Business Review Weekly* put his fortune at between 2 and 3 billion dollars, but confessed that it was only a guess, a conservative one.

'Some assets he owns are known: the modest house in Westbourne Grove, his thirty acres in the Cotswalds, on which stands a not unduly large, converted vicarage, his unvisited sheep station in the Western District of Victoria, with its forty thousand sheep, his rarely used apartment at Mosman in Sydney, his walled fortress-like thousand-square villa on the water near Positano—his Renaissance drawings, his antique furniture, and the Lear jet that he pilots himself. But these, as varied and grand as they may sound, are only trappings of wealth, mere bagatelle.

'His real wealth is concealed in trusts which control huge combines, television channels in deregulated countries, a porcelain factory in Luxembourg, a silver mine in Peru, a newspaper chain in Texas and Nevada, and an insurance company with its head office in Zurich.

'He has been even more secretive about his Australian business holdings. His recent policy in this country has been to take substantial but minority interests in the leading dozen or so industrial and mining corporations. He has kept himself remote from the management of them, even though in some he could be the largest single shareholder.

The fact that the Board well knows that he is sitting on the register may be seen and an incentive to good management.

'He is a man who does permission everywhere and pays tax nowhere. We have a message for you Mr Bencham. Come clean. What have you got to hide? That is the question that an increasing number of people and not just Australians are asking. Come out of your closet, whatever it conceals.'

There then followed a list of places, people and materials that the journalists had consulted. It looked to have been a very expensive exercise and a highly questionable one at that.

The articles, typical as it was, irritated Sandra. If—when, she joined him, she knew that she would have to live with the kind of resentment that Australians held towards success in any field except sport. How wise he had been to refuse to be interviewed, to live his life as quietly and elusively as he had.

Sandra put away the article. It was, at last, the time for practicalities. For a time she thought about the actresses and aristocrats. What had Lucy said? 'Courtesans, *demi-mondaine* escorts.' All the same. Sexual temps. That was probably right. She could live with that.

Chapter 11
The Last Dance

Fifty, it was just a number. It didn't mean anything. Jack's insistence that he give her a birthday party was in kind with the hypocrisy with which they had lived their lives. The invitations engraved on their thick, fine paper had long gone out and been responded to. The caterers had been engaged, and soon they would come to erect the marquee on the lawn.

She wished Dan were here now. Always the magician, he would spirit the problems away. No, not yet: but soon, and then nothing would stand in his way. There were yet things to be done, and worse, much to be endured.

She should travel light. Her life would be different now. She would need new clothes to match her new existence. Property, her car, her shares, these would be for Dan to manage.

The children, well, she had thought a lot about them. Her daughter would berate her, because she would have the least entitlement to do so. Her son, she hoped he wouldn't be hurt. He shouldn't be, she told herself over and over again. There could, however, be no turning back. They would both have to take their chances.

Lucy would applaud. She might even be able to do something for Lucy, some large commissions for interiors overseas, holidays by Lear jet. The others, the lunchers, well they'd have something to talk about.

All of this was to postpone the real task, to tell Jack that it was over. He would not want to believe it. He wouldn't believe it. She had rehearsed the argument in her mind a dozen times since she had taken the decision. For any woman to reject Jack was unthinkable, he who left women behind him like driftwood on a beach. The gossip columns would have a field day. She would away by then, like Dan, impervious to their gibes.

Her mind turned to Jack. She thought back over the years of disappointments, of insensitivities, of intentional slights and hurts, of indifference, and of betrayal. It would never improve. Each bleak year would follow the other until the grave. And as Jack would grow older, as his jogging route grew shorter, his young registrars came to eclipse him, and the middle-aged Adonis grew into a satiric gargoyle, and as she might fight and lose, and have her temporary successes with abstention from the wine, their life would descend into a black and meaningless round of words and appearances by rote. She was determined. The time had come.

How disapproving her father would have been. Her mother—well. Too late for her too. So much must be accepted. In a curious kind of way though she could almost feel sorry for Jack. Most of his transgressions were out of conceit or negligence. She bore him little particular ill-will, just indifference now.

On the day, all afternoon the caterers came and went. The marquee was erected. For once Jack had dug deep, although she wouldn't be surprised if he tried to get a contribution from her later. Small chance of that with Dan running the finances. The interior of the marquee was draped with a light blue gauze, and the walls were tied back with bows of silver ribbon: silver and blue. She had toyed with the idea of a silver and blue dress but decided against it. Jack couldn't have remembered these were her colours.

Already the drinks were cooling in ice in large polythene boxes. A place had been prepared for a four-piece band who had been engaged to play the songs of her youth. They had come earlier in the day to set up the sound equipment. The heavy tropical clouds had gradually dispersed during the afternoon and a gentle breeze now rustled the leaves. Jack was behaving in a very officious way. He thought himself a skilful organizer. He shouted and strode around the garden as the temporary dance floor was brought in and laid beyond the far end of the swimming pool. He tried to tell the electricians how and where to rig up the coloured lights. They gave him short shift.

Lucy arrived while it was still light.

She told Lucy her plans. Then she told her about the letters.

'Are you sure?' Lucy asked. 'How many letters has he really written to you? You're not imagining this? Did he really say he'd come? It's a fantasy.'

'No, it's true.'

'I was very clear in my letter. I still have to to pack.' Sandra was shoeless in her petticoat. She was striding up and down the bedroom, half made up and suddenly desperate.

'You should have told Jack, before this, all this Cecil B. de Mille stuff.'

'I haven't had your experience with this kind of thing. Look, get me a drink please.'

When Lucy came back with a glass of champagne, Sandra was seated at her dressing table, a little more composed.

'He's the most reliable man in the world. Something must have come up. My fiftieth birthday. My most, most important birthday.'

'You must tell Jack.'

'Leave it Lucy. How could I tell him with all of this going on?' The band could be heard tuning up in the garden. It was twilight now. Jack, like a child, thrilled by the novelty of new toys turned on the coloured lights that bathed the dance floor in a pale blue glow.

'Ring him up then if it's true.'

'I'll finish dressing first. God, is that the time?' She hurriedly finished her make-up and pulled on her long dress. Jack had insisted that the party be formal.

The band was now into the first bracket o songs. The pianist practised a passable imitation of Frank Sinatra singing 'I Did It My Way'. Jack was still outside. He had been intercepted by a few unusually punctual guests.

Sandra felt disoriented and faint. Lucy took her arm a she came down the steps of the old timber house.

She spoke distractedly to the early guests and thanked them for their good wishes. The invitations had made clear that there were to be no presents, but the offerings of wine and books and various useless articles in shiny wrapping paper were beginning to build up.

As if from a long way she heard a voice singing, 'There's a messenger here.' A man in grey trousers and shirt with a red pocket with the words World Wide Messages embroidered on it, asked Sandra to sign for an envelope. Nobody else, except Lucy, paid any attention. It would be no more than a birthday message from a guest who couldn't come.

Sandra excused herself. It wasn't difficult. The collective talk was almost as loud as the band, and guests milled around, telling the same stories and repeating the same gossip in lowered or raised voices, depending on the proximity of the subjects of their conversations.

She took the precious letter upstairs. In the bedroom she tore away the envelope. The letter was written in the same accountant's hand that had never changed.

My Darling Sandra,

You will always be that, I want you to know that. You must also know that I anguished long over what I have done. However, the time had come for me. I could no longer lay any claim to you. To have written as I have in the past must have been a dreadful and presumptuous intrusion into your life. What right did I have, I finally asked myself, to take you away from your children and all the familiar people and places that are your life?

All those years ago when I tried to come into your life, I told myself that your ideas and standards were narrow and exclusionary. I was a very judgmental person. I hope that I have ceased to be so. I used to tell myself, and I think you, that a life of the kind that your parents pre-ordained for you could not possibly be a happy or a contented one. Talk about presumption. I had plenty of that as a prospectless young student with only ambition to his name.

I think I was wrong. As for your marriage—who can see inside and understand a marriage? Not me certainly. I have no qualifications for that. You still have your marriage. You have stayed together. You told me of the party. He must have feelings for you. You could never, I finally realized, leave your family. And nor you should.

Sandra, last night I married Gillian Lamense, who is, as you would know, an opera singer. She is thirty six, so although the age difference is there, it is not so great that we will not have much in common. You have your children. It cannot be wrong for me to want desperately to have children of my own. It is not that I wish to start a dynasty. I don't believe in them. Your children, at their age now, could never be my children. Gillian wants children too. She knows that at her age she cannot have long to conceive and bear healthy infants.

I told Gillian about you. I do not think she can understand what you have meant to me. It is probably better that she does not. It is better too that she not know what an inspiration you have been to me, how I was driven—yes driven—to succeed not only by my own ambition, but also so that I might one day be acceptable to you.

The time has come therefore for me to acknowledge that we can never be together. As a groom my heart should be light. It is not. It is heavy because I now must accept what I hoped for is impossible.

I will try to be a good husband to Gillian. I will always be your friend. You must think of me as that, forever, to be called on for help or support, financial or otherwise.

Be happy, be contented and, I almost forgot, happy birthday.

Love Daniel

Sandra started to sob. Her sobbing drowned out the band and the vocalist who was singing 'Kisses sweeter than Wine'.

THE END

www.ingramcontent.com/pod-product-compliance
Ingram Content Group Australia Pty Ltd
76 Discovery Rd, Dandenong South VIC 3175, AU
AUHW020136130726
429791AU00003B/96

9 781925 333602